Footsteps in Time

FOOTSTEPS IN TIME

A TIME TRAVEL FANTASY

by

SARAH WOODBURY

Footsteps in Time: A Time Travel Fantasy
Copyright © 2011 by Sarah Woodbury

This is a work of fiction.

www.sarahwoodbury.com

Cover image by Christine DeMaio-Rice at Flip City Books
http://flipcitybooks.com

To Anna

A Brief Guide to Welsh Pronunciation

c   a hard 'c' sound (Cadfael)

ch   a non-English sound as in Scottish "ch" in "loch" (Fychan)

dd   a buzzy 'th' sound, as in "there" (Ddu; Gwynedd)

f   as in "of" (Cadfael)

ff   as in "off" (Gruffydd)

g   a hard 'g' sound, as in "gas" (Goronwy)

l   as in "lamp" (Llywelyn)

ll   a breathy "th" sound that does not occur in English (Llywelyn)

rh   a breathy mix between 'r' and 'rh' that does not occur in English (Rhys)

th   a softer sound than for 'dd,' as in "thick" (Arthur)

u   a short 'ih' sound (Gruffydd), or a long 'ee' sound (Cymru—pronounced "kumree")

w   as a consonant, it's an English 'w' (Llywelyn); as a vowel, an 'oo' sound (Bwlch)

y   the only letter in which Welsh is not phonetic. It can be an 'ih' sound, as in "Gwyn," is often an "uh" sound (Cymru), and at the end of the word is an "ee" sound (thus, both Cymru—the modern word for Wales—and Cymry—the word for Wales in the Dark Ages—are pronounced "kumree")

Prologue

Llywelyn

"How can you leave Gwynedd undefended, my lord? Without you, we can't hold back the English."

Goronwy stood with his back to me, gazing out the window at the courtyard where a dozen men prepared to ride out on a scouting mission. I didn't envy them, for rain lashed their faces and the temperature hovered just above freezing. It was cold for November, even here by the sea.

I put aside the letter I was writing and gave Goronwy, my steadfast friend through nearly fifty years of governing and fighting, my full attention.

"Dafydd will hold the north for me, and you with him," I said. "You may travel with me as far as Castell y Bere, but not beyond that. I need you to watch Dafydd and rein him in if necessary."

"Dafydd." Goronwy swung around to face me. "Traitor isn't too strong a word to describe him. You can't deny it."

"I don't deny it. Dafydd follows always his own desires, usually in direct opposition to mine. I can't trust him to remain true to Wales or to me, but I can trust him to remain true to himself. For now, his interests and those of Wales coincide." I picked up my pen and twirled it in my hand. "It's not Dafydd's loyalty that concerns me, but the Mortimers."

"The Mortimers!" Goronwy's tone for them matched the one he'd used for Dafydd. "We've heard rumors only. They hold Buellt Castle for King Edward and no amount of persuasion is ever going to talk them out of it."

"So Marged said."

"You still want to risk it? You listen to neither her nor me. If you go south to meet them, I fear you meet your death."

"I do listen, Goronwy," I said. "That's why you're staying here, in case I don't return. The men will follow Dafydd if they know you stand with him."

Goronwy rubbed his face with both hands. "There's nothing I can say to persuade you not to make this journey?"

"If we are to defeat the English once and for all, if I am to rule Wales in fact as well as name, I must control the south. The Mortimers' allegiance would strengthen my position and shorten the war. Surely you can see that I must meet them?"

"If it were true, I would see it, my lord; but I don't believe they will betray England. Not all men bend with the wind as easily as Dafydd."

"Some bend; some break." I picked up the letter and saluted Goronwy with it. "This time either Edward or I will break. I know only that I can bend no longer."

Goronwy took a deep breath. "May I take my leave, my lord?" he asked.

I nodded. Goronwy bowed and left the room. I gripped my pen, reading over the words I'd written, and signed my name at the end: *We fight because we are forced to fight, for we, and all Wales, are oppressed, subjugated, despoiled, reduced to servitude by the royal officers and bailiffs so that we feel, and have often so protested to the king, that we are left without any remedy* . . .

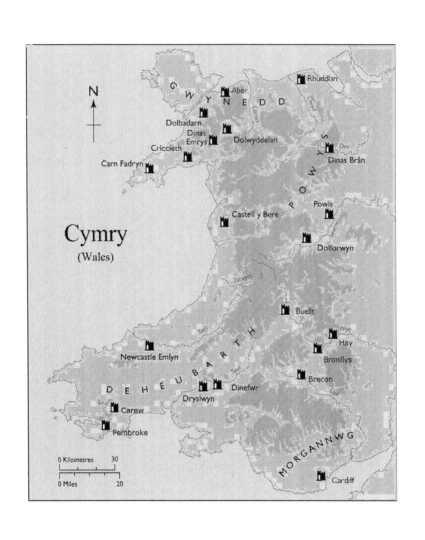

N

Rhuddlan

GWYNEDD

Aber

Dolbadarn

Dinas
Emrys

Dolwyddelan

POWYS

Dee

Criccieth

Dinas Brân

Carn Fadryn

Castell y Bere

Powis

Cymry
(Wales)

Dolforwyn

Ystwyth

Buellt

Wye

Teifi

Hay

Newcastle Emlyn

Bronllys

DEHEUBARTH

Dryslwyn

Dinefwr

Brecon

Carew

Pembroke

MORGANNWG

0 Kilometres   30

Cardiff

0 Miles   20

Part One

1

"**D**o you want me to come with you?"

Anna looked back at her brother. He'd followed her to the door, his coat in his hand.

"Okay," she said, trying not to sound relieved. "You can hold the map."

The clouds were so low they blended into the trees around the house and Anna tipped her head to the sky, feeling a few gentle snowflakes hit her face. They walked across the driveway, the first to leave tracks in the new snow.

"You're sure you can handle this?" David asked, eyeing the van. It faced the house so Anna would have to back it out.

"Christopher's waiting," Anna said. "It's not like I have a choice."

"If you say so," David said.

Their aunt had asked Anna to pick up her cousin at a friend's house, since she had a late meeting and wouldn't make it. Ignoring David's skeptical expression, Anna tugged open the door, threw her purse on the floor between the seats, and got in the

1

driver's side. David plopped himself beside her with a mischievous grin.

"And don't you dare say anything!" she said, wagging her finger in his face before he could open his mouth. He was three years younger than she, having just turned fourteen in November, unbearably pompous at times, and good at everything. Except for his handwriting, which was atrocious. Sometimes a girl had to hold onto the small things.

"Which way?" Anna asked, once they reached the main road. The windshield wipers flicked away the new snow, barely keeping up. Anna peered through the white for oncoming cars and waited for David to say something.

David studied the map, disconcertingly turning it this way and that, and then finally settled back in his seat with it upside down. "Uh . . . right," he said.

Anna took a right, and then a left, and within three minutes they were thoroughly lost. "This is so unlike you," she said.

"I'm trying!" he said, "but look at this—" he held out the map and Anna glanced at it. One of the reasons she'd accepted his offer, however, was because maps confused her under the best of circumstances. "The roads wander at random and they all look the same. Half of them don't even have signs."

Anna had to agree, especially in December, with the leafless trees and rugged terrain. She drove up one hill and down another, winding back and forth around rocky outcroppings and spectacular, yet similar, mansions. As the minutes ticked by, Anna clenched the wheel more tightly. They sat unspeaking in their heated, all-wheel drive cocoon, while the snow fell harder and the sky outside the windows darkened with the waning of the day. Then, just as they crested a small rise and were taking a downhill curve to the left, David hissed and reached for the handhold above his door.

"What?" Anna asked. She took a quick look at him. His mouth was open, but no sound came out and he pointed straight ahead.

Anna returned her gaze to the windscreen. Ten feet in front of them, a wall of snow blocked the road, like a massive, opaque picture window. She had no time respond, think, or press the brake, before they hit it.

Whuf!

They powered through the wall and for a long three seconds a vast black space surrounded them. Then they burst through to the other side to find themselves bouncing down a snow-covered hill, much like the one they'd been driving on, but with grass beneath their wheels instead of asphalt. During the first few seconds as Anna fought to bring the van under control, they rumbled into a clearing situated halfway down the hill. She gaped through the windshield at the three men on horseback who appeared out of nowhere. They stared back at her, frozen as if in a photograph, oblivious now to the fourth man on the ground whom they'd surrounded.

All four men held swords.

"Anna!" David said, finally finding his voice.

Anna stood on the brakes, but couldn't get any traction in the snow. All three horses reared, catapulting their riders out of their saddles. Anna careened into two of the men who fell under the wheels with a sickening crunching thud. Still unable to stop the van, she plowed right over them and the snow-covered grass, into the underside of a rearing horse.

By then, the van was starting to slide sideways and its nose slewed under the horse's front hooves, which were high in the air, and hit its midsection full on. The windshield shattered from the impact of the hooves, the horse fell backwards, pinning its rider beneath it, and the airbags exploded. By then, the van's momentum had spun it completely around, carried it across the clearing to the edge, and over it.

It slid another twenty feet down the hill before connecting with a tree at the bottom of the slope. Breathless, chained by the seatbelt, Anna sat stunned. David fumbled with the door handle.

"Come on," he said. He shoved at her shoulder. When she didn't move, he grasped her chin to turn her head to look at him. "The gas tank could explode."

Her heart catching in her throat, Anna wrenched the door open and tumbled into the snow. She and David ran toward a small stand of trees thirty feet to their left, and stopped there, breathing hard. The van remained as they'd left it, sad and crumpled against the tree at the base of the hill. David had a line of blood on his cheek. Anna put her hand to her forehead and it came away with blood, marring her brown glove.

"What—" Anna said, swallowed hard, and tried again. "How did we go from lost to totaled in two point four seconds?" She found a tissue in her pocket, wiped at the blood on her glove, and began dabbing at her forehead.

David followed the van tracks with his eyes. "Can you walk up the hill with me and see what's up there?"

"Shouldn't we call Mom first?" Their mother was giving a talk at a medieval history conference in Philadelphia, which is why she'd parked her children at her sister's house in Bryn Mawr in the first place.

"Let's find out where we are before we call her," David said.

Anna was starting to shake, whether from cold or shock it didn't really matter. David saw it and took her hand for perhaps the first time in ten years. He tugged her up the hill to the clearing. They came to a stop at the top, unable to take another step. Two dozen men lay dead on the ground. They sprawled in every possible position. A man close to Anna was missing an arm and his blood stained the snow around him. Anna's stomach heaved and she turned away, but there was no place to look where a dead man didn't lie.

But even as she looked away, it registered that the men weren't dressed normally. They wore mail and helmets, and many still had their swords in their hands. Then David left at a run, heading along the path the van had followed. Anna watched him, trying not to see anyone else. He crouched next to a body.

"Over here!" he said, waving an arm.

Anna followed David's snowy footprints, weaving among the dead men—every one butchered. By the time she came to a halt beside David, tears streamed down her cheeks.

"My God, David," she said, choking on the words, her voice a whisper. "Where are we?" Heedless of the snow, Anna fell to her knees beside the man David was helping to sit upright. She was still breathing hard. She'd never been in a car accident before, much less one that landed her in the middle of a clearing full of dead men.

"I don't know," David said. He'd gotten his arm under the man's shoulder and now braced his back. The man didn't appear to have any blood on him, although it was obvious from his quiet moans that he was hurt.

The man grunted and put his hands to his helmet, struggling to pull it from his head. Anna leaned forward, helped him remove it, and then set it on the ground beside him. The man looked old to have been in a battle. He had a dark head of hair, with touches of white at his temples, but his mustache was mostly grey and his face lined. At the moment it was also streaked with sweat and dirt—and very pale.

"Diolch," he said.

Anna blinked. That was *thank you* in Welsh, which she knew because of her mother's near-continual efforts to teach them the language, although Anna had never thought she'd actually need to know it. She met the man's eyes. They were deep blue but bloodshot from his exertions. To her surprise, instead of finding them full of fear and pain, they held amusement. Anna couldn't credit it, and decided she must be mistaken.

The man turned to David. "Beth yw'ch enw chi?" he asked. *What is your name?*

"Dafydd dw i," David said. *My name is David.* David gestured towards Anna and continued in Welsh. "This is my sister, Anna."

The man's eyes tracked back to Anna and a twitch of a smile flickered at the corner of his mouth. "We need to find safety before night falls," he said, still all in Welsh. "I must find my men."

Now *that* was equally ridiculous and impossible.

Pause.

Anna was trying to think what to say to him, anything to say to him, when someone shouted. She swung around. A dozen men on horses rode out of the trees near the van. David settled the man back on the ground and stood up. At the sight of him, the lead rider reined his horse. The others crowded up behind him.

They all stared at each other, or rather, the men stared at David. They seemed frozen to their horses and Anna looked up at David, trying to see what they saw. He had turned fourteen in November, but his voice hadn't yet changed so he hadn't grown as tall as many of his friends. At 5' 6", he was still four inches taller than she, however. David had sandy blonde hair, cut short, and an athletic build, thanks to his continuous efforts in soccer and karate. Anna's friends at school considered him cute, in a geeky sort of way.

"What is it?" she whispered.

"I don't know," David said. "Is it our clothes? Your hair?"

Anna touched her head, feeling the clip that held her hair back from her face. The bun had come lose and her hair cascaded down her back in a tangled, curly mass.

"They're looking at *you*, David, not me."

The man they'd helped moaned and David crouched again beside him. His movement broke the spell holding the horsemen. They shouted, something like "move!" and "now!" and their lead rider climbed the hill and dismounted. He elbowed Anna out of the way, knocking her on her rear in the snow, and knelt beside the wounded man. This newcomer was about David's height, but fit the description Anna had always attributed to the word 'grizzled.' Like all these men, he wore mail and a helmet and bore a sword. He had bracers on his arms—*where had I learned that word?*—and a surcoat over his chain mail.

He and the man held a conversation while David and Anna looked at each other across the six feet of space that separated them. Despite her comprehension earlier, Anna couldn't understand a word. Maybe the man had spoken slower for their benefit, or in a different dialect from what he spoke now. The men must have decided something, because after more shouting, other men hurried up the hill, surrounded the downed man, and lifted him to his feet. He walked away—actually walked—suspended between two men who supported him on either side.

David and Anna sat in the snow, forgotten. Anna's jeans were soaking wet, but stiff from the cold, and her hands were frozen, even in her gloves.

"What do we do now?" David asked, his eyes tracking the progress of the soldiers.

"Let's go back up the hill," Anna said. "We didn't drive that far. There must be a road at the top."

David gave her a speaking look, which she ignored. Anna took a few steps, trying not to look at the dead men whom she'd managed to forget for a few minutes, and then found herself running away across the meadow. She veered into the wheel tracks of the van. David pounded along beside her until she had to slow down. They'd reached the upward slope at the far side of the meadow. The snow was deeper here because men and horses hadn't packed it down; her feet lost their purchase on the steep slope and she put out a hand to keep from falling.

Anna looked up the hill. Only a dozen yards away, the van tracks began. Beyond them, smooth fresh snow stretched as far as she could see. It was as if they'd dropped out of the sky.

More shouts interrupted her astonishment and Anna turned to find horsemen bearing down on them. She looked around wildly but there was nowhere to run. One man leaned down and in a smooth movement, caught her around the waist. Before she could think, he pulled her in front of him. She struggled to free herself but the man tightened his grip and growled something she didn't catch, but could easily have been *sit still, dammit!*

"David!" Anna said, her voice going high.

"I'm here, Anna," he called. The man holding her turned the horse and they passed David, just getting comfortable on his own horse. Dumbstruck, Anna twisted in her seat to look back at him.

All he did was shrug, and Anna faced forward again. They rode across the meadow and down the hill, reaching the bottom just as the wounded man got a boost onto a horse. He gathered the reins while glancing at the van. Anna followed his gaze. It sat where she'd left it. It was hopeless to think of driving it, even if they had somewhere to go.

The company followed a trail through the trees. A litany of complaints—about her wet clothes and hair, about her aching neck and back from the car crash, and most of all, her inability to understand what was happening—cycled through Anna's head as they rode.

Fortunately, after a mile or two (it was hard to tell in the growing darkness and her misery) they trotted off the trail into a camp. Three fire rings burned brightly and the twenty men who'd ridden in doubled the number of people in the small space. The man behind Anna dismounted and pulled her after him. Although she tried to stand, her knees buckled and he scooped her up, carried her to a fallen log near one of the fires, and set her down on it.

"Thanks," Anna said automatically, forgetting he probably couldn't understand English. Fighting tears, she pulled her hood up to hide her face, and then David materialized beside her.

"Tell me you have an explanation for all this," Anna said, the moment he sat down.

He crossed his arms and shook his head. "Not one I'm ready to share, even with you."

Great. They sat unspeaking as men walked back and forth around the fire. Some cooked, some tended the horses staked near the trees on the edges of the clearing. Three men emerged from a tent thirty feet away. Their chain mail didn't clank like Anna imagined plate mail would, but it creaked a little as they walked. Someone somewhere roasted meat and despite her queasiness, Anna's stomach growled.

Nobody approached them, and it seemed to Anna that whenever one of the men looked at them, his gaze immediately slid away. She wasn't confused enough to imagine they couldn't see her, but maybe they didn't want to see her or know what to make of her. Anna pulled her coat over her knees, trying to make herself as small as possible. The sky grew darker and still she and David sat silent.

"Do you think we've stumbled upon a Welsh extremist group that prefers the medieval period to the present day?" Anna finally asked.

"Twenty miles from Philadelphia?" he said. "Bryn Mawr isn't that rural. Somehow, I just can't see it."

"Maybe we aren't in Pennsylvania anymore, David." Anna had been thinking those words for the last half an hour and couldn't hold them in any longer.

He sighed. "No, perhaps not."

"Mom's going to be worried sick," she said, choking on the words. "She was supposed to call us at 8 o'clock. I can't imagine what Aunt Elisa is going to tell her." Then Anna thought, *stupid!* She whipped out her phone.

"It says 'searching for service'," David said. "I already tried it."

Anna doubled over and put her head into David's chest. Her lungs felt squeezed and her throat was tight with unshed tears. He patted her back in a 'there, there' motion, like he wasn't really paying attention, but when she tried to pull away, he tightened his grip and hugged her to him.

Eventually, Anna wiped her face and straightened to look into his face. He met her eyes and tried to smile, but his eyes were reddened and his heart wasn't in it. Looking at him, Anna resolved not to pretend that all was well. They needed to talk about what had happened even if David didn't want to. *How many books have we all read where the heroine refuses to face reality? How many times have I thrown the book across the room in disgust at her stupidity?*

"What are you thinking?" she asked him.

He shook his head.

"We could leave right now, follow the trail back to the van," Anna said. "It couldn't be more than a few miles from here."

David cleared his throat. "No."

"Why not?" she said.

"What for?"

"I want to climb to the top of the hill we came down and see what's up there," she said. "I know the tracks of the van disappeared, but we had to have driven down that hill from somewhere. We couldn't have appeared out of nowhere."

"Couldn't we?" David said. He sat with his elbows resting on his knees and his chin in his hands. When Anna didn't respond, he canted his head to the side to look at her. "Do you really think we'll find the road home at the top of that hill?"

Anna looked away from him and into the fire. *No . . . No more than you do.* "You're thinking time travel, aren't you?" she said.

"Time travel is impossible."

"Why do you say that?"

Anna's abrupt question made David hunch. Then he straightened. "Okay," he said. "If time travel is possible, why don't we have people from the future stopping by all the time? If time travel is possible, all of *time* itself has to have already happened. It would need to be one big pre-existent event."

"That doesn't work for me," Anna said.

"Not for me either," said David. "It's pretty arrogant for us to think that 2010 is as far as time has gotten, but these people's lives have already happened, else how could we travel back and relive it with them?"

"So you're saying the same argument could hold for people traveling from 3010 to 2010. To them, we've already lived our lives because *they* are living theirs."

"Exactly," David agreed.

"Then where are we? Is this real?"

"Of course it's *real*," he said, "but maybe not the same reality we knew at home."

"I'm not following you," Anna said.

"What if the wall of snow led us to a parallel universe?" he said.

"A parallel universe that has only gotten to the Middle Ages instead of 2010?"

"Sure."

"You've read too much science fiction," she said.

David actually smiled. "Now, *that's* not possible," he said.

Anna put her head in her hands, not wanting to believe it. David picked up a stick and begin digging in the dirt at his feet. He stabbed the stick into the ground between them again and again, twisting it around until it stuck there, upright. Anna studied it, then reached over, pulled it out, and threw it into the fire in front of them.

"Hey!" David said.

Anna turned on him. "Are we ever going to be able to go home again?" she asked. "How could this have happened to us? Why has this happened to us? Do you even realize how appalling this all is?"

David opened his mouth to speak, perhaps to protest that she shouldn't be angry at *him*, but at that moment, a man came out of the far tent and approached them. Instead of addressing them, however, he looked over their heads to someone behind them and spoke. At his words, two men grasped David and Anna by their upper arms and lifted them to their feet. The first man turned back to the tent and their captors hustled them after him. At the entrance, the man indicated they should enter. David put his hand on the small of Anna's back and urged her forward.

She ducked through the entrance, worried about what she might find, but it was only the wounded man from the meadow, reclining among blankets on the ground. He no longer wore his armor, but had on a cream colored shirt. A blanket covered him to his waist. Several candles, guttering in shallow dishes, lit the tent, and the remains of a meal sat on a plate beside him. He took a sip from a small cup, and looked at them over the top of it.

The tent held one other man, this one still in full armor, and he gestured them closer. They walked to the wounded man and knelt by his side. He gave them a long look, set down his cup, and then pointed to himself.

"Llywelyn ap Gruffydd," he said.

Anna knew she looked blank, but she simply couldn't accept his words. He tried again, thinking they hadn't understood. "Llywelyn—ap—Gruffydd."

"Llywelyn ap Gruffydd," David and Anna said together, the words passing Anna's lips as if they belonged to someone else.

Llywelyn nodded. "You understand who I am?" he asked, again in Welsh. Anna's neck was having a hard time bending forward and she barely got her chin to bob in acknowledgement. She was frozen in a nightmare that wouldn't let her go.

David recovered more quickly. "You are the Prince of Wales," he said. "Thank you, my lord, for bringing us with you. We would be lost without your assistance."

15

"It is I who should be thanking you," he said.

Anna had allowed them to continue speaking, growing colder and colder with every sentence. Llywelyn eyes flicked to her face and she could read the concern in them. Finally, she took in a deep breath, accepting for now what she couldn't deny.

"My lord," she said, "Could you please tell us the date?"

"Certainly," he said. "It is the day of Damasus the Pope, Friday, the 11ᵗʰ of December."

David's face paled as he realized the importance of the question, but Anna was determined to get the whole truth out and wasn't going to stop pressing because he was finally having the same heart attack she was. "And the year?" Anna asked.

"The year of our Lord twelve hundred and eighty-two," Llywelyn said.

Anna nodded. "You remember the story now, don't you, David?" she said in English, her voice a whisper because to speak her thoughts more loudly would give them greater credence. David couldn't have forgotten it any more readily than she could. Their mother had told them stories about medieval Wales since before they could walk—and tales of this man in particular. "Llywelyn ap Gruffydd was lured into a trap by some English lords and killed on December 11, 1282 near a place called Cilmeri. Except ..." Anna kept her eyes fixed on Llywelyn's.

"Except we just saved his life," David said.

2

It just wasn't possible. None of it. David stared into the fire. The kindling popped and the sparks flew above the trees. In his head, he went over the trip from Aunt Elisa's house, crossing the black abyss, watching the men go under the wheels. It didn't look as if Anna had yet absorbed the fact that she'd driven the van into three people and killed them. David glanced at her out of the corner of his eye. He wasn't going to remind her if she hadn't thought of it. She tended to be rather single-minded, and right now other things were more important.

Can we really be in the Middle Ages? If he and Anna were really in the Middle Ages, everything David had ever thought was true might not be. *What about the laws of physics? Mathematics?* David could understand Anna's anger and despair, but didn't know what to tell her.

He looked up as a lone man rode off the trail to the right, stopping at the edge of the clearing, his horse lathered. Two men-at-arms ran to him as he dismounted. One grabbed the horse's reins and led it away, towards the trees where the rest of the horses were picketed, but the other walked with him to Llywelyn's tent and disappeared inside.

Llywelyn ap Gruffydd. David repeated the name, trying to recall everything his mother had ever told him about Wales or he'd gleaned from the bits of her research he'd paid attention to. It *was* her specialty after all. His mother should have been there instead of him and Anna. She'd *kill* to have been there instead of them.

David ran his hand through his hair, clenching his fists as if that would help him sort out his thoughts. They'd arrived in Wales smack in the middle of a war between the Welsh and the English. In fact, Llywelyn's death tonight would have nearly ended it.

Llywelyn had traveled south to Cilmeri to try to bolster support for his cause while his brother, Dafydd, was supposed to continue Llywelyn's campaign in the north. Instead, in the old world, Llywelyn died when the Mortimers lured him away from the bulk of his army. They ambushed and slaughtered him and eighteen of his men. Edward then killed or imprisoned all of Llywelyn's family. Once Edward caught Dafydd, he had him hanged, drawn, and quartered before dragging what remained of his body behind a horse through the streets of Shrewsbury.

Edward crushed Wales so completely and successfully, it may not have been possible for Llywelyn to have held it together even if he'd lived. *What is going to happen now?* David shook his head at the thought that he and Anna were going to have a front row seat in finding out.

"I cannot *believe* this," Anna said.

After their meal of meat and bread, she and David had curled up facing each other, with the blankets pulled to their chins. "This can't be real. How can we be in the thirteenth century?"

"It isn't very warm, is it?" David said, shifting uncomfortably to find a spot that was slightly less rocky. The woolen blankets were scratchy and the ground *really* hard—that one year in boy scouts when the winter jamboree occurred in the middle of a snowstorm had not prepared David for sleeping outside without even a tent.

"No central heating, no pasteurized milk, no antibiotics! David! We could die out here from a hangnail!"

"It's worse than that," David said. "They don't have a lot of stuff we depend upon, but in addition, nobody here knows anything about the way the world works. The printing press wasn't invented until the 1430s, we've got the Inquisition coming up in another two hundred years, and we are nearly five hundred years from the Age of Enlightenment. Don't even get me started on the black plague." David closed his eyes, trying to push these thoughts away.

"But—" Anna said.

David kept his eyes closed, resolutely ignoring her. She grumbled to herself but didn't bother him again and eventually they fell asleep. Both of them woke some time later. But where David was merely cold, Anna trembled and gasped for breath. The top blanket had slipped, so he pulled it over their shoulders and shifted to his side. "You were dreaming," he said, watching her through slitted eyes. "Want to tell me about it?"

19

She didn't answer at first, and he thought she might be punishing him for his earlier silence, but then she must have decided she didn't need to keep it from him. "It was a jumble of men on horses, riding fast, and bloody swords swinging my way," she said. "It wasn't really coherent." Anna tried to hold back sobs, her fist stuffed in her mouth.

At home, whenever they'd had bad dreams they'd always gone to Mom. Since their dad had died before David was born, she'd slept alone in a big bed in the room next to his. Not that David had gone to her in several years, but whether he was two or ten, she'd roll over and tuck him in beside her for the rest of the night. This time Mom was too far away to help. There was only David and he was afraid he wasn't going to do Anna much good.

David turned onto his back, Anna's head on his shoulder. She fell asleep again, but David lay there, awake and restless. His feet kept twitching; it was strange to go to sleep while wearing shoes. At least he wore waterproof brown hiking boots, pulled on at the last minute before he left the house because of the snow. His sneakers would have looked ridiculous in thirteenth century Wales.

David turned his head to study the other men. Every so often he caught the glint of the fire off metal and realized that a sentry had passed by, patrolling the camp near the edge of the woods. At one point, the soldier who'd been with Llywelyn in the tent pushed open the flap and came out. He stood, his hands on his hips, helmetless, surveying the sleeping men. For a moment it seemed that his eyes met David's, but he was too far away, and it was probably just a trick of the light.

A man lying on the ground to David's right grunted, scratching his chest in his sleep, and another thought occurred to David—one that nearly made him choke: If this was the Middle Ages, then he was responsible for Anna. It was his job to protect her, maybe even from men such as these. In this world, a woman had no rights or status without a man, whether father, husband, or brother. *How can that man be me?*

David hardly ever talked to her, really. She was three and a half years older and three years ahead of him in school. Their lives almost never intersected in or out of the classroom, not with homework, sports, and totally different friends getting in the way. They took karate together, but that was it. *When was the last time we had a real conversation before today?* David couldn't remember.

More scared than he'd been since Anna drove the van into the clearing, David hugged his sister to him. The stars were fully out now. They were beautiful beyond reckoning and yet, unfamiliar. In the end, there were more than David could count, but he tried.

3

Anna drifted off to sleep with David's arm wrapped around her and found herself back in a nightmare, though this time as her mother.

I enter my hotel room just as my cell phone rings. I think it's Anna and clear my mind, putting away the talk I've just heard on medieval trade. It's not Anna, though, but Elisa whose voice I hear.

"Meg!" she sobs into the phone.

"What is it?" I ask, imagining the worst, as mothers do. And the worst it is.

"Anna and David have disappeared! I sent them to pick up Christopher but they never arrived and nobody has seen them."

"I'm coming now," I say, glancing at my watch. 8 o'clock. "Have you called the police?"

"Right before I called you," she says.

I put down the phone and lean forward over the bed, my hands supporting my weight. My breath quickens and I swallow hard, trying to hold down the panic and the tears. Where are they? What could they be doing? I dial Anna's cell phone number, but her phone doesn't ring, immediately switching to her messaging. I try David's number with the same result. I snap the phone shut, my eyes closed.

It takes me an hour to get to Bryn Mawr from my hotel. The train is late and packed with commuters. I find myself hiding my face from the other passengers in case I disturb them with my tears. I call Elisa every ten minutes, my hands shaking as I dial the phone, but each time Elisa answers with 'I'm sorry'.

Elisa meets me at the station and drives me back to her house. A police car sits in the driveway where Elisa usually parks the van and an officer stands near the front stoop, talking with Elisa's husband, Ted. I get out of the car and the policeman turns to me, eyes narrowed.

"I'll need a description of your children," he says. "Have they run away before?"

I put a hand to my mouth, trying to hold in a cry ...

"Anna!" She opened her eyes. David's concerned face hovered above her.

"Dreaming of swords again?" David asked.

Anna shook her head. "Mom," she said. She massaged her temples with her fingers, still lost in the dream, while at the same time trying to push it away. This kind of dream was always the worst: so tangible and terrible that she always woke up relieved it hadn't happened in real life.

Anna sat up. The stars were gone and the sky was growing paler with the coming dawn. Someone had stoked the fire and men ate near it. Others checked the horses and prepared their saddlebags, but there seemed fewer men than the night before. Anna swallowed, her throat dry, and wondered about a bathroom.

Suddenly resolute, she stood up, studied the surrounding forest, bracing herself for the inevitable, and strode off into the woods.

"Where are you going?" David asked.

Anna waved a hand at him without turning around, "I have to pee!"

Behind her, David laughed, but Anna surely wasn't laughing. Wherever they were going would be better than this, right? Didn't castles have outhouses? And cloth instead of frozen leaves?

David had acquired food by the time Anna returned. He handed her a length of dried meat. She nibbled at it but her stomach had that nauseous feeling that too little sleep can leave. David had no compunctions at all. He laid into his meal with all the enthusiasm of a starving fourteen-year-old boy. Watching him eat, Anna recalled with horror another tidbit about Welsh culture:

David was fourteen and therefore considered a man by Welsh law. Appalling thought.

"Sorry about earlier."

"About what?" Anna asked.

"Laughing at you, I mean."

"Oh," she said.

"We're going to have to stick together," he said. "This is going to be . . ." he paused, searching for the words, "really, really difficult." Anna turned her head to see his face, but he was looking past her. He bowed slightly, and Anna followed his gaze.

Sure enough, Llywelyn himself limped towards them. He held out his hand to David who stood to greet him. David gripped his forearm as Anna had seen other men do. When Llywelyn released him, he turned to Anna and unfolded an expanse of fabric he'd tucked under his arm. He swung the cloak around her shoulders, enveloping her from head to foot. Anna hugged it to her, warm for the first time since they'd arrived.

The men prepared to depart and this time David and Anna got to stay together, with him in the saddle and her riding pillion behind him. They trotted out of the clearing and onto the same path the company had traveled up the day before. When the sun rose, so low in the sky it was barely there, it became clear they were headed north, which made sense if their destination was Llywelyn's home.

"It's beautiful here," David said, after a while.

Although Anna was having a hard time seeing past her own misery, she had to admit that the snow-covered mountains were spectacular.

"No cars, no machines, power lines, houses, or garbage," she said, for once agreeing with him. "But why can't we understand better what they're saying?"

"It's middle Welsh," David said. "Didn't you—" he stopped himself as he remembered who'd been willing to sit through another Welsh language class and who hadn't.

"No," Anna said. "I took German."

"Useful language, German," David said. "Especially about now."

Crap.

That evening, they camped beside the trail as before. This time, Anna needed no help getting off the horse, but then was left alone on the edge of the camp, uncertain. Her rear hurt so badly she couldn't bear the thought of sitting, so she stood and tried to stretch without calling attention to herself.

Once David had seen to the horse, he found her again. "You okay?" he asked.

Anna stared at him for a second, befuddled. *Okay? How could he even ask such a question? Of course I'm not okay and neither is he.* She didn't answer she was so irritated, but then realized he was trying to be understanding, in his limited way, and relented.

"I survived the day and am still upright," she said. David nodded, and awkwardly put his arm around her shoulder. He *was* trying. He didn't stay beside her long, though, because the grizzled man from the day before called him over: "Dafydd!"

David blinked, but did as he was bid. The man stood in the middle of a large open space and held a long stick in his hand, which he tossed to David. He shouted something, the Welsh equivalent of *en garde!* and David brought his stick up as if it was a sword. Anna almost laughed, but stopped herself because nobody else was laughing. A dozen men stood nearby, watching intently. It was unbelievable and right out of a fantasy film. Anna could think of at least three movies where such a scene occurred and was willing to bet David knew them too.

For an hour, David stabbed and parried, twisted and lunged. He looked competent, but as Anna had nothing but the movies to judge him by, she doubted their accuracy. Several men patted David on the shoulder afterwards, however, so perhaps he had done well.

David sat beside her at dinner, disheveled and hot from his exertions. "It was a lot harder than I expected," he said.

"Not quite like the battles you have with your friends?" Anna asked, trying to keep the mocking out of her voice and undoubtedly not succeeding.

David glanced at her, and then smiled. Anna was glad to see it. "I think it's going to be okay," he said. "I think I can do this."

Again his words startled Anna. *Do what? And what about me?*

Her primary concern was what Prince Llywelyn thought about them. She desperately wanted to talk to him because their continued survival depended on his good will. Her mother's stories about the Middle Ages were a far cry from actually living in them.

Anna was particularly concerned about David finding a place here. He was really smart, but would anyone recognize it? The Welsh wouldn't have any use for his computer skills or his encyclopedic knowledge of dinosaurs. It wasn't as if he'd taken any engineering courses and could build them a steam engine; and how was anyone to know how smart he was if all they wanted him to do was learn how to handle a sword? He wouldn't even make a good clerk, since his writing was illegible and when he did write it was in American English, not Latin, French, or Welsh. As an alternative, what did he know about farming? Or animal husbandry?

These problems nagged at Anna constantly. She was too freaked out to worry about herself, but as she lay on the ground beside David after the second day of riding, unable to sleep, David revealed that he was worrying about her.

"They're going to want to marry you off to someone pretty quick, you know," he said.

Anna rolled over and punched him in the side. "So, how's your sword fighting coming?" she asked.

That evening, Prince Llywelyn had graduated David to a real sword. He'd buckled it on immediately and Anna was pretty sure he had it tucked under the blanket with him.

"I'm serious!" David insisted, rolling over to face her. "How are you going to handle that? You're only seventeen!"

"I know, David," Anna said. "I remember from things Mom said that women aren't quite as oppressed in Wales as elsewhere in this day and age, but I don't remember exactly what that means."

"I can tell you what it means," David said. "If Prince Llywelyn thinks you ought to marry someone, neither of us are going to have any say in the matter. You do what your lord says and that's that."

"Maybe when we get to wherever we're going—"

"Castell y Bere," David interrupted.

"How do you know that?" Anna asked.

"I overheard the men talking about it earlier."

Anna glared at him, disgusted. "I don't know why I put up with you. You're going to have middle Welsh completely mastered within the week!"

"Well, maybe . . . not quite . . . and that isn't going to help us tomorrow when we arrive," David pointed out.

"And I suppose you just 'overheard' that too, didn't you?"

Even in the flickering firelight, Anna could see that David was trying unsuccessfully to look modest. "I guess so," he said.

"Maybe," Anna said, "if we learn Welsh fast enough I can talk to Prince Llywelyn about what happened with the van, and tell him what the future would have held for Wales if we hadn't killed those men."

"Maybe," said David. "Either that or he'll think you're a witch and burn you at the stake." And with that helpful thought, he wrapped his arm around her for warmth, and they both went to sleep.

* * * * *

The company reached Castell y Bere the next afternoon. The castle sat on a high promontory with commanding views of the valley below and the mountains in the distance. During the two hours between spotting it and reaching it, it acted as a beacon. Anna's thoughts focused on hot fires and warm food. New snow slowed the trip down and it was a steep climb to the impressive and elaborate main gate. They finally clattered through it into a crowd of men, women, and children who waited to greet the company.

Anna slid off the horse onto packed dirt and looked for David. She caught his eye but Hywel, one of the boys who'd cared for the horses during the trip, grabbed his arm and pointed towards a long, low building squatting against the curtain wall. *The stables?* David shrugged and waved. "Later," he mouthed.

Anna edged away, trying to be inconspicuous, and found a wall to stand against. So many people milled about, all talking at once, that she wished she could hide. Without looking her way, Prince Llywelyn disappeared into the keep with two older men, one of whom had looked at her as if he'd wanted to speak before turning away. *What is to become of us?*

After five minutes of total insecurity, an older woman standing near the entrance to the hall beckoned to Anna. She felt an intense longing to turn around and head back down the road. It had been a long, fairly unpleasant journey, but she'd grown accustomed to it. The familiar seemed infinitely more desirable than the unknown that now faced her.

The woman introduced herself as Bronwen and greeted Anna with a slight bow and a smile. With Anna trailing after her like a lost duckling, Bronwen led her into the keep, across the great hall, down a corridor and up some stairs to another corridor, to a room occupied by several young women. A fire blazed at the far end and Anna stood close to it, grateful to be indoors at last. Bronwen said something to the women and they giggled, before they filed from the room, leaving Anna alone with Bronwen.

Talking the whole time, Bronwen looked Anna up and down and then opened a chest set against the wall. From it, she pulled a dark green dress, surely borrowed from someone else, a girdle, a linen shift, a corset, a petticoat to go over that, stockings, slipper-like shoes, and a cloak, and laid them on the bed.

Anna looked at the clothes. They were pretty and clean, but Anna clutched her cloak to her. She felt awful. It seemed that if she agreed to take off her clothes and put on these, she would cease to be Anna and would become someone even she didn't know. Her clothes were dirty and she'd never worn the same thing for more than two days in a row, much less four, but these clothes were *hers*.

Her hands clasped in front of her, Bronwen waited. There was no help for it. Anna undressed completely, shivering despite the fire. Bronwen clucked her tongue at Anna's underclothes, which must have seemed totally bizarre to her, but once Anna removed them, Bronwen dressed her from the inside out. Then she sat Anna on a stool and began to brush her hair. Anna was so tired she settled into it, to the point that her head fell forward with every stroke.

Bronwen braided Anna's hair in two braids and twisted them onto the top of her head. To this, she pinned a piece of cloth that went from ear to ear but left Anna's face uncovered. Anna stood and Bronwen walked around her to get a view from all sides. She tweaked the dress here and there, but it fit very well. Anna wondered whose dress it was and if the owner begrudged the loan. If she did nothing else, Anna resolved to find her and thank her as soon as she could.

Finally, Bronwen nodded, satisfied. She took Anna's arm and steered her through the door and back down the stairs to the entrance to the great hall. When they reached the doorway, however, Anna found it impossible to enter. At least a hundred people sat at the tables, and every single one was looking at her. Prince Llywelyn sat at a raised table at the head of the room. Two long tables perpendicular to his extended down the hall. David was near the head of one of them, with space left beside him. Trying to ignore the looks she was getting, Anna hurried over to him and sat down.

"Where did you go?" she said. "Is everything okay?"

"I think so. Hywel took me to the stables to take care of my horse and then he showed me to a room where I could wash. He even brought me these clothes," he said, looking down at himself.

Anna inspected him. He wore a cream-colored tunic, a deep blue over-tunic that matched his eyes, and a pair of brown pants, along with his own brown leather boots, which were out of place, but not too dramatically different. David had cleaned his face and hands, but a ring of dirt adorned his neck where he hadn't scrubbed, and his hair really needed a wash. Anna decided not to mention it.

"What are we eating?" she asked, noting that most of the diners were nearly finished.

"We have some kind of meat, along with vegetables I've never seen before. And wine," he said, significantly.

"Have you had any?"

"Nope."

"Do they have water?"

"I don't know," he said. "If they have a well the water ought to be fine."

He tapped the man next to him, and introduced him as Bevyn. Anna greeted him and then couldn't help staring. He had the most humongous set of mustachios she'd ever seen, not that she'd seen any before arriving in Wales. For some reason, Welsh men wore mustaches but no beards, not even in winter. Bevyn's mustaches grew long, thick, and immaculately curled along each cheek. It was an amazing sight and Anna found herself fighting the giggles. *Okay, just a little punchy here, don't mind me.*

David said something to Bevyn that Anna didn't catch, except for the "dŵr", meaning 'water'. Bevyn replied, twisted in his seat, and signaled to a serving boy who ran off and came back with a pitcher of water and a cup. It was marvelous what knowing the language could do! Anna was going to have to contrive some way to keep David around.

She ate a full portion of food and before long, felt hot and sleepy, even without the alcohol. Anna tried to stay awake by examining other individuals in the room: what clothes they wore, their hair styles, their position at the tables, trying to imagine what their stories were. Thankfully, there was a lot of laughter and talk and nobody was paying any attention to the two of them. After what seemed like hours, Prince Llywelyn got to his feet. The hall quieted and he began to speak.

He told a lengthy tale, mentioning their names several times which prompted everyone to look at them again. David studied Prince Llywelyn and ignored the others. Anna wanted to slump in her seat but refused to succumb to the urge. At last, Prince Llywelyn finished and silence descended on the hall. Abruptly, David got to his feet and pulled Anna with him.

"He wants us out there. Just do what I do!" he whispered.

They walked around the table to stand in front of Prince Llywelyn. David bowed, and belatedly Anna made what she thought was a curtsy, thankful for her 'princess' period between the ages of six and eight when it was something she'd practiced in front of a mirror, for just such an occasion. She guessed it was acceptable because Prince Llywelyn took a step and held out both hands, slightly apart. David knelt on one knee and put his hands between Prince Llywelyn's.

Prince Llywelyn spoke a few words and murmur of approval went around the hall. Then it was Anna's turn. Then Prince Llywelyn sent them back to their seats, and signaled for music to begin. Anna and David settled on the bench again.

"What do you think that speech was about?" she asked. "What did we just do?"

"I think Prince Llywelyn gave some version of how we came to be on that hill with him," David said, "and we pledged our allegiance to him. Hopefully, we're his responsibility now, because I hate to think about being thrown out in the cold."

"I'm pretty sure that as long as we don't betray Prince Llywelyn, he'll take care of us."

"Let's hope so," David said.

"What do you think will happen next?" Anna said.

"I don't know," David said. "I'm as much at a loss as you."

4

"Keep your guard up," Bevyn said.

Dutifully, David raised his wooden sword above his head, two hands on the hilt, ready for another attack by Dai, a boy bigger than he was (as most of them were), and nearly two years older.

"Now!" Bevyn said, and they met in the middle of the practice ring, set in the courtyard of the castle. The courtyard sloped in a northerly direction, and as Bevyn had taught, David tried to maneuver onto the higher ground

Anna might have been having difficulties with the whole sewing thing—she'd spent the last twelve evenings complaining about living here: having to spend all day in the women's solar, the gossip she didn't understand, the lack of showers, the lack of Mom, which David could appreciate—but David didn't see how it could compare to what he had to deal with every day. Not only was he having to learn three new languages at once: Welsh, French, and the god-awful Latin, but he actually had to *fight* boys every day—and have the adults in authority think it was perfectly fine.

So, David was a black belt in karate. *Okay, yeah—that was really helpful.* David *knew* how to fight, both fairly and unfairly, and he wasn't having trouble holding his own in hand-to-hand combat. In fact, nobody wanted to fight him anymore and Bevyn was having him teach the boys a few things. It was the sword fighting and the quarterstaff that were another matter entirely.

"*Thwack; thwack; thwack.*" Their swords met, little splinters flying off as they hacked at each other. David had done all right that first session around the fire on the road to Castell y Bere, but in the daily grind of squire practice, his inadequacies and inexperience were bare for everyone to see. There were *rules* for how to swordfight, attacks and counter attacks and strategy, none of which he knew.

Dai's weapon smashed into his fingers. "Merde!" David swore in French and dropped his sword as, despite his exertions, his hands were freezing in their fingerless gloves and only more painful now that Dai's attack had nearly severed them. Once he became a knight—*Ha! If I became a knight, as if the thought wasn't entirely ludicrous under the circumstances—* David would wear gauntlets to protect the back of his hands, but no one had issued him any yet, the worse for him.

"You became distracted by your footing," Bevyn said. He gestured to the ground where David's sword lay and David bent over to pick it up. "You were not attentive."

"Yes, sir," David said, resisting the temptation to roll his eyes, knowing that Bevyn was right. Every one of these boys had at least five or six years of experience in sword fighting on him—

lightsaber fighting with his friends didn't count—and David was woefully behind.

"Try again," Bevyn said.

Dai and David faced each other. Dai was sweating despite the cold, and perhaps because he so badly wanted to beat David. Dai was the boy David had dropped to the ground that first day at wrestling and he'd not forgiven him.

They hacked away at each other for another ten minutes, ending in a draw this time. Finally warm enough, David pulled off his woolen jersey and stood in his linen tunic. It was soaked with sweat and steam came off his torso.

Bevyn nodded, gave David a quick nod of his head, and slapped his hand on David's left shoulder as he passed, heading to the keep. "Good," he said.

David turned to watch as Bevyn strode across the courtyard.

"He said 'good'?" Owain, a tall lanky boy, came to stand next to David. "He never says 'good'! The best I've ever gotten is a grunt. Christmas must have gotten the better of him!"

David shrugged. "Maybe he's encouraged by the fact that I managed to hold onto my sword. He's happy that I don't appear completely hopeless."

"You're not hopeless," Owain said. "Dai is second only to Fychan in ability with the sword. You've been with us only a few weeks and you're younger than any of us. It will come."

"Thanks, Owain," David said, surprised at the sudden camaraderie of shared experience. He'd felt so alone since they'd arrived at Castell y Bere, isolated in his difference and lack of Welsh, scrabbling so hard to catch up he'd not even thought he could make friends.

The two boys turned to walk together toward the stables where their horses waited. Mom had indulged Anna with a 'horse phase' for about a year when she was eleven, and David had been given riding lessons too. There was a big difference, however, between riding sedately around a ring and galloping across the Welsh countryside with a shield in one hand and reins in the other. So much of what the boys were learning had to do with riding using no hands at all, just signaling with the knees.

David loved his horse though. He was big and black—bigger than he wanted now, but Bevyn was convinced David would grow a lot taller and Taranis would fit him then. David only knew that he was proportioned all wrong, with too long legs and a ridiculously short torso. He was as short as Anna when he sat down, but his shins alone were three inches longer than hers! *Humiliating.*

With only thirty men-at-arms housed at Castell y Bere, they were under-manned, and the stables, a long, low building which hid the postern gate, was only half full. The stable boys worked hard all day long, trucking manure and hay out of the stables, making clean beds for the horses, cleaning them, brushing them, and saddling them—and yet, for Hywel, born a poor shepherd boy, this was an advancement, and would provide him with a secure future for his entire life.

If Llywelyn lives through this war, that is.

Typically, all the men and boys threw themselves at the food when it appeared at dinner, and were in bed not long afterwards. Books and movies of medieval times often depicted feasting in the great hall as a long drawn-out affair, and while the meals could last for a couple of hours, people didn't usually eat that whole time. It was just that there was nowhere else to go in the castle, so people sat around, munching and drinking until it was time to sleep, often on the floor of the great hall itself. David had done it a couple of times, when the barracks were particularly cold, and thought it not so bad, especially compared to sleeping on the rocky ground outside.

Taranis whickered as Owain and David walked into the stables. David stroked his nose, telling him what a good boy he was.

"What did you say?" Owain asked.

"I told him he was beautiful and fast and we would have a fine ride today," David said.

"Tell him so in Welsh," Owain said. "He's a Welsh horse and needs Welsh words."

David ducked his head, embarrassed. *There is too much to learn; too much I do wrong by instinct, and no time to make it right.*

"Let's go, boys!" Maredudd, Bevyn's second in command, shouted into the stables. One by one, they led the horses out of their stalls, across the courtyard, and down to the first gatehouse (Castell y Bere had two), situated on the western approach to the castle. Because of the uneven ground, horsemen usually didn't mount until they were near the gate. It was as easy for a horse to misstep and go lame as it was for a man to turn an ankle, and the horses were, quite frankly, more valuable than boys.

As always, Cadair Idris rose high to the northeast of the castle, a spectacular mountain peak in a country of beautiful mountains. Clouds circled it and David wondered about the possibility of more snow. They would ride on patrol regardless of the weather. Rain or snow made no difference if the Welsh were to keep the English at bay.

This day, however, was a special day. Everyone had breakfasted on the remains of the Christmas feast, and now the boys, along with a dozen noblemen *and* Prince Llywelyn, were going to hunt boar, apparently a tradition the day after Christmas. Anna's comment when she'd heard about it resounded in David's ears: *That sounds about right. Good will and peace to all men, and now, let's kill a giant pig!*

Christmas had not been wonderful, other than the singing, which David had enjoyed. Anna's misery at her own predicament, no presents, followed by thoughts of Mom's lonely Christmas, had pretty much put paid to anything in the way of good cheer for him.

Prince Llywelyn stepped out of the keep just as Hywel brought his horse from the stables. Everyone mounted—eight boys, ranging in age from fourteen to eighteen, Bevyn, Maredudd, Prince Llywelyn, and the other noblemen most of whose names David had a hard time remembering (they were all named either Owain, Gruffydd, Hywel, or Rhys anyway, as were their fathers)—and headed down the long, twisting road to the valley floor below

Castell y Bere. Trackers, handlers who would control the hunting dogs, and stable boys who'd hold the horses once they found the boar, came too.

They rode in two lines, each paired with another rider. Dai and Fychan always led the group, and today David maneuvered to a position that allowed him to ride with Owain. He was perhaps two years older than David, the son of one of Prince Llywelyn's cousins. Genealogy was incredibly important to the Welsh, but that (and Latin verb forms) was something David was having a difficult time getting his head around. Plus, as with Latin, he didn't care. As far as was relevant here, David had no genealogy at all, so it always made for awkward conversation.

In what village were you born?

Uh.

Who was your grandfather on your mother's side?

Uh.

Fychan had taken to whacking David up the back of the head on his way by, while saying "Who's your da? Who's your da?" When David didn't answer, he would sneer and say, "Dafydd hasn't got a da!" For all practical purposes, that was true in both this world and the old one, which certainly didn't make David feel any better. While his mother had been married to his father, even if David were illegitimate it would have been okay here, as long as his father acknowledged him. David didn't even have that consolation.

They reached the valley floor and reformed the group, as it had become stretched out in too long a line. Amazingly, Prince

Llywelyn himself approached and aligned his horse with Owain's. Owain and David bowed their heads, a little awed to have him in such close proximity. He looked well, with no apparent after effects of the fight at Cilmeri.

Prince Llywelyn spoke. "The English are known to have quartered in the north for the Christmas feast, and the scouts report that we should remain undisturbed today," he said.

David glanced at Owain, but he seemed struck dumb by this conversation opener, so it was left to David to keep it going. "Will we meet them soon?" he asked.

"Soon enough," Prince Llywelyn said. "Is your spear sharpened?"

"Yes," David said. "Bevyn tells us we're ready."

The Prince nodded. "I would have you watch yourself today," he said. "A boar is a dangerous beast and not the easiest first hunt."

"If I were Bevyn, I wouldn't want to rely on me," David said. "I don't know enough."

Prince Llywelyn raised his eyebrows. "Then I suggest you learn faster," he said. He spurred his horse away.

Owain sputtered at Llywelyn's back, perhaps wanting to protest on David's behalf, but it merely left David speechless, not only at his words, but at the wink that had taken some of the sting out of them.

"Twice in one day?" Owain said, once the Prince was out of earshot.

"What do you mean?" David asked.

43

"First Bevyn and now the Prince took the time to speak to you today. I've lived among the Prince's entourage for three years and that's the first time he's looked at me directly."

"And you didn't answer!" David said.

"Of course not! What was I supposed to say? He was talking to you anyway."

"Why?" David asked, finally putting voice to the question that had nagged him since that first sword fighting experience on the road from Cilmeri. *Why are they bothering with me? Why am I not a stable boy like Hywel?*

Owain shrugged. "Because you're smarter than the rest of us combined?"

Like that counted for anything? The lessons with the priest after breakfast, other than the impossible Latin, were the basics: reading, writing, and arithmetic. It was astounding, really, that they were learning anything academic at all, but it was important to the Prince that the future knights of his household were even mildly educated. That David was learning to speak, read, and write three unfamiliar languages simultaneously was incredibly challenging for him, but that wasn't what was impressive to the Welsh. The nobility learned multiple languages routinely.

It was his ability to do all the math in his head as well as his grounding in philosophy that startled them—just the fact that David had *heard* of Plato and Aristotle and could describe their philosophical positions. He knew how to *think* and discuss abstractly. It was all thanks to his mom, really, but David couldn't tell them that.

At first, David didn't even speak up in class, partly because he didn't know this middle version of Welsh well enough, and partly because he didn't want them to think he was smart and send him in the direction of becoming a priest or monk. David might not think sword-fighting was the best job ever, but it was better than sitting in a scriptorium for the rest of his life, copying books. Then again, they'd seen his handwriting, so probably that job was a non-starter from the beginning.

The company headed north from the castle, crossing a stream about a quarter mile from the road. Taranis got wet, but only up to his knees. David made a mental note to make sure he rubbed him down particularly well when they got home. The riders continued northeast, skirting the mountains that fronted the valley to the north, and following the Cadair River east. They spread out, more than they would have if looking for the English, and kept an eye out for traces of a boar.

Once under the trees, they slowed and the tracker got down from his horse. Owain had told David that they wouldn't be here today unless he'd found the boar last night, in preparation for this morning's hunt. Boars are nocturnal. In winter, the adult males live alone so the intent was to approach his burrow, roust him out, surround him, and let him charge. What could be more fun than that?

A rustling sound came from the right. A thicket screened whatever made the noise, but David turned, finding the spear looser in his hand and slipping in his sweaty palm. David had carried it straight upright, its base resting in a leather cup near his

45

right leg, but now pulled it out and held it, javelin like, in his right hand.

"Steady," Bevyn said. The dogs bayed. Their handlers pulled them back and unleashed the larger hunters—at least one of which was a mastiff.

"Dismount," Prince Llywelyn said. Everyone obeyed, trying to hurry, leading their horses away from the scene and handing them to the servants. David gave Taranis' reins to Hywel.

"Good luck, sir!" he said.

David decided it wasn't the time to remind Hywel that David was no more noble than he was. Heart pounding, David took his place in the semicircle of men, spaced some three feet apart, spears out, waiting for the boar to come out of his bush.

The dogs barked in a cacophony now. They had pushed through the brush to find their prey. The branches rustled and a dog backed through a hole in the bush. Another dog squealed. At the sound, David hefted his spear again, and just to be on the safe side, pulled his sword from its sheath to hold in his left hand. He was near the far left of the circle, with an older man on one side and Bevyn on the other.

"Steady, lad," Bevyn said. "Hold your spear low, not over your shoulder. You open yourself up to his tusk that way."

David shifted position and the next second, a huge boar—maybe five feet long and nearly two hundred pounds of compact, angry pig—burst out of the bushes in front of them, scattering branches and throwing off a dog that he'd impaled. As one, the men crouched to face him. He squealed and grunted, no longer advancing and still distracted by the dogs.

"Now!" The Prince shouted.

Half of the men, including Bevyn, threw their spears at the same time. Yet the boar must have thought the Prince was talking to him because as the men threw, he charged toward the center of the ring of men. Two of the spears hit—one on the right shoulder, another in the left rear. Perhaps because of them, the boar changed direction at the last second and turned toward where Bevyn and David stood.

Bevyn pulled out his sword. David had dropped his in the snow, once he saw the size of the boar. He held his spear with two hands, bracing himself to ram it into the boar because his only alternative was to drop it and run. Another spear hit the boar, low on the right side of his neck. He opened his mouth to squeal. David squealed too, though his throat was so full of spit and fear no sound came out. At that moment, the Prince appeared on David's right and grasped his spear with both hands.

"Ready?"

"Ready!" David said, though nothing could have been further from the truth. He and the Prince threw themselves forward just as the boar charged—and rammed himself onto their spear, straight down its gullet.

The boar's momentum carried it past David, knocking him sideways as he released the spear. David rolled, arms over his head. Boar and boy came to rest no more than six inches from each other. David opened his eyes in time to stare into the boar's brown ones before the life left them.

"Are you all right, son?" Prince Llywelyn fell to his knees beside David, patting him all over to make sure he wasn't bleeding anywhere. David carefully sat up, feeling his arms and legs. His heart still pounded, but he grinned at the Prince.

"I'm alive!" David said, not thinking about who could hear him and how juvenile that sounded.

"I'm glad to hear it," Prince Llywelyn said, in the same dry tone he'd used with David earlier. "First hunt, indeed." He helped David to his feet and handed him his sword. "I suppose Bevyn could rely on you after all."

"Yes, he could," Bevyn said, "and did." He tousled David's hair and then the three watched as the handlers soaked a cloth in the boar's blood to satisfy the hunger of the dogs and call them off the hunt. It turned David's stomach and he glanced away. He didn't want to watch the preparations to move the boar and bring him back to the castle.

"What a great day," the Prince said, looking down at David. He gave him a wicked grin. "Makes one glad to be alive, doesn't it?" Prince Llywelyn walked toward the other noblemen who gathered on the other side of the boar to mount their horses.

"Can you ride?" Bevyn said.

"Am I that pale?" David said.

"Yes." Bevyn whistled to Hywel, who'd been watching and now hurried over with Taranis. "Exhilaration comes first, then chills as the energy drains from you. When it is a man you've killed, the next emotion is revulsion, perhaps nausea, but this is a boar, an evil creature. Don't allow his death to trouble you that way."

"Yes, sir," David said.

Back at the castle, David dismounted, even more exhausted than he usually was after patrol because, as Bevyn had warned, the adrenaline had seeped away, leaving him shivering and weak.

"Go and rest," Owain said. "I'll rub down Taranis."

David shook his head. "Thanks, Owain, but I'll do it. I'll feel better when I'm done."

An hour later, men carrying the boar appeared in the courtyard. For the rest of the afternoon, the kitchen was busy preparing it and then roasting it, with the odor of cooking wafting into every corner of the castle. It was dark outside by the time David found Anna on their usual bench and plopped down beside her. Usually she wrinkled her nose at his smell—sweat and horses and no bath for more than a week—but not today.

"I hear you killed it."

"Prince Llywelyn killed it," David corrected her. "I was merely holding onto the same spear he was when he did it."

"Uh huh," she said, not believing him. "I'm glad your day was more interesting than mine."

"I'm sorry you're so bored," David said.

Anna shrugged. "I'll live," she said.

David stared at her, waiting for more. He'd given her an opening to complain and she hadn't taken it. David had even felt up to listening for once. *I killed a boar today!*

5

David intercepted Anna on the way to breakfast two days later. "How'd you like to learn to ride a horse?" he asked, smiling. "I talked to Bevyn and he said that we could take you out in the mornings after breakfast when the weather is good."

As 'good' in Wales meant 'not raining or snowing', Anna didn't know how often they'd get to ride, but the idea itself was enough to lift her spirits. It was still bitterly cold, but she didn't care. She threw her arms around David's neck and hugged him.

"Yes, please!" she said. *At last, I can* do *something*!

They rode that very day and it was refreshing to be outside, even if Anna's muscles were so sore the next day she could barely walk, much less sit on a horse. She sat the next day anyway, determined to shake off her gloomy thoughts and focus on what she could do in Wales, rather than what she couldn't. *Which is everything.* Since their arrival at Castell y Bere, she'd had no opportunity for exercise, other than walking from her room to the solar, to church, to the great hall, and back again. Her karate instructor would have been appalled.

So that was one good thing in her life, and within the week, Anna discovered another: Prince Llywelyn's only child, Gwenllian. Her mother, whom Prince Llywelyn had married late in life, had died at the baby's birth. Consequently, her caretakers were a wet nurse and a nanny, who were frazzled most of the time because Gwenllian was a fussy child. Although she was six months old, not an infant, she cried at any hour of the day. One afternoon, Anna was sitting and sewing among the women in the solar, listening to Gwenllian's constant wails, when she realized that her head would explode if she had to endure another minute of either sewing or crying. She put her useless work aside and left the room.

Anna went to Gwenllian's chambers and found her wet nurse, Heledd, pacing with her around the room, trying to get her to nurse. The nanny, Mari, was making unwanted suggestions. They looked at Anna as she entered and Anna simply held out her hands for the baby. After shooting a speaking look at each other, perhaps deciding in that instant that she was trustworthy, the nurse handed the baby to Anna and she took her into the great hall. Because it felt like the right thing to do, Anna put Gwenllian onto her shoulder and just by chance, she burped hugely and stopped crying.

"Now that's much better, isn't it?" Anna said. Gwenllian seemed to understand American English perfectly.

She was clearly a bright child, alert and curious, with un-Welsh-like blond, curly hair, blue eyes, and chubby fingers she used to point at anything and everything. They spent the afternoon looking at the huge hearth in the great hall in which a fire burned twenty-four hours a day, poking their noses into the kitchen to steal a biscuit which Gwenlllian managed to spread all over her face, and sitting at one of the tables to watch men play chess while Gwenllian gummed one of the chess pieces.

Two hours later, Gwenllian started fussing again and Anna brought her back to her nanny. The wet nurse had just woken up from a nap and stretched out her arms for the baby. It was a very pleasant day for everyone and from then on, Anna cared for the baby every afternoon. She was happy to do it. It gave purpose to her day, in addition to the riding and Anna's feeble attempts to learn middle Welsh.

David, on the other hand, continued to make great strides towards becoming a man as understood by the Welsh of the thirteenth century. For him, life in Wales was a real life role-playing adventure. His friends at home would have been falling all over themselves to experience it with him—that is until they realized the swords were sharp and a real war was coming, one in which David might well play a part.

Except for the daily ride, Anna usually saw him only at meals. However, one day in early January, she heard a commotion in the great hall. Anna hurried in and saw David and another boy standing before Prince Llywelyn. Bevyn accompanied them, along with the grizzled older man who'd first taught David to fight on the way north from Cilmeri.

The other boy, who was more than two years older than David as well as bigger and burlier, had a black eye and a swollen nose. It was unlike David to get into a fist fight, but it looked like that was what had happened. Bevyn and the older man spoke calmly to each other. David stood quiet, staring fixedly ahead, with his feet spread and fists clenched. He was doing some of the breathing exercises he'd learned in karate.

Prince Llywelyn, standing straight with his hands clasped behind his back, looked from one boy to the other. He spoke to David, who replied. Prince Llywelyn then put a hand on David's shoulder, leaned down, looked him in the eye. Whatever he was saying, he enunciated so clearly had Anna known enough Welsh she could have read his lips. At last, the two boys gripped forearms in sort of a handshake and the group broke apart.

David spotted Anna leaning against the wall and walked over.

"What happened?" she asked.

He half-laughed. "I was in a fight. Can't you tell?"

Anna looked him up and down. "No, I can't," she said. "The other guy sure looks like it, though."

"Fychan and I were fighting with wooden swords," David explained. "I won fairly. No one has ever defeated him before and he was mad about it, I guess. He shouted at Bevyn that I cheated. I tried talking to him, but he wouldn't listen, so I turned around and walked away. Next thing I knew, he jumped me!"

"Uh oh," Anna said.

"Yeah," David said. "He caught me off-guard and I went down on one knee. His arms were around my shoulders, but I threw him off and turned to face him. I heard someone shout at us to stop, but I was seeing red and I think he was too because he rushed at me. He believed he could overpower me."

"Let me guess," Anna said. "He took a swing at you, you blocked his arm, kicked him in the groin, and when he doubled over you came up into his face with your knee."

"Pretty much," David admitted. "I was so mad I was ready to hit him on the way down too, but a couple of the guys pulled me off."

"So what did Prince Llywelyn say?" Anna asked.

"Fychan was in the wrong," David said, "so there wasn't any question that I had the right to defend myself. But Bevyn was concerned that I let my temper get the better of me and the knee in the face was unnecessary."

"It was," Anna said, "especially since you had people calling you off before the fighting started."

"I know," David said. "Then Prince Llywelyn said that a leader couldn't afford to allow anger to affect his decisions, and that I needed to understand that there was a time for making an example of a man, and a time for showing mercy. He didn't object to the way I'd conducted the fight, but that I'd done it while hot, instead of cold. A leader has to be cold in order to mete out true justice."

"A leader, huh?" Anna said.

"You caught that too, did you? I'm not sure what to make of that."

Anna knew. Her brother was going to succeed in this world even more easily than in the old one. She'd feared that no one would appreciate David's talents, but it seemed that here, stripped of the trappings of modern society and with over seven hundred fewer years of accumulated knowledge, it was impossible not to.

* * * * *

As Anna's misery abated, despite the continued absence of hot showers, she became more aware of the increasing activity in the castle. A martial mentality was going around, with men-at-arms moving purposefully through the courtyards and more men peopling the great hall at dinner. David came to her one day to show off his mail armor, though his eyes were hooded with concern. He sat on a bench near one of the tables.

"I may have to kill people," he said. "They expect me to kill people."

Anna had been wondering at what point he'd realize that all the training he was doing would end in actual warfare in which he was destined to participate. She'd hoped he would come to her when it happened. Anna hadn't exactly come to terms with what had happened at Cilmeri, but as it was an accident, she tried not to let it bother her. David would be killing on purpose, knowingly.

"I know," Anna said. "I'm sorry."

David stared at the floor. "Do you see an alternative?"

She'd been thinking about this since David's first mock sword fight with a stick. She shook her head. "We're in the wrong time," she said, "but even in our time it's not immoral to fight if you have to—if you are attacked, or to protect people. You would be defending your people against invaders. If the English defeat us, Wales ceases to exist as a separate country."

"True," he said, and then continued softly. "Killing will change me. It harms the soul of anyone who does it."

"Yes," Anna said. "It does."

But there was nothing they could do about it. Wales was at war. On three separate occasions, a lone man arrived, his horse steaming, having ridden hard from a distant castle. King Edward of England wasn't finished with the Welsh, not by a long shot, even if he'd failed to kill the Prince. Anna's impression was that Prince Llywelyn was waiting for something. She didn't know if the problem lay with his allies, including his own brother, or a change in English strategy.

One day, in the second week of January, David and Anna came back late from their ride, with darkness almost upon them by the time they rode through the gate. David had duties to attend to and hurried through the grooming of his horse, leaving Anna alone in the stables.

After he left, she deliberately delayed her own return to the great hall. *Wouldn't it be great if I had something important to do that needed my immediate attention?* She combed her horse's mane again and again. He was a gentle fellow, ironically named Madoc for a great prince of Wales, though he was little bigger than a pony. Bevyn had decided he would suit her, and Anna was very happy with him. As a child, she'd dreamed of spirited horses and begged for one of her own, but at seventeen, the reality of them was entirely different. Small and gentle was just fine with her.

Anna was giving Madoc a farewell pat when an odd creak came from behind her. She looked around Madoc's head, but couldn't see anyone except a groom raking hay in one of the stalls. The torch light revealed no unfamiliar shadows.

"Hello?" she called, in Welsh.

An arm slipped around her waist and a gravelly voice said. "Hello, missy." Alcohol fumes wafted past as the man hugged Anna to him.

"Excuse me," Anna said. She batted at the man's hand, but he didn't let go. The stable boy stood twenty paces away and their eyes met. He dropped his broom and raced out the stable door.

Great. I would've liked some help. The man slobbered disgustingly in Anna's ear. She didn't know who he was, didn't recognize his voice, and didn't care. Taking matters into her own hands, Anna stepped to her left, her right hand clenched in a tight fist, and swung it into the man's groin. As he bent over in reflex, she turned and met his face with a strong punch from the left. The man collapsed to the ground, groaning.

Anna poked him with her toe. She'd never done karate in a dress and was glad to see it still worked. She was turning to leave when David burst through the stable door, followed by Prince Llywelyn and Goronwy and a small crowd of people. As it turned out, the stable boy hadn't abandoned her but had gone for help instead.

"He doesn't look good," David said, in English.

"He was drunk," Anna replied. "It wasn't much of a challenge."

"Is he a member of the garrison?" David asked Prince Llywelyn.

Goronwy answered. "He was sent off today, for drunkenness while on duty. He will hang for touching Anna."

Anna opened her mouth to protest, but Goronwy and the Prince had their heads in close conference.

"Hang?" she whispered to David.

"When you make a mistake here, Anna, the price is very high."

Two men-at-arms helped him to his feet while he continued to moan.

"Come on," David took her arm. "There are some things you don't need to watch."

Anna shrugged out of his grip. "I'm not a delicate flower, David! I've as good as killed that man. Shouldn't I watch the result?"

"And what would have happened if you hadn't stopped him?" he demanded.

Oh, I see the problem. David thought this was *his* fault, for leaving her alone in the stables.

Anna stepped closer and gripped David's tunic. David brought his head down to hers. "I hate this, David. So often I hate this."

"I do too, Anna, but we just don't have any choices."

* * * * *

Nobody but Anna seemed to care about the death of the man and the escapade earned her some distinction among the women for a few days. One of the girls, Gwladys with whom Anna usually got along asked what she'd done to him. When Anna demonstrated, Gwladys stared at her, not so much appalled, as amazed. Her assumption, shared by most of the women, was that other than screaming and struggling, there was nothing they could do to stop a man once he had his hands on them. If Anna could have explained better in Welsh, she would have told them that being the 'weaker sex' didn't mean you couldn't fight if you had to.

Unfortunately, things settled back into their old, dull routine pretty quickly and Anna found herself painfully ripping out the stitches on yet another pathetic embroidery project. As usual, desultory conversation went on around her. Over the last week, she'd noticed that she was better able to follow conversations, and in this case, understood enough to know that it had to do with people and places she'd never heard of.

Then one of the girls Anna's age said, ". . . the green dress anyway. It was mine."

"Hush, Elen," her mother replied. "It's not your place to question the orders of Prince Llywelyn."

Elen refused to be silenced. "I don't see why we have to be so nice to her," she said. "She's stupid and ugly. Look at her, she can't even sew a straight stitch."

Anna tried to cover her surprise at this speech by dropping her needle. She didn't want anyone to realize she at long last understood them, not when she was finally hearing something

60

interesting. She *had* thanked Elen for the loan of the dress, after all. Head bent, Anna continued to sew.

Elen's comment was met with disapproval, to Anna's relief. "She's beautiful and you know it," Gwladys said. "You're jealous that she has found favor with Prince Llywelyn. He will find a husband for her who's more important than the one you marry."

Now another woman spoke, "There have been rumors . . ."

Have there? Prince Llywelyn has found a husband for me? Anna was appalled, but at the same time, all ears.

"There are no rumors," Elen's mother said stoutly.

"That's all very well for you to say," complained Elen. "Father was with the Prince at Cilmeri and *knows* all about them. But he won't tell me until he has the Prince's permission. I don't see why it is such a secret. Silly cow."

Shocked silence followed the last statement. *Such gossip! Were the women like this all the time and I hadn't known it? Perhaps it was a blessing not to know middle Welsh.*

"I want to know what this language is they speak," declared a woman sitting across from Anna. "It's very strange, unlike any English I've encountered."

"And what about Prince Llywelyn?" said another. "I heard she healed him at Cilmeri with a touch of her finger!"

That was news to Anna.

"She's a witch!" Elen said, triumphantly.

"Don't be ridiculous!" Gwladys said. "She's not a witch. If she were, do you think she'd be sitting there, taking abuse from you?"

With that, Gwenllian and her nanny came into the room, interrupting the discussion. With reluctance, since Anna was eager to hear more, even if it wasn't nice, she rose and took the baby. Deciding that discretion was indeed the better part of valor, Anna left the room and went into the great hall. She'd just settled on a bench against the wall when a group of men strode in, her brother amongst them and gathered around a table upon which pieces of parchment lay. Prince Llywelyn came out of his study and joined them. They talked and gestured over the papers and once again, Anna was astonished to find that she understood them.

One man said, "Our men have reached Dafydd at Dolwyddelan Castle. Others are coming every day. What are the total numbers now?"

"Many thousands, Cadog," the Prince replied.

"When do we join them?" another man asked. "We can't allow Edward to come this far into Gwynedd."

David turned to look at Anna cradling a sleeping Gwenllian, and said in English. "Anna, could you come here for a minute?"

Surprised, Anna rose. David made room for her in front of the map. "What is it?" she asked.

David spoke in English. "Do you remember what Edward did after—" he stopped with a glance at Prince Llywelyn. "You know."

"Edward moved down the northern coast and then headed inland," she said. "But the Prince—" here too, she stopped. Anna didn't think he could understand her but didn't feel comfortable saying *the Prince was dead* when he was standing right in front of them. She looked at David. "Do you think it's time we talked to Prince Llywelyn about Wales—about the future of Wales? Do you think he would speak with us, away from all these people? In the solar, there's already discussion that I might be a witch."

David put an arm over Anna's shoulder and together they faced the Prince. In Welsh, David asked, "Could we have a moment of your time, my lord—in private?"

* * * * *

Anna gave Gwenllian to her nanny and then joined Prince Llywelyn in his study. David, Goronwy, and another of Llywelyn's lieutenants, a young man named Tudur, were there when she arrived. Prince Llywelyn dismissed Tudur and Goronwy and then indicated that David and Anna should sit in two chairs on one side of a table. He sat down across from them, stretched out his legs, heaved a sigh, and fingered the papers in front of him. Then he straightened, apparently having come to a decision.

"It is time for me to tell you what you need to know," he said.

David and Anna looked at each other in confusion. They'd imagined themselves telling him the very same thing.

"It begins and ends with Marged, your mother, who became my friend many years ago." Prince Llywelyn used her formal name, instead of "Meg" which everyone called her at home.

"What?" Anna asked.

"What did you say?" David stared at the Prince, his jaw on the floor. "You knew our mother?"

Prince Llywelyn held up his hand. "Let me get this out," he said. "You may have wondered why I've not expressed more curiosity about your sudden arrival in the meadow at Cilmeri, or pressed you, despite your lack of Welsh, concerning your strange chariot. In truth, it was not the first such vehicle I have seen, and you aren't the first of your kind I've come across. Your mother came to me fifteen years ago, after the death of her husband. You were with her, Anna, and she appeared in front of me one day, just as you and Dafydd did last month."

Prince Llywelyn held out his hands, upturned towards them. "I've put off telling you this because I haven't known how, but maybe I'd better just say it," he said.

Anna nodded, trying to be encouraging.

"We loved each other," he said. "The result was you, Dafydd. You are our son."

"What?" That was Anna again. David said nothing, just stared at Prince Llywelyn, his face pale. Was he angry? Afraid? Hurt? Prince Llywelyn's story seemed impossible, a delusion.

The two continued to gaze at each other in silence. "Please tell me," David said at last.

Prince Llywelyn eyed David carefully, but took encouragement from his calm words. "It was close to this time of year, late in the day, and already dark," he said. "I stood alone on the ramparts at Criccieth, a seaside castle built by my grandfather. One moment, I was alone with the sea and the birds, and the next, your mother appeared in her blue carriage, her 'Honda,' lights shining from the front. She came out of the woods near the shore and slid down a slope toward the sea. The vehicle became mired in the marsh, and began to submerge. Marged had lost control of the vehicle in her world and slid through a barrier into this one. At least that's how she described it to me.

"Astonished, I raced down the steps, out the postern gate, and onto the shore. Marged had lost consciousness, and her baby—that was you, Anna—was crying in the rear seat. Without knowing how I knew to do it, I opened the door of the chariot and pulled you both free. Soon after, the car sank into the mire and disappeared. I imagine it would still be there, if you knew where to look."

Prince Llywelyn held David's eyes as he spoke, though it seemed as if he saw not David, but the past. Anna kept glancing from the Prince to David. David tended to be unforgiving when other people fell short of his expectations, even Mom. And this was so out of character for her. As far as Anna knew, she hadn't dated *anyone* after their dad died. Or rather *her* dad died.

"Your mother stayed with me for less than a year," he said, "almost until your birth, Dafydd. Then one day, I awoke to find her gone and Anna with her. None claimed responsibility for her leaving, or had seen her go."

"She left? Just like that?" asked David.

"We ransacked the castle and searched the surrounding countryside for her to no avail. She left me as quickly as she had come."

"But how do you know that I'm your son?" David asked. "You've never seen me before, and I am with Anna, not my mother."

Prince Llywelyn smiled. "It's obvious to anyone with eyes. You, of course," he said, turning to Anna, "look just like your mother. I'm sure others have told you that many times."

Anna nodded. It was true.

"And you, Dafydd, look much like my father, Gruffydd, and my older brother, Owain. My men noticed it as soon as they saw you standing in the clearing at Cilmeri—thus the rumors which have spread about your identity."

"I heard of these rumors, just today in the solar," Anna said to David, not able to render this in Welsh. "I thought Prince Llywelyn was arranging a marriage for me."

"Whatever you have to tell me about the fate of Wales," the Prince continued, "I already know through Marged. She warned me of the treachery at Cilmeri; she knew of Edward's deeds and that with my death the dream of an independent Wales would also die."

"But why didn't you do anything about it?" David asked. "If not for us, you would have died, just as our history books say."

"It's one thing to know something, it's another to avert the course of the future," Prince Llywelyn countered. "These last fifteen years I've worked to shore up my castles and consolidate my power—and resist the advances of the English. But each time I tried to do something that seemed to lead toward a different future, others who knew nothing of what I knew would move to ensure that my efforts failed. My own kin betrayed me more than once."

"That doesn't explain your presence in that meadow," David pointed out.

"In early November," Prince Llywelyn said, "The first rumors reached me that the powerful Mortimer family might consider defecting to my side. On the eighth of December, after our great victory at the Menai Straits, I received a note suggesting exactly that. They offered a meeting outside of Buellt. Your mother had warned me against the meeting, but still, I couldn't pass it up."

"So, you went to the rendezvous," said David.

"Yes, and found it a trap, and one which I allowed them to spring on me," Prince Llywelyn said. "I did not, however, bring my entire army with me to the south, even though the English thought I did. This small thing I could and did control. The men you met that first day were my entire party, save those who died on the hill before you arrived. The bulk of my army has now reached my brother Dafydd at Dolwyddelan Castle. If Edward chooses to sweep down the valley of the Conwy, he will find a larger force than he expects prepared to stop him."

Anna had been leaning forward, hanging on the Prince's every word, and with that sat back, heaving a sigh of relief.

"At least you could do something to change the future," she said.

"If you hadn't appeared when you did, I don't know how much difference it would have made," Prince Llywelyn said. "I felt I had to take a chance with the Mortimers, despite your mother's warning. Unfortunately, I was as unprepared this time as in your world. That's the reason, however, that when your chariot appeared in the meadow, I knew you, even before you gave me your names.

"So, Dafydd," Prince Llywelyn said, "may I greet you as my son?"

David sat frozen to his chair, and then sprang up. He met the Prince half-way around the table. The Prince lifted him off his feet and hugged him. When Prince Llywelyn put David down, he looked at Anna.

"Do you remember anything of your time in Wales?" he asked.

"My first memories aren't until David was a baby," Anna said, "except . . ." She paused, thinking hard, " . . . did I know Goronwy then?"

Llywelyn smiled. "You did," he said. "And you called me Papa. You liked me to put you on my shoulders. You would grasp my hair with your fists to hold on."

Anna gazed at him through several heartbeats. "I don't think you want to carry me anywhere, but I will call you 'Papa' again, if you'd like," she said.

"Yes," he said, smiling. "I'd like that."

Then she skipped back to what he'd said before and jumped to her feet, unable to sit still. "Wait! Wait!" she said, in Welsh, of which she'd understood more in the last five minutes than in the previous five weeks. "You're saying that Mom and I lived here for a time and then disappeared. Could that happen to David and me? Could it happen to Mom again?"

"When I was with her, we talked about it," Prince Llywelyn said. "She had no idea why it had happened in the first place, much less how to make it happen again, or how to prevent it."

"And now it's happened to us," said David. "That's an amazing coincidence."

Prince Llywelyn looked from David to Anna, amused. "Do you believe in coincidences?" he asked. "I confess, I no longer do."

6

I am Prince Llywelyn's son. I am Mom's *and Prince Llywelyn's son.* David awoke alone—suddenly alone—in his own, solitary, single, never-to-be-shared-with-anyone room in the castle, and found himself choking on semi-hysterical laughter. No longer the son of a man he'd never met, and whom hardly anyone in his family remembered much about or spoke of, he was the son of the Prince of Wales. *I am a Prince of Wales!*

Admittedly, one of David's first actions upon entering the room was to throw himself upon the bed, spread-eagled, and rejoice in the comfort of the down mattress. Then, he imagined himself going up to Fychan and mentioning, offhand and casually, that he was late for sword play today because he'd just left his father in his office where they'd had discussed important business. His *father*.

Despite his fantasies, dinner the night before had been the most awkward meal of David's life. Anna had joined the high table too, sitting between him and Goronwy. She'd seemed completely relaxed and had talked animatedly with Goronwy, whose usually severe expression had been transformed by his joy that Anna remembered him.

David, for his part, hadn't known how to act. He didn't know how to *be* a son; how to *be* a Prince of Wales. Prince Llywelyn—*Father*—had asked David to sit beside him, and he'd done so, but he'd knocked over his water glass, dropped parsnips down his front, and generally made a fool of himself within the first five minutes. Father had then grabbed David's arm as he was reaching for his cup and held it.

He smiled, though his eyes were serious. "Are you a different person from this morning, son?" he'd asked.

"No," David said, "and yes. I don't know how to be a prince."

"Don't think of it that way," Father had said. "Just be my son."

"I don't know how to be that either," David said. "I've never had a father."

"Then be the man you were this morning," Father said. "That man *is* a Prince of Wales."

That was an oddly comforting thought, other than his use of the word 'man', which was still taking some getting used to. Then Father spoke again. "When your mother returned to your world, she didn't marry?"

Anna stilled beside him at the question.

"No," David said.

"Ahh," Father said, and sat back in his chair. Then, under his breath, David thought he heard him mutter, "Good," but wasn't sure. *Did he still think of her too, or was it just that now I was here, he was thinking of her?* He *had married someone else.*

Anna poked David's leg under the table and leaned closer. "His whole life, Wales, and the Middle Ages is what Mom studies!" she said. "She talks about him all the time and nobody suspects a thing!"

"There's no way we could have known," David said, "but it feels like we've been blind."

"It was your heritage," Anna said, "but she couldn't tell you anything about it."

"And how does it make you feel?" David asked her, suddenly concerned. "We're only half-siblings now."

"I'm still your older sister," she responded, starch in her voice. "Don't think just because you're the Prince of Wales that it makes any difference to me."

Father overheard. "You're a princess, my dear," he said. "I'll not hear otherwise."

Anna's ducked her head and focused on her food.

Ha! "Accept it, Anna," David said, leaning close again. "It might get you out of some sewing."

She didn't say anything after that, but she was smiling.

* * * * *

The next morning, David was pulling on his shirt, knowing he'd slept far too late, when a tentative knock came at the door.

"Come in!" David said.

72

Owain and four of the other boys from David's contingent pushed open the door and stood hesitating in the doorway. David straightened and they studied each other for a long ten seconds.

Owain was the first to speak. "My lord," he said, and David felt that the words came awkwardly to his lips. They felt awkward to *hear*. "Sir Bevyn requests your presence at the practice ring."

David raised his eyebrows. "Is that what he said?" he asked.

Owain shifted from one foot to another. "Um, no, my lord."

"So what he really said was 'tell his lordship to get his noble ass out here right now or I'll make him wish he'd woken earlier, Prince of Wales or no Prince of Wales.'"

Despite themselves, everyone laughed. David laughed with them and waved them into the room. He'd tried to do Bevyn's accent and gruff voice and gotten it nearly right. Now, with the tension broken, the boys spread out. One stoked the fire in the grate, another sat gingerly upon the mattress.

"I think we'll sleep with you from now on," a boy named Gruffydd said. "This is much nicer than the barracks."

"Why didn't you tell us you were Prince Llywelyn's son?" Owain asked. Everyone stopped moving. David looked up from pulling on his boots—no longer the twenty-first century ones, but a new pair the cobbler had finished last week. *What a question!*

"I didn't know," he said. "My mother never told me." David and Llywelyn had discussed how to respond to this before they parted after dinner and had decided that they'd hit as close to the truth as they could.

The boys looked nonplussed. "Why not?"

"I can't ask her," David said. "All I know is that she sent me here to be with the Prince, and he waited to tell me until he thought the time was right."

"No wonder you're so smart." That was Owain again. David didn't want to hear that, though, because dwelling on their differences would only create a bigger barrier between them and him. They were all noble too, but there was the nobility—and then there was the Prince's son. David might have only been a prince for twelve hours, but he knew enough about it to know *that*.

Bevyn waited for them in the courtyard, his hands on his hips, and a distinct smirk on his face. If David was expecting deference, he didn't get it.

"You're late," he snapped.

"I'm sorry, sir," David said. "I've not slept by myself here before, and didn't realize that I wouldn't wake in time."

"You missed mass and breakfast," Bevyn said. "Here." He threw David a roll. "Come," he said.

"Thanks," David replied to his back. He inspected the food and saw there was both cheese and meat inside. As always, Bevyn treated David with a complicated mix of causticity and muted affection.

"Where are Fychan and Dai?" Gruffydd asked from behind David.

"Gone," Bevyn answered, "along with a dozen others. We're gathering at Dolwyddelan." He looked back and his sneer was almost a smile. "In two days' time, we all will leave here to join them—even you, Gruffydd."

Everyone saddled up. As David mounted Taranis, a stranger led his horse from the stables. Bevyn trotted over to introduce them. "Prince Dafydd," he said, "please meet Mathonwy ap Rhys Fychan, your cousin. Lord Mathonwy, this is Prince Dafydd."

"My lord," Mathonwy said, bowing, "please call me Math."

"Dafydd," David said. They grasped forearms in greeting.

"It is my honor to serve you," Math said.

And then David realized that Math meant what he said. "My father brought you here to watch over me, didn't he?" David asked.

"Yes," Math said, as if there was nothing more to it than that.

Yet David didn't have to ask why. *I am a Prince of Wales.* Math mounted his horse and rode out of the gatehouse at David's side. David tried to think of something to say. Math was a lot older—maybe twenty, six feet tall, with black hair, blue eyes, but no mustache. That was unusual enough to comment upon, but David thought the first question out of his mouth shouldn't be, "why don't you have a mustache?"

Instead, David said, "So you're my cousin?"

"I am the son of Prince Llywelyn's sister, Gwladys. She died at my birth, and I lost my father ten years later. I've lived in your father's household since then. I've just come from the north, from

Ewloe, one of the castles I hold for your father against the English."

"When did my father send for you?"

"I received word of your arrival the day after Christmas, but it took some time to make a proper disposition of my men. Ewloe is only a few miles from Hawarden and Flint, both of which the English once held and would like to hold again. Edward himself sits at Rhuddlan, waiting for the weather to clear."

"Are you a knight?" David blurted out. Math certainly looked it, with well-polished mail armor, sword, and leather bracers worn with use.

He laughed, but not *at* David. "Yes," he said. "And someday, that fate will be yours, God willing."

As they rode down the road to the valley floor, David kept glancing out the corner of his eye at Math. He sat very straight, his hands on the reins *just so*, his shield held at exactly the right angle. Without saying anything, David tried to copy him. David had a sense, all the same, that Math was watching him and knew what he was doing. David decided he didn't care. Father wouldn't have brought Math to Castell y Bere if he didn't trust him, and if he didn't think David had something to learn from him.

"Today we ride west," Bevyn said above the clopping of hooves and the murmur of boys, "to the sea."

David's ears perked up at that. He hadn't yet seen the sea, even though it was fewer than ten miles from Castell y Bere. They forded the River Dysynni, to the northwest of the castle, and then followed a trail that followed the north bank of the river. When the river cut south, the trail continued west to the sea and the village of Llangelynin. They rode without stopping through what in the summer would be rich farmland, and less than an hour later reached the beach.

David breathed in the sea air. His eyes strained forward across the water, but the low clouds hanging on the horizon blocked the view of Ireland.

And America.

"The sea is in my blood," Math said. "My family's lands lie in the south, at Dinefwr Castle in Ystrad Tywi but I was born at Aberystwyth, in the old castle that Edward destroyed. That castle sat on a headland, overlooking this sea, and was beautiful, not like the half-finished ruin that Edward thought to build."

"Who has it now?" David asked.

"Gruffydd ap Maredudd. During Holy Week a year ago, we took Aberystwyth, Hawarden, Flint, Llandovery, and Carreg Cennen in one night. We've won and lost these and more in the last year, but Aberystwyth is still ours."

"Were you there?"

Math laughed again. "No. The rebellion was all your uncle's idea at first, you know. Your father didn't join the fight until nearly summer. We've had some defeats and a few victories, most notably at the Menai Straits in November. Edward has waited two months to attack again. It will come, and I pray we will be ready."

"I don't know that I'm ready," David said.

"You are," Math said, "else your father wouldn't be letting you fight."

Bevyn spoke above the murmuring of the boys. "We will split up, today," he said. "I've a new lesson for you. You'll need to find your way home without my help."

"Now that's going to be interesting," Math said. He tipped his head to David and Owain, indicating they should ride with him.

Llangelynin didn't have much of a beach and within an eighth of a mile of the shoreline, a rocky escarpment rose over two hundred feet above it, forming a ridge of land that descended only slightly to the farmland on the other side. Further east, the land fell nearly to sea level, before rising again to the foot of the mountain range of which Cadair Idris was the highest peak.

Two miles north, however, which is probably why Bevyn suggested they take that route in the first place, the escarpment receded and it was possible to ride around it inland.

"So the first step is done," Math said. "Now tell me the direction of Castell y Bere."

David thought about it and pointed southeast.

"No," Owain said. "It is directly east, perhaps ten miles."

Math shook his head. "Make it five and you'd be correct," he said. "We rode south from the castle along the Dysinni, before cutting east. Five miles riding is less than an hour's work, but there's a twelve hundred foot mountain between us and the castle. Should we go over it?"

Owain and David slowly shook their heads, both thinking harder now. "No," David said. "We go around it."

Math nodded. "North or south?"

"South," Owain said, more confident now, "back to the Dysinni."

"Yes," Math said. "The first rule of travel through unfamiliar territory is to stick with what you know. We *know* there's a mountain between us and the castle; we know that Cadair Idris rises above us to the northeast." He pointed, and Owain and David turned to look, but the cloud cover had descended even further.

"And," Owain finished, "we know the river passes by the castle." He held out his hand as a snowflake fell into it.

"So we pick our way between the ridge that runs along the sea, and the one that rises between us and the castle," David said, wishing for the ease of a GPS unit, or at worst, a map and compass.

Math nodded. "You must always remain aware of the land through which you're traveling. Ridges, rivers, mountains, wind, sun—all will inform you of your location. If the snow falls," and now he looked up to check the sky, "you have the wind to guide you. Your great-grandfather built Castell y Bere were he did, Dafydd, because it guards a primary route for travel and trade into the mountains behind it, and is one of the most defensible locations in Wales. An army can approach the valley over which it presides only from the east or west. By following the intersections of roads, ridges and the river we can determine the direction we must travel."

"Even in snow?" Owain asked.

David checked his cloak. It was dusted with white.

"Even in snow," Math said, "though it's much less pleasant than when the sun and wind are at your back. If we were anywhere but here, we might have to stop and find shelter, rather than risk becoming lost in the mountains."

With one last look at the grey sea storming onto the shore, David turned inland and led Owain and Math along the curve of the ridge east, and then southeast through the blowing snow. The wind was behind them at first, and then became more swirled and directionless as the escarpment rose between them and the sea.

The clouds descended until they couldn't see ten feet in front of them. "It's going to get dark before we're home," Owain said.

They plodded on, hoods up and cloaks tugged tight. They reached the river an hour later and turned east towards Castell y Bere. Then, just as David thought they were on the home stretch, Owain's horse slipped awkwardly on uneven ground the snow had hidden.

"I'm sorry, my lords," Owain said when he dismounted. Although the horse's leg wasn't broken, he couldn't put his weight on it.

Math dismounted too. "It's a sprain only," he said, feeling the horse's hock. "We'll have to lead him."

The horse's head bobbed down with every step, but he walked the rest of the way. Even as they neared the castle, they would have missed it if beacons hadn't shone from the ramparts. They followed the light, wending their long way up the road to the castle gate. When they reached it, Prince Llywelyn was standing under the raised portcullis, his cloak blowing around his shoulders and his hands on his hips.

"Father," David said, dismounting in front of him.

"Son," he replied, but only glanced at David once before looking over his shoulder to Math.

"All is well, my lord," Math said.

David's eyes went from his father, to Goronwy, to Bevyn, both of whom stood slightly behind the Prince. Something was wrong and it took him a moment to realize that each them was holding himself very tightly. Prince Llywelyn's jaw was set and his eyes narrowed. *Angry at me? Why?*

"My lord," Goronwy tried, and David had a sense that this was not his first entreaty.

"What happened?" Father said, his voice flat and emotionless. "You're the last to arrive."

"Owain's horse slipped and strained his leg," David said. "He could barely walk."

"It's only five miles from here to the sea," Father said.

"As the crow flies," David said. "We followed the ridge south, and then had to turn northeast again along the Dysinni. We must have come at least double that distance." David tried to keep defensiveness out of his voice, but probably failed.

Math stepped forward, rescuing him. "It is better that he becomes a little lost here, my lord, and learns to read the landscape close to home, before he attempts it elsewhere where he'll have no choice but to find his way alone."

Father's face remained rigid.

81

Now it was Goronwy's turn. "If you don't allow Dafydd experiences such as this, you do him a disservice."

"That's why you brought me here, Uncle," Math said, "to keep him safe and I have done so."

"You told me to ensure he learned what he needed to know, sire," Bevyn said. "I apologize if I misunderstood your intentions."

"You didn't," Father said, finally. He stepped towards David and wrapped his arm around his shoulders. "It was I who was unprepared."

7

Prince Llywelyn, David, and a host of men rode out of
Castell y Bere, in the third week of January, 1283. What's more,
David rode at the head of the company, at Prince Llywelyn's side,
acknowledged as his son. Somehow, after that afternoon in Papa's
study, without any overt acclaim, word had spread. By dinner,
everyone in the castle had known David's true identity. Instead of
anger, there was general contentment, if not a palpable sense of
relief. Prince Llywelyn had been wise to give his people time to
become acquainted with David's character, so that now their
response was a genuine, "Of course he is! We knew it all along!"

Before he left, Anna found David near the stables,
adjusting his stirrups (because he'd probably grown two inches
over night). Putting her arms around his waist, she squeezed him
tightly and pressed her face into his wool cloak.

"Be safe," she said.

He turned and hugged her to him. "I will."

Anna let go to look up at him and he smiled, with eyes that
were bright with excitement. Anna's were bright with tears

because what she really wanted to say was *don't go and leave me here by myself!* But she didn't say it. She fought her tears, swallowed hard, and stepped away. She even managed to smile.

"This isn't a computer game, remember. That sword is real!"

"I know it!" he replied, and mounted his horse. Once seated, he turned serious and reached down to take Anna's hand. Sliding his fingers through hers, he leaned close.

"Don't worry, Anna," he said in English in case others were near enough to overhear. "Father isn't going to put me in the front lines the first day on the job. This week we've talked more about the future of Wales. He says that Wales exists now under a sentence of death. Each day he lives is a reprieve of sorts, and he's determined to live until he sees me grown. Unlike his father, or grandfather, he has no other son. I won't fight unless I have to."

He squeezed her hand and let go. Back straight and eyes forward to where Prince Llywelyn waited near the castle gate, David brought his horse through the ranks of cavalry, which parted respectfully. When he reached the head of the lines of troops, he approached his father and bowed his head. Prince Llywelyn smiled, more with his eyes than with his mouth, but his face looked as bright and excited as David's. He reached out to David and they clasped forearms, as they'd done that first morning after he and Anna had arrived. With that, a huge cheer went up from the men and women in the courtyard.

Anna's lips trembled and she put a hand to her mouth as the tears began to fall. She pulled up her hood to hide her face, but Gwladys tugged it back down.

"He'll want to see your face as he leaves," she said. "You must smile and wave at him. From this distance, he cannot see your tears and you must pretend they're not there."

Without replying, Anna held up a hand as Gwladys had suggested and was glad of her advice, because just then David turned for one last look. Anna smiled and waved and he raised his own hand in salute.

And then he was gone.

Anna watched until the entire company had ridden away. Then she turned to Gwladys, put her head on her shoulder, and wept. Gwladys held her and patted her back until she quieted.

Anna took a deep breath. "I'm sorry, Gwladys," she said. "I don't know why I'm so upset."

"Are you afraid for his life?" she asked. "Surely you know he'll be well protected."

"It's not that," Anna said, and she realized that she *wasn't* crying out of fear for David, and not even for herself. She was crying because what she'd witnessed was one of the most magical things she'd ever seen, or thought to see. David had found his father, and Prince Llywelyn his son, to the acknowledgment of all, and with this the world was a completely different place.

Gwladys set off towards the great hall, but when Anna held back, turned with a questioning look. Anna shook her head. She couldn't go back inside, back to her embroidery and her baby tending.

"I'm going for a ride," she said.

"Are you sure?" Gwladys asked. "It's very cold today."

"I'm sure," Anna replied, and headed towards the stables.

"You won't go alone?" Gwladys called after Anna.

"I'll take a groom with me," Anna said, over her shoulder. "There's no need to worry. I'm only going for a ride, not into battle!"

Anna gave her a little wave and Gwladys went inside. Anna reached the stables and passed many empty stalls before she found her horse. She looked around for someone to take with her, but all her usual companions had left with the cavalry. The only person available was Hywel, the boy they'd met that first day in Prince Llywelyn's camp. Anna called him to her. He looked like he'd grown two inches in the last month, just like David.

"Would you be free to ride with me today?" Anna asked.

"Yes, my lady!" he said. "I would be honored."

As he saddled the horses, Anna reflected that he seemed as infected by the excitement of the day as everyone else. It was a good thing she was going out so she couldn't dampen anyone else's good mood.

As they rode from the castle, the wind was brisk, but as always, the scenery was spectacular and Anna's spirits rose. The mountains loomed above them in all their splendor and she resolved to ride every morning, regardless of the cold. *David will be fine. Wales will win out. All will be well.*

Anna rode with Hywel for the next two days and tried not to be gloomy. On the third day, they were on their way home, leading their horses through the trees instead of riding because the branches were heavy with snow and lower to the ground. Anna probably could have ridden Madoc through them because both of them were short, but Hywel's horse wasn't as gentle as hers and had a habit of trying to brush Hywel off. The warriors had left this particular creature behind because of that habit, and they'd regretted bringing him multiple times already. They hurried now because they'd left for their ride late, well after noon, and it would soon be dark.

All thoughts of time vanished, however, as they ducked under some particularly low branches. A shout of laughter followed by the words, "You are a fine fool!" came through the trees.

Anna froze. She couldn't believe it. It was English—a weird sort of English with unfamiliar vowels, which would probably be written something like 'Yow ar a fyn fole' by the medieval-obsessed people Mom hung out with, but understandable to Anna, nonetheless.

They waited, hardly daring to breathe and praying that the men weren't coming their way. More laughter and murmurs were followed by the sound of men relieving themselves in the bushes— a most distinctive sound and, sad to say, one Anna had grown accustomed to hearing over the last weeks.

After another minute the feet tramped away, moving to the east. Hywel leaned towards Anna. "We must return to the castle!"

Anna thought for a second, and then shook her head. "Here," she said, handing him Madoc's reins. "Stay here! I must follow those men."

"My lady, no!" Hywel said, shocked. "You cannot! They're English!"

"Yes, Hywel, I know," Anna said, "but before we go home I must find out how many there are, where they're camping, and perhaps even what they're up to. By the time we find someone to help us, they may have hidden themselves in the woods and it'll be too late."

Anna took a step in the direction the men had gone but Hywel reached out and grasped her arm. "My lady!" he said, even more anxious than before. "I can't allow it. I'll go. You return to the castle and raise the alarm."

"You don't speak English, Hywel," Anna said, trying to remain patient, though she was worried that the men might disappear before she'd worked this out with Hywel. "I do." Then she saw his fear and his sincerity and thought better of her plan.

"All right," she said. "We'll go together."

Hywel tied the horses to a nearby tree and they set off, single file. Anna let Hywel lead, in concession to his masculinity and the fact that he knew these woods better than she did. He found the footprints of the two men without any trouble and they followed them another quarter of a mile before they saw signs of more men and horses. They reached the bottom of an incline and, looking up through the trees, spotted a group of men at the top, moving about in a purposeful way.

They crouched behind a bush and looked at each other, not really knowing what to do.

"We wait," Anna said.

Hywel nodded, fortunately without asking Anna to explain what they were waiting for. *A chance. A break.* They burrowed into the bush and tried to keep warm, wrapping their cloaks close. One thing Anna had found hard to get used to in Wales was the constant chill. Whether outside or in, unless she was close to a fire, she was cold. Even wrapped in a cloak, with two layers of stockings and woolen leggings under her dress, she couldn't defeat it.

Anna occupied herself with fruitless speculation about what the English might be planning. Some kind of attack on Castell y Bere seemed likely, but it seemed equally impossible for them to have brought enough men this deep into Gwynedd for a frontal assault.

The sun began to set. Darkness would make their journey back to the castle more treacherous, but it would allow them to sneak closer to the camp and perhaps learn something about what the English were doing in Wales. Anna worried that Gwladys would miss her soon, but had no remedy for that. After what seemed like hours, but was probably only forty-five minutes, it was dark enough and Hywel stirred.

"Lady Anna, it is time," he said.

They crawled from the bush and Anna followed Hywel up the hill, crouching low and moving slowly. It was hard for Anna to keep on her feet in the slippery snow. She lost her footing more than once, falling to her knees and silently cursing, before struggling upwards again. Once at the top, they found themselves on the edge of the camp but well out of the firelight.

Hywel squatted behind a prickly bush and gestured to Anna to stay behind him. She peered over his shoulder at the camp which bustled with men, all wearing unadorned, white surcoats, perhaps in an effort to blend in with their surroundings. Anna counted forty men and an equal number of horses, but few tents. Apparently, most of the men would spend the night on open ground, as they had during the journey from Cilmeri with Papa.

A small group of men conferred around one fire. They spoke quietly, without laughter. One of them had a big red beard and by that alone Anna would have known he wasn't Welsh. He signaled to three others waiting near a tree to join him and when they walked to him, the bearded man rose to his feet. He spoke, the men nodded, and then broke away. One of them headed for the horses and the other two walked straight towards Anna and Hywel.

The two friends looked at each other, trying not to panic, and shrank lower against the bush. Fortunately, the men didn't see them but veered towards the trees just to their right. They stopped about fifteen feet from where Anna and Hywel hid and when Anna realized what they were doing, she closed her eyes in dismay. *Men must have amazingly small bladders!* She couldn't block out the noise, but then didn't want to, because the men spoke to each other and she could hear them clearly.

"So this Rhys will give us the castle as easily as that? We can walk in before dawn and take it?" the first man asked.

The other man snorted. "These Welsh traitors will sell their own mother if the price is right," he said. "They're good for nothing. Their women can't even heat a man's bed."

The first man laughed. Anna was glad Hywel couldn't understand the words, even if there was no mistaking the tone.

"That Welsh princess will be like the rest. Better that after tomorrow she spends her life under Edward's thumb!"

Anna swallowed a gasp. She couldn't believe it. She knew from her mom that the English *had* kidnapped Gwenllian in the old world after Papa died. And here it was, happening right in front of her.

The two men finished their business. The instant they reentered the firelight, Anna backed down the hill, tugging on Hywel's cloak to get him to come with her. She didn't want to wait to find out more. Hywel caught her urgency and slid after Anna. When they reached the bottom, they ran hand in hand through the snow, keeping each other upright. It took twenty minutes to find their horses in the dark forest. Hywel untied the reins and threw Anna up on Madoc's back. She started to protest, but he shushed her and took Madoc's lead. Anna lay flat against the horse's neck to avoid the low branches on the trail as Hywel led them home, his horse following behind.

Less than an hour later the bulk of Castell y Bere came into view and Hywel stopped. Anna looked up at it, uncertain what needed to happen next. Hywel led the horses off the main path.

"Can you tell me now what was said?" he asked. "You think we're in danger?"

"One of the Englishmen said that a traitor named Rhys will turn the castle over to the English before dawn," Anna said. "Do you know of whom he speaks?"

Hywel coughed, choking on his fear. "Rhys is the captain of the castle garrison that remains," he said. "If he's a traitor, then it would be a simple matter for him to let the English in. They could even enter through the front gate! No one would be the wiser until the castle was under English command." Hywel contemplated the wall in front of him. "Did they name other traitors? Did they say anything else?"

"I'm afraid I didn't hear, Hywel," Anna replied. "They said some unpleasant things about Welsh women, but after they threatened Gwenllian's life, I didn't want to stay and hear more!"

"Gwenllian!" Hywel said.

"We must stop them!" Anna said.

Hywel looked down at his feet, then scuffed at the snow, revealing the fallen leaves moldering underneath. "I don't know how, Lady Anna," he said, refusing to look at her, his voice sad and regretful. "I'm only a stable boy and I don't know whom we can trust if we can't trust Master Rhys."

Unfortunately, he had a point. Anna knew many of the women, but all the men with whom David and she had ridden from Cilmeri were with the Prince at Dolwyddelan. As a matter of fact, Hywel was the only male at Castell y Bere with whom she had any acquaintance at all.

"Then we must get her away," Anna said, trembling more from anxiety, than cold. "We have no choice. And we'll have to do it tonight because we don't know exactly when they'll come. It's likely they'll move quickly, rather than risk detection so close to the castle."

Hywel rubbed his face with both hands. "By the saints, how can we?" he asked.

"If I find a way to take Gwenllian out of the castle, will you come with me?" Anna asked. "Will you help me?"

Hywel took his hands from his face. "Of course, my lady," he said. "I don't see any other choice either. If you misunderstood their intentions, Prince Llywelyn will have my head, but if you heard correctly, and we do nothing, I may die anyway. I would rather die on the road with you, than cowering in the stables having turned Prince Llywelyn's daughters over to the English."

"Good," Anna said, relieved. "Now we must return to the castle. Tonight, when all is quiet, I'll bring the baby and, hopefully, her wet nurse, to the stables. We can leave by the postern gate. Perhaps with so few men available and treachery on his mind, Rhys won't have as many guards posted."

"I would rather not trust to hope!" Hywel said. "But I'll find provisions for the journey to Dolwyddelan. That's where we're going, right?"

"Where else?" Anna said. "Do you know the way?"

"I know it," Hywel answered. "I was born in the forest just south of Dolgellau. If we can get there, we can hide ourselves off the main road in the remains of the shepherd's hut where I was born."

"How far is that from here?"

"More than ten miles. It's nearly forty miles to Dolwyddelan. If we had fast horses . . ." Hywel's words trailed off.

"But we only have Madoc," Anna said, "and we shouldn't take the main road."

"No," Hywel sighed, and then straightened his shoulders. "We should go in. I will meet you near midnight. Say your prayers before you come."

"I'll do that, friend," Anna said. She placed a hand on his shoulder. "Thank you for helping me. Thank you for trusting me."

Hywel bowed, as gracefully as any courtier, and led the way through the still-open gate into the courtyard of the castle.

8

There was something about sleeping on the road again, this time in a tent David shared with Math, that kept him in a constant state of anticipation. It was cold, it was snowy, and he loved it. Before noon on the third day out from Castell y Bere, the keep of Dolwyddelan appeared above them. It guarded the pass into the Conwy Valley. In the old world, it was here that Dafydd ap Gruffydd, Llywelyn's brother, had retreated after Llywelyn died at Cilmeri. Uncle Dafydd had escaped before the English took it, but it only delayed the inevitable.

An hour later, they clattered through the gateway. Dolwyddelan was smaller than Castell y Bere, with only two towers (instead of Castell y Bere's three). Regardless, the courtyard seethed with men and horses, a fraction of the thousands of men camped in the valley just to the north of the castle. Llywelyn ap Gruffydd had an army.

"Come, son." Father stood at David's stirrup, his hand on Taranis' neck. "You must meet your uncle before he marches."

Father's fifty men wouldn't strain the provisions of the castle because at least two hundred cavalry and a third of the foot soldiers were preparing to move out at that moment, heading north and then east to the Clwyd River. Father believed (and Anna concurred) that Edward would head west from Rhuddlan Castle along the north shore of Wales, before advancing south towards Dolwyddelan through the Vale of Conwy. He had thousands of foot soldiers and hundreds of knights and men-at-arms and the Welsh would meet him somewhere between Dolwyddelan and the coast.

"Yes, sir," David said. His heart beat a little faster at the thought. He and his traitorous uncle would be fighting together; fighting against the English. David decided that the latter fact alone was enough to make his heart pound, and that he shouldn't worry about meeting a man who'd proved false far too many times (he'd even once tried to assassinate Prince Llywelyn), even if he was on Father's side now.

They entered the great hall, with its massive fireplace set against one wall. Many men must have slept there the night before, but now it was nearly deserted, except for a small group of men gathered around a table at the far end.

They all looked up as David and Llywelyn entered and Father lifted his hand to greet them. One man, dark like Father, broader in the shoulders but not as tall, separated himself from the group.

"So, you've come," he said.

"Yes," Father said. "It's time to face what King Edward has in store for us."

"The King left Rhuddlan last night with seven thousand men." The man reached Father and they clasped forearms. Then they both turned to David. "Your son," the man said.

David held out his hand. "Uncle Dafydd," he said. "I'm glad to finally meet you, sir."

"You share my name, I believe," Uncle Dafydd said.

"Yes, sir," David said.

Uncle Dafydd nodded, pleased it seemed. He probably didn't know that David had been named for the other Prince Dafydd, David's great uncle, who'd ruled Wales from 1240 to 1246.

"The weather remains cold, even on the coast?" Father asked.

"Yes, for now," Uncle Dafydd said. His expression was so fierce, David had to stop himself from taking a step back but then he realized that the emotion was not directed at Father, but at Edward.

"You have reason to believe a change is coming?" Father asked.

Uncle Dafydd nodded. "Another week, maybe less, and we'll see a thaw. The fishermen assure me of it."

"Well, they would know," Father said. "When do you leave for Denbigh?" Father asked, and David realized that was his third question in a row. David couldn't think of another time his father had asked anyone so many questions. Even if the conversation seemed unnatural and stilted to David, he could see how it could be a deliberate strategy on Father's part to show his confidence in his brother.

It better not be misplaced, Uncle Dafydd. You're the one who fought beside Edward all these years.

"Within the hour," Uncle Dafydd said. "As we agreed, my men and I will ride north and east to take Denbigh from Lacy. In anticipation of a thaw, we will then cross the Clwyd and besiege Rhuddlan until it falls. You must prevent Edward from returning north with his full force, or this entire endeavor will fail."

"We will," David said, surprising himself. The words had just popped out. Uncle Dafydd's tone had bothered him—as if somehow he supposed that Father didn't know what he was doing. Of course, David had *no* idea what he was doing, but Uncle Dafydd didn't know that and David sure wasn't going to tell him.

Father put a hand on David's shoulder and nodded at Uncle Dafydd. "We are agreed then," he said. "Leave Edward to me."

On the road, Father had confessed to David that he'd joined Uncle Dafydd's rebellion initially out of a sense of despair. In June of last year, Father had lost his wife and with her, at well-past fifty, any hope of a son to carry on his rule. He loved Gwynedd, loved Wales, felt a kinship with the land itself. He spoke of this love with a passion, not too different from patriots in America, hundreds of years later.

"Did Mom ever talk to you about the American Revolution?" David asked him later, once they were alone in his chamber which, unusually, they were sharing because the castle was so full.

"She explained to me that your country has no kings and had won the right to govern itself from England at the point of a sword. She didn't discuss the details," he said. He sat in a chair and stuck out his foot. David obliged as his squire.

"Well," David said, grunting with the effort of removing the boot, "our circumstances here are much the same as the Americans of that time. We were taxed, subject to unfair laws, and forced to suffer indignities imposed upon us by the King of England and his soldiers."

"And they were still doing this five hundred years from now?" Father asked. "Why am I not surprised?"

David straightened and dropped the boot to the floor. "The first president of our country was a man named George Washington. He was hard pressed through a long winter, with little support and fewer men. Many were dying from infectious diseases and dysentery. He feared that many of the men wouldn't re-enlist at the New Year unless he had a victory to show them, so he concocted a bold and unexpected plan."

"Ha," Father said. "I like the man already."

"On Christmas night, he rowed his men across the Delaware River and force-marched them to a town called Trenton, where the English mercenaries were sleeping off their meal. Washington's men attacked shortly after dawn and completely routed the enemy. Nobody suspected that they would attack on Christmas night—and in such bitterly cold weather."

Father stretched out his legs towards the fire and put his hands behind his head, leaning back in his chair. "Your Uncle

Dafydd tried something like this, with great success, on Palm Sunday last year," Father said. "Unfortunately, Christmas is past."

"It is bitterly cold, though," David said. "I understand that five years ago, during King Edward's march through Wales, he cleared the land of trees and settlements so that we couldn't ambush him—so we couldn't use what in the modern world we call 'guerilla warfare'."

"Yes," Father said. "I assume he will do so again, yet I'm loathe to meet him on the open field. He has more cavalry than we do, more soldiers in general, and more experience with moving armies great distances."

"Yet, the English are far from home," David said. "They'll be marching with their supply lines stretched out behind them. They expect to besiege us and force us to sue for peace. What if we were to divide our men into small groups and attack them at night? They may have cleared the trees around their camps, but they still have to sleep, and we know the terrain."

"My castles are my strength," Father said. "I am loathe to abandon Dolwyddelan."

"I didn't mean that you should," David said. "But we can maximize their weaknesses. How many rivers does Edward have to cross to reach us here?"

"About eight."

"How far can our archers shoot? I've heard many times that they are the best in the world. I'm suggesting that we use them; that we plan a systematic, guerilla-like attack to whittle down the English numbers and demoralize them at the same time.

We can blow through the English at their most vulnerable moments—when they ford rivers and at night. Yes, we need Uncle Dafydd to take Rhuddlan, but even more we need to drive the English away."

Father sat up straight, his hands gripping his knees. "I like it," he said. "I'll like it even more if it starts to rain as promised."

"Why?" David asked.

"Because the rivers will rise, the ground will become as soggy as a bog, and his men will be camping in the rain without a fire or succor."

"Of course, then, so will we," David pointed out.

"Yes," Father said. "But we like it." He was looking at the fire as he said these words, but then glanced over at David. He was only half-joking. "Our men will know that the weather is our ally."

Pause.

"How worried are you?" David asked him.

"It may be a near thing," he said. "This isn't a comfortable world you've fallen into, my son." He hesitated. "We may not live through this."

"I know," David said, though he'd not spent a single moment thinking about it. He couldn't.

"Don't think on it," Father said. "We've still several days and many miles between us and Edward. We'll prepare as best we can, and pray, and wish for the kind of luck that we've rarely had in the past, but seems to have found us here at last."

* * * * *

Uncle Dafydd and his men vanished into the east. David had a moment's pang that he was gone forever, defecting again to Edward. Uncle Dafydd had already done it twice. That's the kind of thing one cannot forget or forgive, no matter how sincere Uncle Dafydd seemed now.

Father introduced David to more of his men, many of whom had walked or ridden to Dolwyddelan from every corner of Wales. David stayed at his side, and when he wasn't with him, he was with Math or Bevyn. Father had decreed that David was to captain a company of men: foot, archer, and horse. It wasn't that David felt ready, but as Prince of Wales, it was expected, and anything less from him would have invited comment and implied a lack of trust in his son on Prince Llywelyn's part.

Their third morning in Dolwyddelan, Goronwy strode into the hall, a messenger at his side. "He's coming," Gorowny said. Nobody had to ask who 'he' was. "He has reached Llansanffraid, hampered only slightly by the weather, but has not attempted to force the Conwy, as it continues to snow even along the coast. He's halted the majority of his men, but sent his laborers along the path he intends to follow south, clearing the forest and rousting the common folk in his path."

"Total war," David said, from his seat on the dais.

"What's that, my lord?" Math asked from his position by the fire.

"Edward seeks to destroy not only our army, but to completely subjugate our people by terrorizing the countryside, hoping to drive men away from their allegiance to Father."

"It won't work," Father said. "It only emboldens us." He paced in front of the dais. "Edward understands neither me nor my people. We have held on to what is ours since November, and we will not give it up. Not without a fight."

Struck by Father's emotion, David threw out the ending of Patrick Henry's speech from the start of the American Revolution, which he'd had to memorize for school. Translated into Welsh, it sounded even more poetic and his voice rang a bit louder than he intended as he recited the words: "Is life so dear, or peace so sweet, as to be purchased at the price of chains and slavery? Forbid it, Almighty God! I know not what course others may take; but as for me, give me liberty or give me death!"

Math gazed at David, his eyes bright but Father clenched his fist and banged it on the table. "Yes," he said. "That's it exactly. If I cannot have one, I will take the other." He strode down the hall to the front door and flung it open. "We will watch them." Father turned back to his men. "And when Edward comes, we will be ready."

9

Anna took a deep breath and knocked on Gwenllian's door. Before she could knock a second time, Mari, Gwenllian's nanny, whipped the door open. Her color was high. Beyond, Heledd suckled the baby, but it looked like she was squeezing her so tightly it was a wonder that Gwenllian wasn't crying. Anna had walked in on a fight.

Mari sneered at the sight of her, but at the last second she seemed to remember who Anna was and, if possible, got even redder. She curtsied.

"Excuse me, my lady," she said. "I'm clearly not wanted here!" She brushed past Anna into the hall. Anna turned to watch her go and then looked back at Heledd.

"I'm sorry, my lady," she said. "We've had a difficult day and, I confess, we missed your help with Gwenllian. The only time she didn't cry was when she nursed, and Mari believes I should not nurse her as much as I do. She says it spoils her. She says she won't return until I apologize for disagreeing with her."

Anna wasn't really listening to Heledd. She was thinking about how to get the baby and her nurse out of the castle at midnight, when Anna caught the last of Heledd's words.

"She said she wouldn't return?" Anna asked. She didn't think the nanny to a princess of Wales could choose to abdicate her responsibilities like that. "Surely not."

Heledd shrugged. "That's what she said. I say good riddance. I'm tired of her constant arguments and complaining."

"Tired enough to bring the baby on an adventure with me?" Anna asked.

"What did you say?" Heledd said, probably thinking Anna had mangled her Welsh again.

Anna closed the door. Gwenllian had fallen asleep and Anna pulled a stool up next to Heledd and sat down.

"I need you to listen to me and try to keep an open mind," she said. "I wasn't able to take the baby this afternoon because I was riding in the forest. Hywel was with me and we encountered two English soldiers."

"What!" Heledd gasped. To her the English were the equivalent of the bogeyman. Although she was wet-nurse to a princess, she was very inexperienced in the world. Her baby's father hadn't married her, and her baby had died two days before Gwenllian's mother, which is why Heledd had become the baby's wet-nurse.

"Listen!" Anna said. "Hywel and I followed them to their camp and I overheard a conversation between two soldiers. They

105

plan to capture the castle through treachery, and take the princess away to a prison in England."

Heledd held the baby closer, already panicked.

"They can't! I won't let them!"

"I won't let them either, Heledd, but there's only so much we can do. A traitor inside the castle is going to allow them to take the castle without a fight. Hywel and I have a plan to escape with Gwenllian before the English come. We need you to come too. Will you do that?"

Heledd's breaths came in gasps. "Leave Castell y Bere?" she asked. "And go where?"

"To Prince Llywelyn at Dolwyddelan," Anna said. "We need to keep Gwenllian safe and at the same time, warn the Prince about the English."

Heledd looked down at the floor, chewing on her lower lip as she thought. Anna held her breath, hoping she'd agree. Anna didn't pressure her but simply sat and waited. At last Heledd looked up and nodded. She hunched her shoulders, as if already oppressed by cold and fear.

"What do you want me to do?" Heledd asked.

* * * * *

Shortly after midnight, Heledd and Anna, with baby Gwenllian in her arms, traversed the back stairway, tiptoed through the kitchens, and walked into the frosty night. The sky was full of stars, but the moon hadn't yet risen. Starlight glinted off the patches of snow in the courtyard. Without the Prince, his attendants, and soldiers, only a skeleton staff remained at the castle, and most of them were asleep.

Anna led Heledd to the stables, behind which was hidden the postern gate. Hywel, as promised, was ready with warm blankets and provisions for their journey. Heledd carried a few possessions and all four were as bundled as comfort allowed. They were traveling light in an effort to put as much distance as possible between them and Castell y Bere before the English came.

They wanted to reach Hywel's hut before morning when a general alarm might be raised. Though it made Anna feel guilty, she'd lied to Gwladys, telling her that she was going riding early in the morning. Thus, it could be quite late tomorrow before anyone noticed their absence, especially if the English did come at dawn and put the castle into an uproar. They should have at least eight hours. Surely they could travel ten miles in that time?

Hywel had the forethought to wrap Madoc's hooves with cloths. The horse made only a muffled clopping sound as Hywel led him out of the back of the stables along the path that descended to the postern gate. Anna lifted the latch and the door opened easily. She raised her eyebrows at Hywel, who grinned. He'd oiled the hinges. The trio filed through the doorway and Anna pulled the gate closed. The latch clicked, and they stood silent, outside of Castell y Bere, gazing west at the valley below.

Hywel put a hand on Anna's arm. "Do you see the shadow?" he asked.

Anna strained to see but couldn't make anything out.

Hywel watched for another ten seconds. "Perhaps it's the English," he said. "We should hurry."

Heledd and Anna followed Hywel and Madoc northeast along the outer castle wall until Hywel reached a large bush, through which he and the horse disappeared.

"Hywel?" Anna called, as softly as she could. "Where are you?"

"Here!" he said, popping his head out from the bush, which was actually two bushes that Hywel had pushed between. He held the branches apart for Anna and Heledd to walk through them and Anna found herself at the start of a narrow, but well-worn trail that led down the side of the hill from the castle.

"The lads and I take this path when we go to the swimming hole in the summer," Hywel said, satisfaction in his voice. "It's safer for us now. And quicker."

The terrain away from the castle was very rocky, but grassy paths wound between the boulders and outcroppings, and Hywel led them down to the valley floor as surely as if it were daylight.

"You've done this before in the dark, haven't you?" Anna asked.

"Of course," he said. "Not often in winter, with the ground so snowy and slippery, but my friends and I often slip away late when our duties are done and come to bed after midnight."

"And the guards?" Anna asked, for Castell y Bere usually had the full complement of men in residence.

"They either don't know or turn a blind eye." Hywel shrugged. "They were young once too and they remember how it was."

Shaking her head at all she had to learn about castle life in Wales, Anna hugged Gwenllian closer to her in the sling she'd fashioned from a long strip of cloth. Gwenllian may have been a fussy baby during the day, but she slept at night, and for that the entire castle was grateful. She slept now, her little head resting on Anna's chest where she could hear her heart beat. Anna was warm enough at present and she hoped that Gwenllian was too.

They'd left the castle through a western door, and the path they'd taken wound to the north. Upon reaching the valley floor, Hywel headed towards the main road. Somewhere ahead Cadair Idris dominated the landscape. Looking back up the hill the castle was silhouetted against the stars. In truth, it should be impregnable. All it took to defeat a castle was a traitor within the walls.

They walked, silent and alert, hoping the shadows Hywel had seen from the top were anything but English soldiers on their way to take the castle. Anna had never walked more than five miles at one time, and double that, on snow-covered ground, in a dress, was aggravating and difficult. Hywel appeared confident and she'd long since decided to trust him completely, but he couldn't shorten the distance they had to travel.

They stopped only twice that night: once, when Hywel boosted Heledd onto Madoc's back because she was falling asleep on her feet, and a second time when Gwenllian woke with a little cry and needed Heledd to nurse her. Thankfully, this kept the baby happy and she went back to sleep without further fuss.

In the end, they made less than two miles an hour, for the sky was beginning to lighten as Hywel's hut came into view. He left the women in a stand of trees and went forward alone to determine if it was empty. All five of them, including Madoc, crowded into the hut. They were too exhausted to miss the fire Hywel feared to light. Except for Madoc, everyone threw themselves onto the hard-packed floor. Anna slept for the first time in over twenty-four hours, with the hood of her cloak as a pillow.

But she didn't sleep long because Gwenllian was ready to be awake. She sat up and began demanding attention. Mutely, Heledd handed her to Anna and lay back down. She was asleep instantly and as Anna looked from her to Hywel, she sighed. Both her friends were no less tired than she was, and there was no reason for all of them to be awake. Holding Gwenllian on her hip, Anna rummaged through Hywel's packs, still on Madoc's back, for food.

Hywel had done himself proud. He'd procured bread, dried meat, and even, bless his heart, three apples. They were spotty and pitted, and never would have passed muster in a modern grocery store, but they looked good in thirteenth century Wales. Anna took out some bread and one of the apples, and carried them and Gwenllian to a spot on the floor of the hut. Anna sat Gwenllian on her cloak and gave her a hard crust of bread to chew on. She gummed it while Anna ate an apple. Seeing that Gwenllian was temporarily happy, Anna closed her eyes and leaned her head against the wall. It was cold. Anna found she couldn't care.

Somehow the day passed. The hut was situated more than a mile from the main road. Hywel believed that no one who wasn't looking for it would find it. In this, he was right, and the companions spent the day uneventfully. Eventually, darkness fell again, though at that time of year it would have been just past four o'clock. Anna woke both Hywel and Heledd, only to find that Heledd was feverish. Hywel and Anna looked at each other in dismay.

"Don't worry," Heledd herself said. "I'm well enough to keep going. I'll ride with Gwenllian on Madoc."

Neither Hywel nor Anna said anything, but Anna spirits fell further. Hywel helped Heledd onto the horse, and this time she carried Gwenllian too. The baby was awake, and Anna hoped she'd be happy to ride where the motion might lull her to an early bed time. They set out into the snow.

After they'd gone two or three miles, Heledd spoke. "I feel a bit better!" she said. "I can walk now, if you like."

"No!" Hywel and Anna said together.

"You're still sick," Anna said. "Please stay on Madoc."

"All right," Heledd said. "But it's boring just sitting and riding, and Gwenllian is wet."

"Can you ride and change her at the same time?" Anna asked.

Heledd looked at her askance, but dug into her pack and pulled out some clothes for Gwenllian. It was quite an operation and Anna was glad it wasn't her up there. She walked a little ahead to talk to Hywel.

"Do you think it's really thirty miles to Dolwyddelan?" Anna asked.

"At least," he replied. "We should walk without stopping, if we can."

"If we can," Anna said. At two miles an hour, it would take fifteen hours if they walked straight through the night.

"If Heledd can make it," Hywel said.

Anna looked back at her, content now with Gwenllian nursing in her arms.

"If Heledd can make it," she echoed.

They'd traveled less than half the distance, perhaps twelve miles by Hywel's reckoning, when Heledd's fever worsened. The roughness of the terrain had forced them onto the road so at least walking was less difficult; Anna took the once-again-wakeful Gwenllian from her. Shortly thereafter, Heledd rested her head on Madoc's neck, hung her arms on either side of him, and fell asleep astride, her dress scrunched up around her thighs, exposing her woolen leggings. It was an amazing feat and Anna was envious, having not slept herself for two days.

Looking at Heledd, Anna had to face that their task might well be hopeless. Eighteen more miles could be eighteen hundred for all the difference it would make. Anna was a coddled child of the twenty-first century, deluded in imagining this journey was possible. What did she know of Wales and horses, and travel on foot at night in the middle of winter? Snow is utterly beautiful when one is inside a centrally heated home in Pennsylvania. It's freezing and awful when one is walking beside a feverish friend on a pony, two days into a trek across medieval Wales.

Clouds hovered near the ground and it was so dark Anna couldn't even see her feet. Eventually, Hywel took the initiative and led them off the road because Anna was too depressed and exhausted to do it. Within a few paces, he found a shelter of sorts in the craggy rocks. Anna thought of Sam, from *The Lord of the Rings,* who says: "If this is shelter, then two walls and no roof make a house!" At least the hobbits had Aragorn and Gandalf to lead the way. Here it was only Hywel and her, stumbling about in the dark.

They lifted Heledd off Madoc's back and huddled together to keep warm as best they could. That Gwenllian was relatively content, Anna took as a small miracle, but they needed a much bigger one as compensation for the terrible state Heledd was in. She burned fiery hot and they couldn't get her warm, even with her nursing Gwenllian, snuggled between Hywel and Anna.

The next morning, when Hywel and Anna woke, they didn't have to speak to know the truth, but what could they do but go on? Miserable, cold, and hungry, they set out again, braving the open road and daylight for the relative speed they offered. Heledd hung onto Madoc for dear life. After they'd traveled some hours, the situation began to worsen, if that was even possible. They felt, and then heard, pounding hooves behind them. Hastily, they pulled Madoc off the trail and into the trees. Within minutes, three riders passed at speed. Anna couldn't believe the English would make their presence so obvious this far into Gwynedd, but then, Castell y Bere had been unprepared for their treachery either.

Shortly after the riders disappeared, it began to snow. It started slowly, gradually building to a constant, thick, heavy downpour, coating the companions' cloaks and hoods. Anna hugged Gwenllian to her, trying to shelter her from the worst of it. They plodded another mile, with the wind picking up with every step.

Then Heledd spoke. "I'm quite warm now, really," she said.

Anna whipped around in time to see her begin a slow tumble off the horse. Moving fast, Hywel caught her as she fell, and then laid her on the ground. At first, Anna could only stare at her dumbly. Heledd didn't move and Anna could hardly comprehend the enormity of the disaster into which she'd led her friends.

My fault, my fault, my fault. The litany rolled on in Anna's head as she shifted Gwenllian in her sling and knelt to hold Heledd's hand. It was cold beyond imagining while her forehead was so hot it could have melted snow. Appalled, Anna pulled back Heledd's cloak and put her ear to Heledd's chest. She was breathing, but shallowly.

Swallowing hard, Anna tried to marshal her thoughts. Hywel leaned down to speak in Anna's ear but the rushing in her ears was so loud she couldn't make out his words, other than that they were urgent. Desperate, Hywel grabbed Anna by the shoulders, hauled her to her feet, and pushed her to one side so he could get to Heledd. He picked her up, staggering under the burden. Anna watched him numbly, hugging Gwenllian to her chest.

And then Anna saw what Hywel had feared: a man on a warhorse, coming at them out of the whirl of snow.

"My lord!" Hywel said. "Please help us!"

Anna blinked and her eyes cleared. The man wasn't English as she'd feared, but a Welshman, and a knight at that, complete with sword, mail hauberk, cloak, and mighty horse. He was young, with dark hair, dark blue eyes, and the fair skin that revealed his Celtic ancestry. Anna had seen him with David in the few days before the army left for Dolwyddelan and tried to remember his name. *Rhys, probably, or another Gruffydd.*

The knight approached and leaned forward to scrutinize their faces. "Who are you?" he asked.

Anna fumbled for the words, for Welsh always abandoned her when she was stressed. "I'm Anna, with Gwenll—"

"The Prince's daughters?" the man asked.

"Yes, yes!" Anna said, nearly collapsing with relief.

"Praise be to God!" the man said. "Riders from the south brought word that you were either dead or taken by the English! They captured Castell y Bere, slaughtered the garrison, and turned the rest out into the snow. They burned the bodies and the castle and left all in ruins. None of those left alive knew what became of you."

"Slaughtered the garrison . . . Gwladys . . ." The world began to darken around the edges and Anna swayed. She gritted her teeth, determined not to pass out.

The man leaned down and gave her his forearm. Confused, Anna stared at it. Obviously the man was insane.

"Take my arm," he said, patiently. "I am Mathonwy ap Rhys Fychan, nephew to Prince Llywelyn. I will take you to Dolwyddelan."

Now Anna reached for him and with a heave, he pulled her in front of him without even squashing Gwenllian. While she tried to get comfortable, the knight dismounted and took Heledd from Hywel. "Get on the pony," he ordered.

Hywel leapt on Madoc and the man passed Heledd to him. Then he appeared in the saddle behind Anna again. His hands grasped her waist and he lifted her, seemingly without effort, and settled her side-saddle in front of him. Gwenllian stirred and Anna patted her back to calm her.

"You're not well," Mathonwy said. "The air is cold, yet your face is hot and flushed."

Anna put a hand to her forehead and felt the heat of fever. "How did you find us?" she asked.

"Word reached us this morning of the fate of Castell y Bere. Your father sent scouts to determine how far into Gwynedd the English have pushed, as well as to seek word of you."

"Hywel and I stumbled upon the English encampment while we were riding," Anna said. "We overheard their plans and fled the castle before dawn, the day of the attack, with Heledd, the baby's nurse." Anna paused to look back. "Is she still living?"

"Yes," Mathonwy said, "though she's very ill. You too are fevered and I must get you all to the Prince quickly. It won't take long. We're not far from the castle."

As he spoke, Mathonwy gathered the reins in one hand and Anna with the other. She rested her head against his chest and closed her eyes. She told herself it was only for a moment but she was running hot and cold at the same time and just wanted to sleep.

They rode through the blowing snow and Anna would have dozed off, but for Gwenllian's increasing restlessness. She was hungry and Anna was sure her clothes were wet beneath the blankets. Anna pulled her woolen hat further over her ears, tucking in stray blonde curls in the process.

Finally, a shout came from Dolwyddelan's ramparts. Mathonwy tightened his grip on Anna and urged his horse faster. Another shout came and the gate to the castle burst open. Half a dozen men cantered toward them, David in the lead. Relief flooded through Anna at the sight of him and she sat up straighter. David turned his horse to ride beside Mathonwy.

"My lord Prince," Mathonwy said.

Anna canted her head to look at David. He glared at her. "Anna," he said.

She flopped a weak hand at him. "You're angry again," she said. "Don't be angry."

David had the grace to look chastened. "I thought I'd lost you," he said.

"I did what needed to be done," Anna said. "I'm sorry you were worried."

"Sorry?" he said, his voice rising again. "We lost a castle and a dozen men, but somehow we didn't lose you or Gwenllian. I can't understand how it is that you're here, safe, with Math."

"It was a long road, David, and Heledd is very ill," Anna said. "Hywel helped too—I couldn't have made the journey here without him."

David glanced back at Hywel, who looked up, his eyes clear and awake, despite the deep shadows under them.

"Let her be, my lord," Mathonwy said. "She's ill too."

David seemed to gather himself. "Thank you, sir, for rescuing my sister."

"I believe she rescued herself, my lord," Mathonwy replied. "I merely came upon her at the last pass."

"I was about to give up," Anna said.

"I don't believe that, my lady," Mathonwy replied. "Maybe you would give up for yourself, but not for Heledd or Hywel or Gwenllian." Anna tipped up her chin to look into Math's face. He smiled down at her. "You are too much of a Welsh princess to give up."

Anna began to reply that she wasn't really a princess—not even Welsh for that matter, though she didn't think she should go into that just now—when they clattered across the wooden bridge that led through to the gates to Dolwyddelan Castle.

As on that first evening at Castell y Bere, people filled the bailey. Prince Llywelyn waited at the top of the stairs to the keep and hurried down the steps to greet them when they rode in. Mathonwy bowed his head. One of the women hurried over and reached up to take Gwenllian from Anna. Grateful, Anna passed her off, but as Mathonwy dismounted behind her, Anna found herself falling off the horse. He caught her before she'd fallen far, and even though Anna thought to stand, he wouldn't have it. With her in his arms, Mathonwy led the way into the great hall, David and Prince Llywelyn following behind.

10

The rain had poured down all night long, plunking on David's helmet until he thought he'd go mad at the constant noise. Fortunately, the rain was so loud, the English couldn't hear the unnatural sounds of rain on metal. All six thousand of Father's army had moved in the night and spread out along a ridge facing west, so as to overlook the Conwy Valley all along its length. The sun had begun to add a hint of light to what had been a very dark night, and would rise fully within the hour. Father had hoped to attack sooner, but no one—Welsh or English—had been able to see his hand in front of his face until five minutes ago.

In summer, the Valley had some of the richest farmland in north Wales. At the moment, it was a fifteen mile-long bog, in which seven thousand English soldiers camped. Father had assigned David's company to the southernmost end of the English lines. David peered at the them from the trees, a tenth of a mile from where the English had camped.

Although they didn't know it, the English soldiers had set up camp closer to the woods than they should have, further from their fellows than they should have, and with fewer men than they should have had, fewer than one hundred. The men huddled under blankets in the rain, with neither fire nor tents. They had to be praying that the rain would stop but also had to know in their hearts that it wouldn't. This was winter in Wales. The fishermen had been right about the weather, and in another minute the Welsh would begin to make the English pay for their hubris and conceit in attacking Castell y Bere, thinking they could conquer Wales while David's father lived to defend it.

With Anna's arrival in Dolwyddelan, what had started out as a strategy had turned into a mission. Two days ago, the snow had stopped falling. The morning had dawned bright, crisp and clear, unusual for Wales at any time. Taking it as a positive sign, Edward had marshaled his army and headed into the mountains in earnest, following the east bank of the Conwy River. By evening, however, the wind had begun to blow from the southwest and almost imperceptibly at first, the weather began to warm.

It's not uncommon in Wales to have an early thaw after a month of hard winter. Within six hours, the temperature had risen thirty degrees, rain began to fall, and the snow to melt. Edward's advance slowed considerably. Having cleared the path of trees to minimize ambush, the army was forced to march through mud, all the while aware that the mountains, inside which the Welsh remained safe, loomed above them.

Edward then found himself in an even worse situation, because the rivers swelled with the rain and melting snow. Within a day and a half of setting out from Llansanffraid, his men were caught in a flood, the army stretched out nearly the entire distance to Conwy Falls with no way to go either forward or back. On one side was the Conwy River, preventing their advance to Dolwyddelan Castle, and on the other side, half a dozen other rivers, including the Clwyd, all in flood, blocking their retreat to Rhuddlan.

And now they were going to have to deal with the Welsh army. The men of Gwynedd were more than ready to launch an attack on their cold, miserable enemy. It wasn't the soldiers' fault they'd been born English and pressed into the service of the English king. But David couldn't afford to feel sorry for them. If his men were truly to send Edward packing, they would have to make him pay first.

"It's time, my lord," Bevyn said. "We must start the attack in a moment."

David nodded and followed him to where they'd staked the horses, well back in the trees. The English soldiers had sent out scouts of course, many of them, but the Welsh had ambushed and killed them all (they hoped) by an hour ago. Now the soldiers at every campsite in the valley would be wondering where their scouts were, and worrying.

David mounted Taranis and pulled his sword from its sheath. The plan was simple. Llywelyn had four hundred archers in the woods tonight, each with twenty arrows—more than enough to kill every man that Edward had brought within three minutes of shooting, though they'd never be that lucky. What they could surely do was sow panic.

David's company comprised twenty-five mounted men and a dozen archers, hidden in the trees and gullies on the other side of the hundred yards of cleared space that separated the woods from the encampment. A hundred yards was nothing to an archer, who could fire upwards of ten arrows a minute. In one minute, then, the dozen archers could shoot seventy-two arrows. They were aiming (quite literally) for accuracy and they were going to hold themselves to a steady six.

Bevyn and David decided to give the archers two minutes to work, and then the cavalry would charge out of the woods. Their intent was to cut a swath through the English camp, turn around and head back the way they'd come. Their intent, after a pass or two, was not to kill all the Englishmen or to take prisoners, but to disappear back into the woods, leaving a path of destruction in their wake. Ideally, this same scenario would be taking place simultaneously up and down the length of the Conwy Valley. There were at least twenty companies the size of David's, and many others that were larger.

Father commanded a company further north where the English encampments were more numerous and closer together. There, the foot soldiers would be put to use, to run screaming across the cleared space, hacking at anyone in their path, and then retreating to the woods on the other side. The Welsh would take casualties. David's mind shied away from it and perhaps it showed on his face.

"All men must face the time when they see death coming," Math said. "Each must prepare himself for battle as he will. Some become angry, some empty themselves of all emotion, some never conquer that fear and fight afraid."

"What do you do?" David asked.

"I hold an image of those I love in the front of my mind and every slash of my sword is a blow struck against those who stand between them and me."

"I've never been this afraid," David said. "I'm finding it hard to hold any thought at all."

"Empty yourself of everything but this moment, then," Math said. "Give yourself up to your senses. Acknowledge your fear, embrace it even, and you will find you have power over it. Your Father told me that you should meet him at his hunting lodge at Trefriw by noon. I intend to see you do just that."

David focused on his breathing, as his sensei would have suggested. *In and out; in and out; become aware of everything around you, the little noises of the forest, the rain, the stamping feet of the horses, then close the sounds off so that there's nothing but you and your enemy; nothing between you and what you have to do.*

"Fire!" Bevyn commanded. The archers released their arrows which flashed past in the gloomy dawn. David could barely see them, but despite the rain, he could hear them, a rushing sound that ended with screams from the English camp. *Press. Loose. Press. Loose.* Again and again they fired until those two long minutes passed and it was David's turn to fight.

His sword pointed forward as a signal to his men, David spurred Taranis out of the woods. Math held position on his right, as silent as David. Prince Llywelyn wanted the soldiers to hear the hooves, but to have his men appear as ghosts, descending on the English out of the murk.

The clearing sloped downwards as David approached the camp and he crossed it in thirty seconds. The camp was already in chaos from the arrows, with those men who could stand fumbling uselessly for their weapons. David's company hit them head on, Taranis taking down one man with his hooves and David slashing at a second man who failed to get out of the way. David killed him, and then killed another.

Eighty English, a hundred arrows, twenty-five horseman and there's no one left standing.

David swung Taranis around, having come out the other side of the camp, his sword bloody in his hand and sweat mixing with the rain and running into his eyes. His men had destroyed the English camp. Bodies sprawled on the ground everywhere, the same as in the clearing at Cilmeri when Anna drove into it. Men screamed further downstream, hopefully from other successful attacks, while men on the ground in front of David moaned. And still unrelenting, came the *rattity-tat-tat* of rain on David's helmet.

David found Math, still aboard his horse, Mael. Their eyes met and Math bowed his head. "My lord," he said.

David spun Taranis around. "Do we know who's down?"

"Morgan and Rhys," the soldier nearest him answered, "and one horse."

"You, you, and you," David pointed to three men whose names he couldn't remember just now. "Collect them and the horses that are loose."

The men obeyed. Others rode or walked from body to body, collecting weapons or kicking them out of English hands that still clasped them. One of the men David had pointed to slung a body over his shoulder while another helped him boost it onto the back of a riderless horse. David watched, trying to remember to breathe. Then he stood in his stirrups, his sword raised high. "We will withdraw to the west," he said. "We cross the river at Llanrwst."

Llanrwst had a usable ford, even with water this high, and Father meant for everyone to regroup on the west bank of the Conwy River. Although Father had been prepared to defend it, Edward didn't appear to know the location of this ford. David settled in his saddle to wait for the company to reassemble. Raindrops hit his mail links and careened off at odd angles. Math dismounted to stand at his stirrup. He handed David a cloth. David looked at it, uncertain as to what Math meant him to do with it.

"To clean your sword, my lord," Math said.

Oh. Unlike when he'd killed the boar, David felt no sense of jubilation, only a hollow thudding of his heart and a relentless purpose. *Killed the English, check; gathered our dead and wounded, check.* David wiped his sword, focusing hard on cleaning every last speck of blood from the blade. "I feel a little sick," he said.

"Not here, lad," Bevyn said, riding up to David. "We need to move now."

David turned Taranis' head. The ragged band entered the woods and trotted silently south towards Llanrwst. They'd gone a mile and were approaching the ford when another company materialized in front of them.

"Who goes there?" their leader asked, in classic movie-ese.

"Prince Dafydd's company," Bevyn answered, "riding to Trefriw."

"All is well?" the man said, stepping out from behind a tree, his sword loose in his hand.

"Our attack was successful," Bevyn said. He tipped his head at David. "His father would not have him late."

"My lord," the man said and gave way.

Several hundred men jostled to get across the ford, more or less at the same time. Many companies had completed their mission for the night, far more quickly than Prince Llywelyn had hoped. Some had more casualties than David's company, some fewer. It was the foot soldiers who might fare the worst. *And Father. Where is he?*

David rode through the newly established camp at Trefriw and up to the entrance to his father's hunting lodge, dismounting amongst the bustle and activity. Math grasped Taranis' reins when David dropped them. The rain still plunked on his helmet so he pulled it off and tossed it to the ground. He never wanted to wear it again. Anna came down the steps of the lodge, oblivious to the rain, the hem of her brown dress dragging in the mud. Math made a gesture with his hands, palms forward, as if to say to Anna *I've delivered him, safe. The rest is up to you.*

"What are you doing here?" David asked. Both she and Heledd had recovered from their fevers, but David didn't want Anna to get wet and cold again.

"David," Anna said. She held out her arms and after a moment's hesitation, David walked into them. He buried his face in her hair and she wrapped her arms around his waist. He squeezed her tight, trying to both contain and release the emotion inside him. David thought he might even cry, but found himself incapable. He loosened his hold on his sister and Anna studied him, her hand to his cheek.

"What can I do?" she asked. "You're very pale, and a little green."

"Here, lad," Bevyn said. He'd been waiting behind David while he greeted Anna. "I've just the spot." He took David's arm. David wanted to shake him off, but that sounded like too much effort and he allowed Bevyn to lead him away. Before they'd gone two steps, David bent over, his stomach heaving.

Anna moved closer. David wanted to stop her, but his stomach wouldn't let him. "Are you all right?"

"Not yet," Math said, intercepting her, "but he will be, given time. As much as it's possible for any of us."

"It's okay, Anna," David said. "I'll come find you in a bit."

Math tugged Anna away, back towards the entrance to the lodge. "Come," he said. "Let's get you out of the rain."

* * * * *

Edward wasn't a fool by any means. He knew the Welsh wouldn't just roll over and let him take their country, but it had been a long time since he'd been attacked in quite this fashion, and he'd never had quite as bad luck. Twenty-five years before, at the battle of Cymerau, Prince Llywelyn's forces had soundly thrashed King Henry's army, attacking at dawn, showering his men with arrows, ensuring that they couldn't advance any further into Wales. The day after that, the same force had met the English army on the open field and killed more than three thousand of them.

It was summer, then, not winter; in Deheubarth, not Gwynedd; but if the next twenty-five years of losses had taught the Welsh anything, it was not to underestimate the English. King Edward had rallied the men closest to him and had attempted to repel the attack centered on his encampment. Father was late getting to Trefriw because his had been the contingent that had faced Edward. Father hadn't won there, losing perhaps an equal number of men to Edward, but he'd not lost either and had retreated in good order, under cover of more arrows.

Once the entire Welsh force had crossed the Conwy River, Llywelyn had set about ensuring that the English couldn't advance any further south. He placed his archers on the ridges along the west bank of the river and instructed them to fire at will into the English camps. As before, the English tried to regroup, but couldn't advance either forward or back.

"It's over," Math said. "Edward must face the loss of half his men, either to us, to dysentery, or fever, and admit defeat." He stood beside David, two hundred feet above the river at the ridge of Cae Coch, just south of Trefriw, looking east.

"Will he make for the woods?" David asked, gesturing with one hand to the ridge on the other side of the valley where his company had stood hours before to launch the initial attack.

"He can't," Math said. "His men will never obey. They know those woods are full of Welshmen. He'll commandeer boats at Degannwy and pray we haven't taken Rhuddlan."

"But we have," David said. "Uncle Dafydd was true to his word."

"For once." That was Bevyn on David's other side, murmuring under his breath.

"Edward will have to sail all the way to Chester," Math said. "He has no choice."

"This will cost Edward plenty," Bevyn added. "In both gold and men. His barons are not going to be as supportive next time."

"If there is a next time," Math said.

"Whose flag flies there?" David asked, pointing to a red cross on a yellow background."

"Mortimer," Math said. "The same ones who betrayed your father."

Bevyn spat on the ground. "Too bad they weren't on the hill that day when you and your sister drove your chariot into their men," he said.

"Speaking of your sister, my lord," Math said, and then paused. David glanced at him, but he was looking at Bevyn. Math canted his head and Bevyn gave him a grin, before retreating a few steps away.

"What?" David asked.

Math turned to back to David, a look of concentration on his face. "I would like your permission to court her," he said.

Standing on the ridge, with Edward and his men retreating before him, David was overcome by the outrageousness of it all. He couldn't help himself. He laughed.

PART TWO

...EIGHTEEN MONTHS later...

TIMELINE: 1196-1284

1196-1240: Llywelyn ap Iorwerth (the Great) rules as Prince of
Gwynedd and later most of Wales.

1215: English barons force King John to sign the Magna Carta.

Circa 1228: Llywelyn ap Gruffydd born to Gruffydd ap Llywelyn,
eldest (illegitimate) son of Llywelyn ap Iowerth.

1240: Llywelyn ap Iorwerth dies. Succeeded by his legitimate but
younger son, Dafydd ap Llywelyn.

1244: Gruffydd ap Llywelyn dies when a makeshift rope breaks as he
attempts to escape from the Tower of London.

1246: Dafydd ap Llywelyn dies unexpectedly, without an heir.
Llywelyn ap Gruffydd stands in his stead.

1255: Battle of Bryn Derwin. Llywelyn ap Gruffydd defeats his
brothers, Owain and Dafydd, becoming sole ruler of
Gwynedd. Imprisons both brothers.

1256: Llywelyn releases his brother, Dafydd, from prison.

1258: Llywelyn accepts allegiance of Princes of Deheubarth, styles
himself *Prince of Wales.*

1263: Dafydd, Llywelyn's brother, defects to English.

1267: Treaty of Montgomery signed by Henry III, ratifying Llywelyn
ap Gruffydd's claim to the title *Prince of Wales.* Dafydd ap
Gruffydd restored to Llywelyn's favor as part of the treaty.

1268 (January): Marged and Anna come to Wales.

1268 (November): David ap Llywelyn born to Marged and Llywelyn.

1272: King Henry III dies.

1274: Dafydd ap Gruffydd, Gruffydd ap Gwenwynwyn, and Gruffydd's
son, Owain, plot to take Llywelyn's life. Plot is foiled by a

snowstorm, but Owain confesses to the Bishop of St. Asaph's. Dafydd and Gruffydd flee to England. Sensing blood, Edward I demands Llywelyn ap Gruffydd pay homage to him before he recognizes him as Prince of Wales. Llywelyn refuses.

1276: Edward I declares Llywelyn a rebel.

1277: Edward gathers an enormous army and invades Wales. Llywelyn forced to sue for peace, resulting in the Treaty of Aberconwy, which restricts Llywelyn to his lands in Gwynedd and restores Llywelyn's brother, Dafydd, and Gruffydd ap Gwenwynwyn to their lands in Wales (Dafydd in Gwynedd near Conwy, Gruffydd in Powys).

1278: Llywelyn marries Elinor, daughter of Simon de Montfort.

1282: Dafydd ap Gruffydd grows dissatisfied with subservience to Edward and rebels against him. Dafydd is joined by other Welsh lords who are discontented with Edward's rule. Llywelyn, as Prince of Wales, sanctions the revolt and unites much of Wales under his banner.

1282 (June): Elinor, wife of Llywelyn, dies in childbirth. Their daughter, Gwenllian, lives.

1282 (December): Ambush of Llywelyn by Mortimers thwarted by David and Anna.

1283 (January): Edward gathers a second huge army to attack Wales. Is soundly defeated by the resurgent Welsh.

1284 (April): Edward II born.

1

David pushed open the door to the great hall and stood on the threshold. Beyond the entranceway, rain poured down in sheets and made muddy puddles in the courtyard. The water in the air and on the ground reflected the flickering light of the torches that lit the gatehouse of Rhuddlan Castle. "Hey, David," Anna said. "Are you all right?"

"Fine," he said. "Why are you up?" He pulled off his cloak and shook it out, soaking the rush mats spread around him on the floor. He checked for his sword on his left hip. Ever since Papa had knighted him last year, he was never without it, not even in his own hall in the middle of the night.

"I couldn't sleep and didn't want to wake Math," Anna said. "What are you doing out in this?"

"Taranis spooks during thunderstorms," David said. "I wanted to make sure he was all right."

"How was Dyfi?" Anna asked.

"Asleep," David said. "That horse is so placid, sometimes I wonder if she doesn't sleep even when you ride her."

Anna laughed and turned from him, glad to see him well. She was tired enough now to return to her room. Lately, her sleep had been troubled and perhaps the storm was affecting her too, because within moments of laying her head on her pillow, Anna dreamt as her mother for the first time in many months:

I wrap my arms around my waist and lean forward, trying to control my nausea as the plane shudders and jerks. The pilot puts out a hand as if to steady me, and then quickly moves it back to the controls.

"My God, Meg!" he exclaims. "What happened? We should be dead on that mountain! Now, there's nothing but static on the radio and I'm flying by the seat of my pants here. The electronics are good, but what I can see of the terrain looks totally wrong. I don't understand it!"

"Just put her down if you can, Marty," I say. "We can figure out what's going on when we land."

"Put her down!" Marty shouts. "Where!" And then he screeches. The sound echoes throughout the small cabin. The trees we've been flying over give way to a heavy sea, rolling beneath us.

"Jesus Christ!" Marty says as he circles the plane back toward land.

I say nothing, just look out the window at the country below, my chin in my hand. The fog isn't as thick now, but it limits visibility to a quarter-mile. No houses or

*towns are in sight and the land is rocky all the way down
to the shoreline.*

"Where in the hell are we?" Marty demands.

*As we are supposed to be flying from Pasco,
Washington to Boise, Idaho, I can understand his
bewilderment. The land looks familiar to me, however. I
suspect this fact will not comfort Marty in the slightest.*

*"Fly south, Marty," I say, after he circles the plane
for a third time.*

*We can just make out the sun, trying to shine
through the fog. It's very high in the sky. It makes me
think that, temporally, we are in the same late-summer
we left in Washington. Wild-eyed, Marty does as I ask. We
fly on, unspeaking. The land rolls away beneath us. The
rocky coastline gives way to a hilly, grass-covered
terrain, interspersed with stands of trees. Everything is
green. The patches of ground we can see don't include a
city.*

*"We're going to run out of fuel soon," Marty says
softly. "What do you suggest we do?"*

*I sigh. "Just put her down. Find a field. Hopefully
people live among these trees, though I don't see any
smoke."*

*"Smoke," Marty retorts. "I gather I'm not looking
to follow the power lines?"*

"I'm afraid there won't be any power lines."

"You know where we are?" Marty says. He glances at me. "What's going on here!"

I turn to look at him. Watching his face, I say as clearly as I can, "This has happened to me before. I can't explain it, but I'm afraid we've been displaced in space and time, to a world not our own."

"You're kidding me!" Marty snorts. He looks out the windscreen. "Aren't you kidding me?"

I shake my head and sit on my hands so he can't see them trembling. I've prayed for this to happen since Anna and David disappeared. I'd given up hope. "Sixteen years ago, I lived in thirteenth century Wales for close to a year," I say. I look out the window again, trying to get my bearings. "But I can't tell from up here what century this is."

Marty grips the yoke so hard his knuckles turn white. Another minute and the fog thins enough to reveal a small lake with a clearing next to it that looks like a possible landing site. Unspeaking still, Marty circles the little plane, lowering it with every revolution. He lands and brings the plane to a halt. With a twist of his wrist, he turns off the engine, and we're quiet.

"I think I saw power lines to the north, just as we landed," he says.

"No, Marty. You didn't."

"I did. I know it."

I decide not to wait for further recriminations or questions I'm not ready to answer, and wrench the door handle. Pushing it open, I hop out, hauling my backpack from the seat behind me. The lake is a few yards to my right and is as clear as any I've ever seen. Grasses grow almost to the water's edge and wildflowers cover the hills around us. I take a deep breath and gaze up at the sky, now as clear as the air I breathe. The fog is gone. And what does that fog represent? The fog of confusion? The mists of time? I have no answers for Marty.

Before we landed, I too noticed something in the distance that looked man-made, though it wasn't power lines. Hoping to spot it again, I shoulder my pack and take off at a brisk walk, following the south side of the lake. After fifty yards or so, I angle away from the lake and head up a small hill that forms the south side of the little valley. Another ten minutes of hard walking brings me to the top. I stop and turn to look back at the plane. Marty's still seated inside. Then I gaze in the opposite direction and my heart skips a beat.

A long wall stretches before me. Dear God, it's Hadrian's wall. I sink to my knees. This is just too much. I'll have to cross miles of open country to reach Llywelyn, if he still lives in this world. Is time here following the same trajectory as at home? Is it 1284 or a different era altogether? Even if he changed the future as I urged, Llywelyn still may not have survived. The thought is

139

terrifying and hysterical laughter bubbles up in my throat. I try hard never to think of him. Can I really return to him again?

I look down at the plane and am astonished to see it rolling steadily across the grass. I watch dumbly. Surely, he's not going to take off and leave me here? Where exactly does he think he's going to go? To find his mythical power lines?

I shout, though I know he can't hear me over the engine of the plane, and take off at a run down the hill. I've walked too far, however, and I'm only half-way down the slope when his front wheels lift off the ground. Five seconds later, he's fifteen feet above the ground—then thirty—then one hundred. He circles the little white plane around the lake and even has the gall to tilt his wings to wave at me, before heading north to heaven knows where. I watch until he disappears . . .

Anna jerked awake, startled out of sleep by the sudden ending to the dream. She reached out under the covers, looking for comfort, but felt instead an empty space beside her.

"Math?" she said. Anna pushed up on one elbow to survey the room, which was beginning to lighten with the rising sun.

He was at the door, already dressed, but turned back to Anna when she called to him. "I hoped not to wake you," he said.

"Why are you up?" Anna asked.

"Last night's storm is spent, but the Irish Sea is unforgiving. The results are driving towards shore, including many dead. Your brother is hoping that we'll find some people alive and he asked that I come with him to survey the damage."

"I'll come too," Anna said, swinging her legs out of bed.

"Anna," Math said, "there's no need."

Anna walked to him and reached up to clasp her hands around his neck. He wrapped his arms around her waist and pulled her close. "We've talked about this before," she said. "I'm not a glass doll. I'm not broken."

"You tell me this, Anna," Math said, "and I know it's true. But I don't feel it."

"There will be another baby," Anna said. "I was only nineteen last week. I realize that many girls here have three children by my age, but I'm not worried. It's only the old busybodies in the solar who look at my belly and wonder why I haven't yet given you a son."

"Part of me would choose for you to never give me one, rather than lose another in the same fashion. I can handle anything but your tears, Anna."

It was Math, in fact, who'd kept better track of the days and had known Anna was pregnant before she did. Even though she'd assumed a child was inevitable, the responsibility for it had brought her to her knees at first. But then as the weeks progressed, she'd accepted it, and then embraced the growing life inside her as a natural result of the love between her and Math. When the pregnancy, which had lasted all of fourteen weeks, had ended three weeks ago, Anna had sobbed through many days, desolated, while Math had stood by, helpless.

In truth, Anna had needed her mother, but as always, she was in another world and too far away to help. The dream of her was fading now. If Anna focused, she could recall the black abyss and the sense of despair, both of which were very familiar, though she thought she'd conquered her fear of them in the past year. But she couldn't control her dreams and perhaps the miscarriage had brought those feelings bubbling to the surface again.

Math's request to court her had caught Anna completely by surprise. She and David had discussed Papa 'marrying her off' when they'd first arrived in Wales, but Anna hadn't seriously considered it again. She'd thought it ridiculous, really, not only because she was only seventeen, but because she wasn't Welsh, because she was from the future, and because telling Math about who they were and where they were from meant she'd have to commit to *this* life as the only one she was going to get.

As the months passed, Math was persistent in his attentions, and heaven help her, Anna grew to like him—more than like him. She began to miss him when he was off somewhere with David, patrolling the border or fighting the English, and found herself atop the battlements, waiting for a sign of his return. Math was upright and straightforward, honest and trustworthy, a knight in the truest sense of the word. And whenever he looked at Anna, it was with a thoughtful expression, intense and gentle at the same time—as if he saw something in her that was special, and perhaps special only to him.

Finally, it was David who'd intervened, understanding what was going on as only he could. So they'd sat Math down and told him the truth, and he'd shaken his head at Anna, not because he didn't believe that she was from the future, but because she'd been silly to think something like that would make him change his mind about her. Anna had long since changed her mind about him.

"If you help me get dressed, I won't have to wake Nell," Anna said. Her maid slept on the floor in the women's chamber. Nobody there would want to be awakened at five in the morning. Anna didn't like needing a maid at all, but she couldn't do all of the laces up the back of her dress by herself. Anna pushed open the shutter to see what the day looked like. After the heavy rain of the night before, the sky was clear, though more clouds hovered on the western horizon.

With Math's help, Anna got into her clothes, twisted her hair onto the top of her head, and pinned it. Not exactly a 'lady of the manor' look, but they were going to the beach and she could clean up better when they returned.

David was waiting for them in the courtyard, Taranis already saddled. Math boosted Anna onto Dyfi, and then mounted Mael. As always when traveling with David, a dozen other men-at-arms came with them. Even a morning stroll on the beach could turn into something malevolent if English were about and Papa insisted David not take unnecessary chances.

"Hey, Anna," David said. "What's up?"

143

Anna smiled back at him, loving the familiar greeting, though it didn't quite have the same ring to it in Welsh.

"Why should you have all the fun?" she asked. "I need to get out and move around."

"Okay," he said. "But I don't think this is going to be fun."

"Yes," Anna said. "I do realize that, but perhaps I can be of help."

In the nine months that Math and she had been married, they'd made a full circuit of the half a dozen estates which he controlled, plus the two he held for Papa. Because many of the lands were in Deheubarth, they'd been lost in the years since 1277 and had only recently been regained.

In each estate, Math had near total power, sitting as judge and jury in all disputes, overseeing the management of the land, and all-in-all acting as an almost-king. Anna, in turn, was a combination hostess, housekeeper, and substitute mother to the people who worked the land or served in the castle or manor. In the process, she found that everyone expected her to act as doctor when the herbalist wasn't available. Anna had brought her satchel with clean bandages and a water sack. People on the beach this morning might need them.

Rhuddlan Castle, which Papa had gladly made his main power base in north Wales, was a monstrosity, but at this point, one Anna could really get behind. Edward had built it after destroying the old castle—the one in which Papa had made his obeisance in 1277 to his humiliation. Now, if one were to use Mom's terminology, the castle resembled 'the finest example of

Edwardian castle architecture ever constructed.' They rode out of the main entrance at the northwest corner of the castle, above which flew both Papa's banner and David's.

Because the ocean tended to throw its refuse on the beach east of the Clwyd estuary, they didn't cross the river, but headed north along the river's eastern bank until they reached the shore of the sea two and half miles downstream. When they arrived at the beach, even though it couldn't have been more than six in the morning, a dozen people combed the shoreline for whatever the sea had thrown up.

Anna dismounted where the cheat grass turned into beach, which now that the tide was out, was a hundred feet deep. She let Dyfi's reins trail and left her cropping the short grass on the landward side of a dune. As Anna faced the sea, the sun shone from behind her. Logs, broken pottery, and planks that perhaps had once been part of a ship littered the beach, but no bodies that she could see. Anna breathed in the sea air, and Math took her hand.

"Let's walk this way," he said, pointing northeast.

Anna lifted her skirt rather than let it trail in the wet sand and wished for sandals she could easily remove. They crunched along anyway, away from the other people, though behind her Anna could hear David making disposition of his men. It was nice to be alone with Math, with just the seagulls calling and the sound of the surf crashing on the shore. It was hard to believe that a storm had raged here in the night, driving men and boats into the deep. The beach narrowed as they went north, and they followed the shore around a mini-headland that bulged into the sea. Further on, the beach projected northeast again, and it was here that they finally saw the bodies.

Five people lay in the sand, each contorted awkwardly. Anna and Math moved from man to man but all were beyond their help except for the one farthest down the beach whose arm moved as Anna reached him. He had brown hair and beard and wore a long robe. She dropped to her knees beside him and as her shadow loomed over him, he opened his eyes. Crow's feet showed in the corners of his eyes as he smiled up at Anna.

"It's you," he said, in English, and then blinked. Anna sat back on her heels, surprised, and he pushed himself up on his elbows.

"How do you feel?" Anna asked in the same language, uncertain of who he was or what he'd meant.

He blinked again, tipping his head to one side as he studied her. "I apologize, my lady," he said. "I mistook you for someone else." He turned his head from left to right, surveying the beach, but nobody moved along it. The man pushed to his knees, and then stood, swaying, so that Math reached out and caught his elbow to hold him steady.

"I'm Math ap Rhys Fychan," Math said carefully, also in English, "the Prince's nephew, and this is my wife, Anna."

"Aaron ben Simon, a physician, at your service," the man said.

Math nodded, but continued in Welsh while Anna translated for Aaron. "Can you walk with us down the beach? Our

146

horses are near and we can provide you with lodging at Rhuddlan Castle until you're well enough to make your way elsewhere."

"Rhuddlan, is it?" Aaron asked. He looked away, his brow furrowed, focusing first on the water and then again on the beach around him.

"Is something wrong?" Anna asked. "Beyond the obvious, that is?"

"I had a companion, a friend who journeyed on the ship with me. We were thrown into the water together, but the sea pulled us apart as we neared shore. I'd hoped that she too reached land safely, but I don't see her."

"I'm sorry," Anna said, not knowing what else to say.

He nodded and bowed his head, obviously troubled. Math took his arm and the trio walked back around the headland to where David was waiting with the horses.

"Four dead men lie further up the beach," Math said. "This is Aaron, a Jewish physician. I've offered him refuge in the castle."

"Good," David said.

Aaron had bowed when he heard his name spoken, but Anna didn't think he understood the rest of the Welsh, so she reverted to English.

"Please meet my brother, David, Prince Llywelyn's son."

"My lord!" Aaron said. He bowed deeply. "Thank you for your hospitality."

"I'm sorry it's necessary, but you are welcome to stay as long as you need," David said. "Was Wales your original destination, or Ireland?"

"Wales," Aaron said, "though I'd not intended to arrive as destitute as the storm has left me."

"Do you have family here, or someone who is awaiting word of your arrival?" Anna asked.

Aaron shook his head. "My wife and daughter died some years ago. I have a son, Samuel, who remains in England."

"Then why Wales?" David asked.

Aaron couldn't mistake his tone, and hurried to explain. "People of my faith are no longer welcome in England, my lord," he said. "I'd heard that Wales might be more obliging." He kept his head bowed, not looking at David.

David gazed down at him and then looked at Anna. "You heard right," David said.

Aaron's head popped up. "I am relieved to hear it," he said. "Please allow me to be of service to you, or your father."

"We can always use a physician," David said.

"So my companion assured me," Aaron said.

"Companion?" David asked.

But Aaron was looking toward the sea again, and this time he appeared to find what he was looking for, because he took several steps away from David. A small figure—a woman—moved along the beach, coming from the river. Aaron hesitated, peering into the distance and squinting.

"Meg!" he said.

Aaron hiked up his robe and took off at a run towards the woman. She waved and veered toward him. They met half-way up the beach, each taking the other's arms in a decorous hug. Aaron then turned her towards David and Anna. The closer they got, the more Anna's eyes watered; tears poured down her cheeks and blurred her vision.

"Oh my God, it's Mom," David said, his voice choking on the words.

His words released Anna and she raced across the beach, her boots slipping in the sand. Sobbing, Anna threw herself at her mother and knocked her backwards. Meg held her, her cheek against Anna's hair, rocking her as if she were a baby.

"Oh, my darling daughter," she repeated over and over. Anna couldn't stop crying, even when her mother took her face in her hands and kissed her eyes, trying to get Anna to stop. "It's okay. It's me. I'm here," she said. Meg looked past Anna to David, who'd come to a halt five paces away, as if he couldn't believe what he was seeing. "And your brother too." Meg held out one arm and he came into the circle of it, embracing both her children.

"How did you get here?" Anna asked.

Meg shook her head. "Same as always," she said. "I can't believe you're here too. I didn't let myself believe it." David's shoulder muffled Meg's voice.

They hugged and rocked until the tightness in Anna's chest loosened and she was able to relax her hold enough to look into her mother's face. "You must have been through a lot," Anna said.

"Me?" Mom said, and laughed through her tears. "What about you? Have you been here all this time?"

"We have," David said. "Let's get you home." He put his arm around his mother's shoulder and looked at Anna over the top of her head. When he'd last seen Meg, they'd been same height. Anna held tight to her mother's hand as David herded them, along with a very bemused Aaron, back to where they'd left the horses.

"You mentioned that you had known the Prince many years ago," Aaron commented, "but I didn't quite catch that you'd given him a son."

"I couldn't tell you," Meg said, and left it at that.

A few steps further on, Math waited to be introduced. Anna took his hand and pulled him to her mother. "This is my husband, Mom," Anna said. "Mathonwy ap Rhys Fychan."

"I'm pleased to meet you, Madam," Math said, in his most formal Welsh.

Meg stuck out her hand, as if meeting Anna's husband was a perfectly normal thing to do, but then ruined it. "You're married?" she blurted out. Her hand went to her head before Math could take it. "How can you be married?"

Anna tightened her grip on Math's other hand. "I'm sorry you missed it, Mom," Anna said, "but, well . . . you weren't here."

With that, Meg melted again. She started crying; then Anna started crying, and they fell into each other's arms. Math kissed the top of Anna's head and patted her on the shoulder. "We'll leave you a moment," he said, and tipped his head to Aaron who moved past them towards the horses and out of earshot.

Once again, Anna struggled to regain her composure, wiping her cheeks with the backs of her hands.

"How long have you been back here?" David asked. The control in his voice told Anna he was determined to remain on an even keel.

"Beginning of August," Mom said.

"*How* did you get back here?" Anna asked, finally able to calm down enough to marshal her thoughts.

"By plane," Mom said.

Plane? Hadn't I just dreamed of a plane?

"Near Hadrian's Wall."

"Hadrian's Wall?" David asked. "And you made it here all by yourself?"

"I had help," Mom said, "most recently Aaron's."

"Hadrian's Wall is a long way from here," Anna said.

"It is," David agreed. "Father is going to freak."

2

Meg froze, her hand on David's shoulder, her face still. "Father?" she asked.

"He's alive, Mom," David said. "And he's here, at Rhuddlan."

"Oh, David," Mom said. She put the back of her hand to her mouth. "I didn't dare . . . I mean, I hardly dared to even think that he might be, that I might be able to see him again. So you think . . ." she stopped.

"Do I think he'll want to see you?" David said. "Yeah, I know he will."

"But how did you . . . how did you find him? How did you know?"

"We didn't," David said. "Father did, the moment we arrived. We literally drove into his attackers at Cilmeri and saved him."

"He *went* to Cilmeri?!" Meg's voice went high. "He *went* to Cilmeri on December 11th?"

"It's okay, Mom," Anna said, trying to calm her down. "He felt he had to, despite your warning."

"He could have died!" Mom said. She glared at David and then at Anna, and then the two women burst into tears again.

All David could do was stare at them in amazement. They should be *happy*! Two of the smartest, most independent-minded women in all of Wales, both of whom had managed to trek miles and miles across unfamiliar terrain, surviving entirely on courage and nerves, were falling to pieces *again*.

Meg turned to David, her cheeks wet, blinking her eyes to rid them of tears. "This is too much to take in," she said. "You were a child last time I saw you, David, and now you are grown and Anna is married." Meg turned back to Anna. "You got married at what? Seventeen? Eighteen?!"

David tried injecting rationality into the proceedings. "Math's a great guy, Mom," he said. "He can't believe how lucky he is to have her; and the marriage secures a beneficial alliance for Father. It's all worked out really well."

"Besides, I'm nineteen now," Anna said.

Meg stared at them for a second and then gave a laugh that was almost a bark. "See!" she said. "Precisely my point!" And then, more thoughtfully, "Does Math know where you're from?"

Anna nodded. "He *knows*," she said, "but I think he's just beginning to *believe*."

"It's always been impossible to believe," Mom said. "And I'm living it."

"Math is pretty grounded in the here and now," David said. "He told me that if Anna looks Welsh, speaks Welsh, and is acknowledged as Welsh by the Prince of Wales, that is good enough for him."

"I guess there is something to be said for that," Mom said. "We will need hard-headed and practical people in the new Wales."

"Don't you remember when you came to Wales the first time?" Anna asked. "Do you remember what it was like trying to find your way when you didn't speak the language and knew nothing about anything that was important?"

Meg sighed. "I do remember," she said. "I remember very well. If not for Llywelyn, I don't know that I would have survived. Before I knew it, we were in love and I was pregnant with David. I managed to bypass most of the trauma by ignoring it."

"We couldn't ignore it, Mom," Anna said. "It was all so awful at first."

Meg nodded. "I know, sweetheart. That you're standing in front of me, whole and happy, tells me that you and David have done remarkably well, at a much younger age than I was."

"We did have each other," Anna said.

"And we also had Father who knew who we were from the start," David added.

"It would have been different if we'd appeared in Cilmeri and *not* killed Papa's attackers," said Anna. "Imagine trying to make your way in Wales with no help from anyone. We could have starved to death. David could have ended up a stable boy, and me a scullery maid."

"Or worse," Mom said, her expression darkening.

"A lot worse!" Anna agreed. "Imagine if the English had captured us!"

More settled, at least for the moment, they walked back to the horses. David mounted Taranis and pulled Meg up behind him. "So, how did you get from Hadrian's Wall to Wales?" David asked, turning Taranis and heading south to the castle. "Planes, trains, automobiles?"

"Try feet and horses," she said. "And then, of course, the ship."

"Oh, Mom." David said. "How bad was the seasickness?"

"That's how I made friends with Aaron," she said. "He gave me a concoction to settle my stomach, which helped, and then he kept me distracted from my stomach by stories of his family. In the end, though, it didn't make any difference since the storm broke up the boat and dumped us into the sea."

Within a few minutes, they approached Rhuddlan Castle. Meg got very quiet. As they rode in under the gatehouse, David glanced up to see a familiar figure standing at the top of one of the towers. Father looked down at them—and it felt like the whole world paused and took a breath.

"Llywelyn," Mom whispered, gripping the back of David's cloak. "I look terrible! My hair, my clothes are full of salt. I don't even have shoes. He can't see me like this."

David ignored her, not dignifying her concerns with a response. *As if Father will care about those things.* He didn't know if Father knew what he was seeing, but he left the battlements the instant they arrived and reappeared at ground level so fast he must have run most of the way. He crossed the bailey with his characteristic long stride, his head steady and his eyes fixed on Meg, and then halted at her knee. He reached for her and she slid into his arms.

"I never meant to leave you, Llywelyn," she said, shaking her head. "I didn't want to keep your son from you."

He didn't dignify that with a response either. Llywelyn slipped one arm around her waist and brought her close to him while threading his other hand through her hair. "I never for a moment thought you did," he said, and kissed her.

* * * * *

"So what's the story, Mom?" Anna said. She'd whisked her mother off to her room to get cleaned up and into proper clothes and now everyone was back together, ready to listen to what Mom had to say. Seating himself behind his desk, Father pulled up a chair for Mom beside him and waved Math, Anna, and David to a bench on the other side of the table.

"I spoke with my priest," Father said without preamble, "and he sees no reason why we can't get married tomorrow. It's not like we have any consangual relationships."

"None among your advisors will object, Father?" David asked.

"Marged's return is more than they ever dared hope for. Our marriage will secure your legitimacy in the eyes of the Pope and the English nobility, if and when the interdict is lifted."

Mom narrowed her eyes at David. "Has he asked me to marry him, or is he just assuming I will?" she said in English.

"Assuming, I think," David said. "You will marry him, won't you?" David held his breath, against the chance, even after all this, that she'd say no.

"Of course," she said. "I just wondered."

"What are you saying?" Father interrupted, obviously disgruntled at all the English.

"I'm sorry, my lord," Mom said in Welsh, laughing. "I asked David if I'd heard correctly. Am I right that you are asking me to marry you? Because it wasn't entirely clear."

Father swore and thumped his fist on the desk. "You try me, woman!" Events were way out of control for him and his talking to the priest had been an attempt to get things back on track.

Mom studied him. "You're still excommunicate, then," she said.

He took her face in his hands and met her eyes. "And every day we live the best we can, as we hope God would wish."

Mom didn't move, just kept staring at him.

"It's been sixteen years since you pledged yourself to me," Father said. "Will you say the words of marriage in front of my people?"

"Yes, Llywelyn," Mom replied. "I missed you every day we were apart."

"Good!" Father said and kissed her for a long time. David looked away. It was great that his parents were together, but . . . *Enough! Let's move on to the story!*

As if they'd heard his thoughts, they broke apart.

"I want to know everything that has happened to you since you left me," Father commanded.

"Everything?" Mom asked. "That will take a long time, Llywelyn."

"Since I cannot take you to bed, I have nothing else to do," Father replied.

David could feel his face getting hot. Mom gave him a pitying look.

"Papa!" Anna admonished.

Father ignored them both. "Talk!" he said to Mom.

First, Mom explained how she'd left Wales the first time. "I'd gone to you in the night, Anna. You'd had a dream that scared you and woke you up."

"I often do," Anna said. "I don't know why."

Mom nodded. "I took you to the garderobe. When I crouched in front of you, I heard a 'pop'. My water had broken as I went into labor with David. I gasped, and we were gone."

"Just like that?" David asked.

"Just like that," Mom said. "I found myself in the grass outside Grandma's house."

"So, any shock could send us back," Anna said.

"That," Father said, "would be unacceptable."

David agreed. There was no way he was going back now.

"I wish I could reassure you," Mom said. "But how it happens is a mystery to me."

"We'll table it for the time being," Father said.

Mom then talked through the next fourteen years of their lives, until she reached the point where Anna and David disappeared from Pennsylvania.

"My sister called me when you two didn't arrive to pick up your cousin."

"Called you?" Math interrupted.

Mom hesitated, and then explained. "In our time, a person can speak into a machine that transmits her voice to another person far away."

Father exchanged a look with Math, before folding his arms across his chest, not looking at all satisfied.

Mom glanced at him. She patted his knee. "It's called a telephone. I mentioned it once before. I'll explain later."

"You were telling us about Aunt Elisa," David reminded her.

"Yes," Mom said. "At the time she was puzzled, and not a little angry, because you'd left your cousin to languish at his friend's house for hours. By the time she got off work, however, she was genuinely worried. The police came, but they never found any trace of you or the van. You remain, I presume, an unsolved mystery."

"As will you," David added. "I wonder what the authorities are thinking now, with the addition of your disappearance."

"What did you think when we disappeared, Mom?" Anna asked. "Did you think we were dead?"

"Not for more than a moment," Mom said. "During those first heart-wrenching hours when you were missing, I refused to think it, and then, once the police had left and I was alone, I realized I couldn't think it. I was very lonely without you, but I believed you were alive, just alive somewhere else. Though I certainly was aware of the significance of the date you disappeared . . ." Tears welled up in her eyes again. "It's just too good to be true that you're here!"

Anna, also teary-eyed, stood up and hugged her.

Father and David looked at each other. Just as David had thought earlier, the expression on his face said, 'Okay—enough!'

Then Mom began to laugh, her shoulders shaking as she struggled for control. Father looked startled, but David remembered that Mom often laughed during stressful situations. It was the crying that was unusual for her. Mom squeezed Anna's hand and David was glad to see the laughter instead of tears.

"I love you, *cariad*," she said. "This has all been a little overwhelming."

"And you're tired," Father said, "so let's finish this."

"As I told Anna and David," Mom said, "I arrived at Hadrian's Wall."

"But that's hundreds of miles from here!" Father said.

"I know, Llywelyn. I was as horrified as you to discover it."

"You really are from the future," Math interjected. He'd rested his elbows on his knees and looked from Mom to Father, and back. "There are times that I forget where Anna was born, but now . . ." he paused, and then leaned back in his chair.

"Are you okay with this?" Anna asked.

"This is fascinating," he said. "I'm very interested in what your mother has to say. Please continue."

Mom nodded. "I walked along the wall, anxious to avoid meeting anyone. My clothes, of course, were entirely inappropriate, and I was anxious about what time I found myself living in. I only hoped that this was 1284—it could easily have been another era entirely.

"The first evening, I spent in one of the ruined Roman forts along the wall. When I entered it, however, I found that I wasn't alone. A ten year old boy had hidden himself there, frightened; hands tied behind his back, he huddled in a corner."

"You're kidding," David said, reverting to English.

Mom shrugged. "Turns out he was the nephew of Carlisle Castle's castellan, Sir John de Falkes, who crusaded with Edward before being given custody of the region. The boy, Thomas, had been riding with an English patrol—apparently they start them early in war in England—which had come upon a Scottish raiding party and gotten wiped out, with the boy as the only survivor. The Scots had tied him up and thrown him over a horse, but he'd slid off the back into the brush in the dark and gotten away."

"So you helped him get home?" Anna asked.

"I did," Mom said. "We walked all night. By dawn we'd reached the outskirts of Carlisle when we encountered Falkes riding out with his men to look for Thomas. They took me in, cleaned me up, and sent me on my way to Wales, though, in truth, he didn't like that part at all."

"He didn't want you to come here?" David said.

"England *is* at war with us, after all," Mom said. "In the end, however, I convinced him I was harmless and he paid for my passage, if for no other reason than to discharge the debt he owed me for caring for his nephew."

"Chance, luck, and happenstance." Father's eyes darkened and he looked very serious, almost grim. "I don't want to lose you three. I don't want Wales to lose you. How do I keep you here?"

Mom, Anna, and David shook their heads, each solemn.

"I don't know," Mom said.

3

Some people (like Goronwy) remembered Meg well, though their memory must have been of a girl only a little older than Anna, rather than the confident woman she'd become. Admittedly, she looked pretty terrible when she arrived and they might not have recognized her when Llywelyn brought her into the great hall. She and Llywelyn had threaded their way through everyone seated at the tables and disappeared into his private apartments with David, Math, and Anna trailing behind. The fact that Papa and Mom were holding hands was a pretty good give-away, though, that something was up, and by the time everyone had finished talking and came out for afternoon meal, the whole castle was in an uproar.

But it was a *good* uproar.

Prince Llywelyn is marrying Prince Dafydd's mother! He sent for her but before she could reach Wales, her boat was wrecked in the storm! The Jewish doctor saved her life!

At the end of the meal, Mom brought Aaron to Papa. Jews couldn't eat with gentiles, and so Mom had made sure he had food and a place to eat in private. "If it please you, my lord," Mom said. "I'd like to introduce you to Aaron ben Simon, a physician. I told you of his assistance on my journey."

Papa nodded.

"And I'd like to introduce you, Aaron," Mom continued in English, "to my future husband, Llywelyn, Prince of Wales."

Aaron's eyes widened but Papa spoke before Aaron could say anything.

"Thank you for caring so well for Marged," Papa said.

"It is my honor, sir, to meet you." Aaron bowed his head as Mom translated.

"Is it true, Aaron the Physician, that you've come to Wales to find a new life for yourself, away from the persecution in England?"

"Yes, my lord. That is true," Aaron said.

"Marged respects you greatly, and if you would like to remain with us, I offer you the position of court physician. We are in need of someone with your skills."

If Anna had been in Aaron's shoes, she would have been feeling pretty overwhelmed by now, but Aaron had a magisterial air that nothing could suppress. "I would be honored to serve you, my lord," he said. "I lost all that I owned when we were thrown into the sea and this is more than I dared hope for."

After relaying his words to Papa, Mom smiled. "I have a room prepared for you," she said. "Please allow me to have a servant show you to your quarters. Tomorrow, perhaps, we can talk, and see about replacing your belongings. We'll need you to provide us with a list of tools, books, and herbs that will assist you in your work."

"I await your pleasure, Madam," Aaron said.

"Meg," Mom corrected, embarrassed. "I am as I was. My clothing is clean and I'm well fed. That is the only difference."

Aaron looked into her eyes for half a second, and a ghost of a smile played around his lips, before he bowed once more and found a seat at one of the lower tables.

Anna was glad for Aaron that he'd arrived in such a spectacular fashion, as Math wasn't quite as optimistic about the tolerance of the Welsh people as Aaron was. In this case, however, the fact that he came with Mom and had been received by the Prince boded well for him. For Anna's part, she couldn't get enough of Mom and found her eyes drawn to her mother again and again, still not really believing that she was there and this was real.

Wales is full of orphans, but it is a peculiar state of being, Anna had found. Math's mother died at his birth, and he'd lost his father ten years later. David and Anna were half-orphaned when Anna's father died, and fully orphaned for the first weeks in Wales, or so they thought. With no parents in the picture, Anna had found that she no longer felt obligated to please them and their absence instilled a certain sense of freedom, but at the same time, the rock on which she'd built her house had washed into the sea.

One of Mom's anthropologist colleagues had commented that in a certain region of Africa, the standard greeting was: *How is your mother?* And if a person replied: *She is well*, the response was always: *Then it must be well with you.*

And it is well with me, perhaps for the first time since we arrived.

"What are you thinking?" Math asked. Math and Anna had retreated to their room to prepare for bed. Math sat in his chair, his bare feet stretched towards the grate. It was the end of August, but the night had grown cool and he'd lit a fire to take the chill from the room.

"That I'm a different person with my mother here," Anna said.

Math held out his hand. Anna went to him and took it. She knelt on the rug in front of the fire and rested her head against his knee. He stroked her hair with his other hand. "I'm glad," he said. "I've always been a little scared that if you were given a choice between returning to your time, or staying with me, you'd choose to leave."

"Oh, Math." Anna said. He pulled her into his lap so she could rest her head against his chest. "There were times when the decision might have been hard," she admitted. "Maybe even as recently as three weeks ago."

"When you first told me of this traveling in time, I believed *you*, but I couldn't believe *it*," he said.

"I thought as much," Anna said. "Now with Mom's arrival, everything has changed. It's like our old world was *this* close just a moment ago, and now it's gone again."

"Perhaps," Math said, "if you are given the choice to return, you could take me with you."

Anna sat silent, thinking—thinking about what that could mean for them, together and separately. "No," she said. Math sat up straighter, but Anna shushed him with a finger to his lips before he could protest. "It would be more difficult for you to live in my time than for me to live in yours. I would rather stay here with you, than either leave you, or ask you to come with me. Thank you, however, for offering."

Math hugged Anna closer. "I'm glad you want to stay with me," he said, "but in truth, I wasn't planning on giving you a choice."

* * * * *

The wedding wasn't, as it turned out, the next day. Goronwy had objected, not because he didn't want Mom to marry Papa, but because it sent the wrong message to the rest of Wales. To do it right, they needed a *big* wedding, if only to thumb their noses at King Edward and his Church.

Invitations went out to all the lords of Wales, from the tiniest commote to those whose power rivaled Papa's. Thus, it was only a week before David's sixteenth birthday that everyone gathered at Aber, Papa's primary seat in Gwynedd.

The moment Anna had walked through the castle gate for her own wedding to Math a year earlier, she'd nearly swooned with happiness. Aber wasn't a castle in the traditional sense. It had a large ring wall surrounding it, within which were the usual stables and kitchens and a large chapel. However, the two primary structures were an 'H'-shaped building, several stories high that served as Papa's administrative center, and a large manor house that wouldn't have looked out of place in the 18th century. Made of stone and wood with many rooms, it was the warmest place Anna had slept since coming to Wales.

It also, miraculously, had a bath. Papa's forefathers had built Aber over the top of an old Roman villa, meaning it had tunnels underneath it, some of which were walkable, and amenities Anna hadn't experienced since leaving Pennsylvania.

The year before, when Papa had given Anna away, David had stood up with Math. Anna had worn a wine-colored dress (not a white one—that was a later custom) made of the finest carded wool, with floor length drop sleeves and embroidered neckline, sleeves, and hem. It had laced up the back and even had a train. Anna had felt like a real princess, like any girl would want to feel on her wedding day. What had felt the best, for Anna, however, was how *right* it was, like this was the culmination of everything she'd been through in the year since she'd come to Wales. Even though Anna had butterflies in her stomach, she was only nervous about the wedding 'show', not about Math himself. *How could I have met anyone like Math in Oregon?*

Mom's and Papa's wedding was set for a Sunday, after a noon mass, but Papa decreed that the assemblage of nobles should meet in the great hall on Friday. Two years before when the nobility of Wales had assembled, the war with the English had been less than a year old. Now they gathered again, more confident and secure in their power.

Unfortunately for David, he had to participate in the conference. For once, Anna wasn't sorry to be a woman if it meant she didn't have to sit through an all-day meeting, which David later told her consisted almost entirely of pontificating by one baron or another.

Mom, however, had wanted to attend but hadn't been able to defy convention enough to do it. "It isn't that I object to being a woman," Mom said as she and Anna crossed the courtyard, heading back to her room, "it's that I don't really enjoy being a *medieval* woman."

"You don't have much choice, Mom," Anna said.

"I don't have *any* choice," Mom said. "I believed, in the first hours of my walk along Hadrian's Wall, that I could control my destiny. Yes, I was a woman, but I was educated and intelligent, and had struggled and survived on my own in the twenty-first century with two children. Surely this would make a difference? It was appalling to realize it made no difference at all."

"What do you mean?" Anna asked.

"Sir John knew that I'd saved his nephew, that I could read and write, but did he offer me a job as replacement for his thieving steward? Of course not. He sent me to the convent in Armathwaite."

"I can't picture you in a convent, Mom."

Meg smiled. "As far as Sir John was concerned, it was the perfect solution for me—it would get me out of the way, yet be a place for me to stay while I waited for a safe method of travel to Wales. He didn't even *consider* that I might be useful to him and could earn my own way. I was a woman, and thus needed to be taken care of."

"Why couldn't you stay at the castle?"

"Because he thought I was only twenty! Do I look twenty? I tell you . . ." Mom paused, shaking her head. "Women age so quickly here. He looked at my relatively unlined face and soft hands and refused to believe I was thirty-seven and the mother of two grown children."

Actually, Mom had often been mistaken for a college student at home too, particularly when she wore shorts and put her hair in a pony tail. Still, if Anna thought back to the peasant women with whom she'd dealt in the past year, many of them had aged before their time. She remembered one woman in particular who'd given birth to her first child at fifteen, had nine children by thirty, and at thirty-three, when Anna met her, could easily have passed for fifty.

Is that to be my fate, then? How many children will I have before I'm thirty?

"Mom," Anna said. "I've something to tell you."

Meg stopped and turned to Anna. "Oh, sweetie," she said. "I've wanted to ask if you were pregnant, but didn't want to invade your space if you weren't ready to tell me."

"I've been working up the courage to talk to you, and you already know!" Anna said. "How do you know?"

Mom took Anna's face in her hands and kissed her nose. "Because I'm your mom," she said. "It's my job to know these things. I'm happy for you and Math."

"And scared too," Anna said.

"Petrified," Mom agreed. She pushed open the door to the living quarters and they both sighed. *Warmth.* "We need to see about a midwife. When are you due?"

"Early July, I think." They shared a look. "I don't want to lose another one," Anna said in a low voice.

"It happens, sweetheart," Mom said. She hugged Anna to her. "Even in our world, all we can do is pray."

"Can you tell me," Anna asked, easing back, "when you came to Wales the first time and met Papa—can you tell me what happened with you? Papa explained it from his perspective, but . . ."

"Llywelyn rescued us from the car, and from then on he was my entire world," Meg said. "He couldn't have been more different from your father—successful, decisive, thoughtful, intelligent—sorry, but there it is—and I loved him."

"But he didn't marry you then," Anna said.

"I wasn't of noble birth," Mom said. "It wasn't possible. Not in the Church."

"Have you talked with David about it? About . . ." Anna paused, trying to think of how to ask her question without judging.

"About the fact that King Edward would look down on him for being illegitimate?" Mom asked.

"Yes."

They reached Mom's rooms and entered, shedding their cloaks. Gwenllian, so grown up now at two and half, napped in a trundle bed in the far corner. Mom went to her first, her hand hovering above the blonde head, before returning to a seat in front of the fire. "David can be a bit judgmental," Mom said,

"Not to mention hard on himself and others," Anna said.

"That too," Mom said. "He certainly doesn't regret being born and nobody regrets his existence. What was hard for me was being forced to leave Llywelyn; what was hard was raising him by myself. I also know that Llywelyn would have acknowledged him in an instant had he been born in Wales. We were married in our hearts, even if the politics of the time forbade it."

"And what did he say?"

"He was glad that Fychan could no longer humiliate him," Mom said.

Anna laughed. "I told him once that even if we were home, and he lived perfectly every day of his life, he'd still need to learn tolerance for others when they fell short of his expectations."

"What did he say?"

"He said he was trying."

"As Prince of Wales, he needs that skill," Mom said.

4

Something was wrong. David could tell from his father's stance, and from the solidity of Goronwy, as if he'd grown roots and was prepared to stand forever at Father's shoulder. The members of the council were waiting in the great hall. If Father's absence continued any longer, they'd know something was wrong. But still, neither of them moved.

"You said we'd take a short break when the messenger came in, but it's been an hour," David asked, closing the door of his father's office behind him. "What is it?"

Finally, Llywelyn turned. His face showed more lines than David had seen in his face in a while—not since Cilmeri. David's presence had rejuvenated his father. Mom had rejuvenated him, but the spark was gone.

"Dafydd," Father said. The word came out as a croak.

David moved closer and put his hand on his father's shoulder. He wanted to grasp him, to hold him up. He seemed so weak.

"Not you, Dafydd," Goronwy said. "Your uncle."

Christ! "What's he gone and done?" David asked.

"He's left us; defected again," Goronwy said. "To Edward."

"But . . . but . . . that's insane!" David said. "Why would he do that?"

"Why has he done it in the past?" Father said. "Why did he try to kill me once? It seems he can't help himself."

Goronwy and David settled Llywelyn into his chair; then Goronwy turned to David. "Your uncle Dafydd may be irrational, but I've noticed an unhappiness brewing within him these past months as our peace negotiations with Edward have progressed."

"It's me, isn't it?" David asked. He scrubbed at his hair. "My presence steps on his toes."

"Your uncle Dafydd is no longer your father's heir," Goronwy said, "and with every month that passes, you prove yourself more capable of stepping into your father's shoes. Your people will follow you when he is gone."

"So by returning to Edward, he hopes to change the balance of power such that Edward defeats Father entirely?"

"And then places Dafydd himself on the throne of Wales," Goronwy said. "That is my guess, yes."

Crap. That's not going to happen.

Father took in a deep breath and straightened his shoulders. "Right," he said. "What's done is done. This changes nothing for me. It gives Edward no more leverage against us than he had before. My people will not defect to Dafydd any more than they would follow Edward."

"I agree, Sire," Goronwy said. "Edward's negotiators might try to use this to subvert the peace process, but as far as I'm concerned, Dafydd can rot in England for the rest of his life. Edward can keep him and good riddance."

Father nodded. "Both previous treaties required me to take him back if Edward was to sign them. When you speak to the Archbishop next, Goronwy, you tell him that giving Dafydd back his lands in Wales in exchange for peace is off the table. He abandoned his lands and his people twice already. He will not play us for fools a third time. My patrimony will not be held hostage to his treachery."

"Yes, my lord," Goronwy said, and bowed.

The wedding festivities weren't quite as jubilant after that, though the lords who attended were as adamant as Father that this act of Uncle Dafydd's was the final straw: no peace treaty with Edward was going to include Llywelyn's brother ever again. Many had followed Uncle Dafydd on and off over the years; even those who hadn't thought much of him had cheered his rebellion back in 1282; and even more had re-evaluated their views later when Llywelyn took the reins of Wales again.

"But Llywelyn's cause was never your Uncle Dafydd's cause," Mom said, twitching her skirt to adjust its fit.

"Can't you talk about something else?" Anna asked, straightening Mom's train. Anna had described it as a 'rich blue'. David didn't know about that, but he had to admit that it, and his mother, looked very nice. "You're getting married in five minutes!"

David ignored his sister. "Uncle Dafydd thought only of himself; Father, though prideful—"Anna shot a scowl at him, although David knew it to be true, "—thinks first of Wales."

"Who's the English lord who sent that nice note congratulating you?" Anna asked. "Nicholas something?"

"Sir Nicholas de Carew," Mom said. "He has a big castle along the south coast of Wales in Deheubarth."

"He saw the writing on the wall," David said, "and appears to have interpreted it exactly opposite of Uncle Dafydd."

"It helps that he's the son of a Welshwoman and married to another," Mom said.

"Leastways, he's promised to hold the south for Father," David said. "I want to believe him."

"Llywelyn—and probably you," Mom said, eyeing David, "will have to see for yourselves come spring. Your uncle was privy to Llywelyn's strategies, his plans, the disposition of his men and the horses at his disposal, and his vision of the future. All of which he has given into Edward's hands."

Footsteps sounded along the corridor and Goronwy poked in his head. He caught sight of Mom and his eyes widened, and then he smiled. David wasn't sure if he'd *ever* seen Goronwy smile, except maybe at Anna —and especially not like that. "Are you ready?" he asked.

Mom nodded. David, for his part, wouldn't ever forget the conversation he'd overheard—by accident, he swore—the night his mother returned:

"I have chosen you," Llywelyn said. "And that should be enough for every one of my subjects. It is certainly enough for me."

"Are you sure, Llywelyn? Really sure?"

"I love you more than I can possibly tell you."

Mom wrapped her arms around Father's waist and pressed her face into his chest. "Sixteen years is a long time to wait," she said. "But I waited."

"God put you in my path and has swept you along with me for a reason," Father said. "I will never turn my back on what He has given me."

* * * * *

In April, with the onset of spring, David and Llywelyn made plans for a new campaign which would combine two aims: the need to patrol the kingdom and Llywelyn's desire to more fully establish David as his heir, with his own authority, out from under his shadow. David would start by making a circuit of Gwynedd, including stops at Dolwyddelan and Dinas Bran where David would leave the increasingly pregnant-looking Anna. Math was already there, having taken charge of the rebuilding of the castle after the English had tried to destroy it back in 1282.

While David held the north for his father, as Llywelyn had once asked Uncle Dafydd to do, Llywelyn would travel south along the coast of Wales to Deheubarth to see for himself the progress the lords there were making in ridding Wales of the English. After joining Carew and the other power there, Lord Rhys, Father would head east to gauge how the war was going closer to England, in the Marche.

The Marche was the border region between England and Wales (including the traditional Earldoms of Chester, Shrewsbury, and Hereford, as well as Pembroke, Norfolk, and Gloucester in south-eastern Wales). English lords ruled these lands as almost-kings. The Welsh had hated them for centuries. Although he hoped to carry the war into southeast Wales, Father's plan was to contain the English and to prevent them from building up their strength to attack him.

Powys was also of concern for him, partially because it was closer to Gwynedd, and partially because it was controlled by the Welsh lord, Gruffydd ap Gwenwynwyn. Amazingly enough, Gruffydd had taken to the new rule of Wales with passion and vengeance. Gruffydd had actually taken Dolforwyn Castle for Father (who, after all, had built it), and Buellt Castle, near where Anna and David had saved Father's life. Father was apprehensive, however, not wanting to trust all these potentially fair-weather friends too far, and especially not the luck that seemed to be holding.

Looking at the maps, it was hard to remember that Wales was only 140 miles long and 50 miles wide in the middle. It was the roughness of the terrain that made Wales difficult to conquer, not its overall size.

The night before everyone left, Llywelyn called his children and his wife into his study for one last conversation. "Foremost in your mind should be the strengthening of Wales," he reminded them. "Do we have men who are able and willing to more actively join our cause? Who has contacts in England who can spy for us against the English? Just because a man isn't a soldier, doesn't mean he can't serve us."

David nodded, understanding his charge, and the need for it.

"Dinas Bran is ideally located for access to information from England," Anna said.

"You are correct in that. All the Welsh can help, which leads me to my other concern," Father said. "I've spoken with the Bishop about admitting Jews into Wales."

Mom's face lit. This had been of particular interest to her. Although Edward himself didn't yet know it, he was about to start a long-term pogram against the Jews, culminating in his decree in 1290, six years from now, that banished all Jews from England.

"What did he say?" Mom asked.

"He has agreed not to condemn them, and to consider welcoming them. We must go slowly. This idea is new and unprecedented. I realize that your mother looks far into the future, but I cannot always see what she does from where I sit."

Father shifted in his seat. Mom and Anna sat together on a bench against one wall, with David beside them in a chair. Llywelyn's eyes went to each of them in turn. "Foremost in my mind is to unite the people of Wales and the Bishop has promised to promote that idea. The problem with war, as you must know by now, is that it is eminently destructive. Peasants are caught between armies in war. Their crops don't get sown and their children starve. In Wales, unlike in England, all men must be warriors, else we have too few to hold off the English. It is reasonable, then, to ask a man to take sides and the Bishop agreed that he would encourage his priests to try to explain that to their flock."

David shook his head. "How am I to rule after you, Father? There's so much I don't know and don't understand. Half the time I don't even know the right questions to ask!"

Llywelyn smiled. "Son, you will be a great Prince—perhaps even the King of Wales one day. They'll name you 'Fawr', like my grandfather."

David didn't contradict him, having learned by now it was fruitless, but didn't see how that could possibly be true.

5

Meg, David, and Anna left Aber on a clear day that for once didn't have a cold wind with it. Anna could almost believe it wasn't going to rain soon, but as this was Wales, it always did. As the crow flies, it was less than twenty miles from Aber to Dolwyddelan, but they wouldn't be traveling as the crow flies. David intended to take a week to make the journey.

Along the way, they'd stop at every hut and hamlet. David would stand for Papa as arbiter and judge in any dispute, Aaron would attend to any ailments, having improved his Welsh considerably in the six months he'd lived in Wales, with Anna herself assisting. That way, she could also translate for him if he needed it. Mom planned on being, as she called it, Papa's 'Cheerleader in Chief'.

Anna was excited to get moving, but for some reason, Mom was apprehensive and not at all herself. Anna thought at first that she didn't want to leave Papa or Gwenllian, but when she asked her about it, she furrowed her brow and complained about the weather and its effect on her skin. For the first time, Mom had found lines around her eyes and on her forehead. Aaron snorted into his cuff at that and promised to concoct a lotion for her to counteract that as soon as he was able.

Anna turned to look at her and then it dawned on her what day it was. "It's your birthday, isn't it?" Anna asked.

Out of nowhere, Mom gave Anna a brilliant smile that was a sharp contrast to her glum look a moment before. "And if I weren't so stubborn, I would have told Llywelyn and he would've done something for me. But then I might have to talk to all the well-wishers about exactly where I was born, and who my father was, and so far, nobody seems to be asking those questions, at least not to my face. On top of which, I'm thirty-eight and getting old, and can't seem to do the math to figure out in what year I'm supposed to have been born."

"It's 19—" Anna said. "Oh . . . I guess that would be 1247."

"Ha!" Mom said, and looked away but she was smiling.

It occurred to Anna that her mother might be suffering the same way Anna herself had when she first came to Wales. In truth, except for Papa, David, Anna, and sometimes Aaron, there was no one for her to talk to. Mom had plenty to *do* as the Princess of Wales, but as she and Anna had lamented many times, twenty-first century women just didn't fit in well in the Middle Ages. It wasn't so much that men treated women poorly, but that they didn't expect anything important of them, beyond an ability to raise children and run a household (which wasn't unimportant, even if some men dismissed it). Men didn't *talk* to women.

Anna had discussed this with David, and he'd understood, even sympathized. For his part, he had plenty of male friends and acquaintances because they mostly talked about what they'd done that day, or what the plan for the next day was. With the older men, all David had to do was get them going about some battle or other that they'd been in, and there were no awkward silences.

The drawback for the three of them was that beyond superficial conversation, they had little in common with anyone. It wasn't so much that people weren't smart, because many were, especially within their own sphere of knowledge; it was just that they were *ignorant*. Everyone saw the sun rise and set every day, but those from the twenty-first century knew how and why, and the rest didn't.

Anna had the same problem with the girls who lived at court—it was really hard to make friends with them. As soon as she actually tried to have a conversation, it became clear that they didn't know how to *think* about things.

David was young and male, but it even bothered him, since he might have liked a girlfriend. To David's embarrassment, Anna had been present for Mom's lecture on the subject: "Most girls are less interested in *you*, David, than the fact that you are the Prince of Wales."

"I know that, Mom," he'd said.

"Bearing your child would set any one of them up for life."

He'd been mortified and refused to talk about it with Mom anymore. When Anna told Math of it, he'd laughed. "He's a Prince of Wales," he'd said. "Your mother needs to let him do what he wants. More than most princes, I, for one, would trust his judgment."

When they reached the first little village, nestled in the crook of a river, Anna and Meg gazed down at it from their vantage point on the ridge above. "I don't know about this, Mom," Anna said. "I was born in Oregon. How can I be a princess? It isn't like they voted for me or anything. I've lived here for just two and a half years. It isn't like I really understand them at all, yet I sit with Math as the lady of the castle."

"That's one reason for making this trip," Mom said. "We all have the same problem. There's a limit to the changes we can make. This isn't a democracy and never will be, not in our lifetime or your children's. The people are uneducated and thus ill-equipped for self-rule. David's job is to campaign for Llywelyn's vision of Wales. Your job is to support him and counsel Math."

"I don't think that helps, Mom," Anna said.

"Why is it you speak of democracy in Wales?" Aaron asked from behind them.

They turned together as Aaron walked his horse closer. "I apologize for speaking out of turn, but I couldn't help but overhear."

"I was just saying that I'm not well acquainted with the people over whom Math rules," Anna explained. "I didn't grow up here, and both they and I know it."

"Yes, but democracy?" Aaron asked. "There hasn't been a true democratic state since Athens was defeated by Macedon fifteen hundred years ago. Where did you learn of its principles?"

"I don't know if this is a conversation we should be having, Aaron," Mom said. "I realize that there are times when my children and I make you uncomfortable with the extent of our differences, and I'm afraid that this just needs to be one of those times."

Aaron's face took on a look that Anna could only describe as fierce. It struck her that he was deeply insulted. He thought Mom was disparaging his intelligence. Anna wanted to tell him a little piece of truth, but didn't even know how to begin.

David must have thought the same thing, because he prodded Taranis closer. "Listen to me, Aaron," he said. "We are from a country which is governed by a democracy as much as it can be. It's a land where all citizens are educated. My mom taught history at a university. There, I was not known as a prince's son, but as a schoolboy. There, much of the knowledge you've spent a lifetime acquiring, is learned routinely by ten-year-olds. We are here by chance and happenstance. If you can bear it, without thinking us witches or devils, someday I will tell you more. I tell you this now so that you won't be offended by our knowledge or our ideas—or by our secrets."

David pulled at Taranis' head and spurred him forward, leaving Meg and Anna to deal with Aaron's questions David had unleashed.

"Where . . . where are you from?" Aaron stuttered. Anna turned her head, following David with her eyes, not wanting to look at Aaron.

"Every day we travel a little closer to it," Mom said.

The future, Mom means. Except that we'll never reach it, not from here.

6

As the company traveled inland from the sea, the people of Gwynedd flocked to them. With every day that passed, the news of their coming spread. Most days, a following of men, women, and children traveled with them for a few miles and then would melt into the landscape, only to be replaced by others who strode, rode, and sidled out of the forest to walk for a time at David's side. It seemed the entire countryside was on the move.

David's presence was a novelty and it drew people to them. Everyone wanted to touch him, talk to him, and tell him their life story. Of course, David would be Prince of Wales one day, but because he was young and had less authority than an older man, the people showered more welcome and love on him than his father might have experienced.

In the first three days, David mediated everything from a dispute over a fishing line, to a marauding bull, to a marriage contract for a young couple whose fathers couldn't agree on price. *That* was not something David had encountered in twenty-first century America!

But marauding bulls aside, David thought being the Prince of Wales was okay. The thirteenth century would never give him a life of luxury and ease, but he'd adjusted to it. He was busy. He was needed. For the first time in his life, he had both parents in the same place. Perhaps David was too young to be a knight, really, but he *was* a knight, and he would do his duty as the Prince of Wales. For the most part, that aspect of the job was within his scope.

Although the responsibilities of command had ceased to be quite as intimidating, the need to kill other men was another matter. It wasn't really that life was worth less here, though it was, but that lives were taken more easily here. Babies died. Children died. Women died in childbirth all the time, though Mom and Aaron were working on that. David had overheard her and Anna talking about it, and David tried not to dwell on the worry he heard in Mom's voice. Anna was happy and optimistic, but Elinor, Gwenllian's mother, had died in childbirth and David didn't think that knowledge was ever far from Mom's mind.

The men with whom David worked generally avoided thinking about death too, not out of fear, though there was that too, but because it went without saying that death rode at their shoulders every day. Sometimes, through the loud talk and bravado, a soldier was able to admit his fear—and that men died from the most minor injuries and illnesses in addition to dying in battle.

David had never been as sick and scared in his life as when his company attacked the English at the Vale of Conwy. Bevyn had told him that the first time he lost it, the men would respect him and understand. He'd been only fourteen then, after all. But there was a fine line between disliking the need to take a life, and being thought weak. Weakness is unforgivable in battle. That was David's new reality. And that was something that haunted him constantly. Killing, like anything else, became easier the more a man did it.

What kind of man will I be when it begins to come easily? What kind of prince can I be if it never does? Can God forgive me for offenses that I repeat over and over, and can I ever forgive myself?

Now David understood why the Catholic Church prescribed confession. A man could tell a priest his sins and walk away clean every time.

When they reached Dolwyddelan, people set up huts, tents, and even a small fair where summer grazing normally took place. David had thought that their stay would be something of a rest, but there were even more demands on his time and more people who wanted to see him. Meg tried to ease the burden, but only the women wanted to talk to her.

They followed the same procedure after the company left Dolwyddelan, following the thirty-five mile spine across Gwynedd to Dinas Bran. The Roman road on which they'd traveled to get to Dolwyddelan didn't go that way, so they took the Welsh track that was as old as the hills it wended between. Each day, they set up camp in the early afternoon and spent time with whatever inhabitants were in the area, before moving on the next day to another location.

David had followed the same routine every day after the evening meal. In the hours between dinner and bed, he would walk among his men, sharing food or a joke with one group or another. He'd read once that this was good practice for a commander, and a good commander was what he was trying to become. Bevyn knew this was his habit. At the end of every evening, David would walk a short distance from the camp to a nearby stream to wash before returning to the tent to sleep.

The third night out from Dolwyddelan, David left the circle of tents and strolled under the trees and down a little hill to a creek. After he washed, he turned around to find Marchudd next to him. Marchudd was a member of David's guard: a relatively young man, perhaps ten years older than David, who kept to himself for the most part.

"My lord," Marchudd said. "If you'll come with me, there's something I think you should see."

Not wanting to offend him, David followed him thirty yards further downstream. At a small ford, Marchudd stopped. David looked inquiringly at him, waiting. Marchudd's eyes focused on something behind David. Before David could turn—

Thunk!

David awoke, trussed, a gag in his mouth and his head pounding.

"You fool!" a voice said. "You hit him too hard. If he can't ride, we're lost."

"If he can't ride, we'll kill him and have an end to this farce," Marchudd said.

Hearing that, David forced himself to focus. He lay in the bed of a cart that jolted along a trail in the dark. David surveyed the sky above him. Scattered clouds blew among the stars, although no moon showed. Despite the darkness, David's captors seemed to know their way well enough.

"The King wants him alive!" the first voice protested. "I want my money."

David strove to hold himself still, but his captors must have sensed a change in him.

"Make a sound and I'll kill you right now. Nod if you understand."

David nodded, groaning inwardly. He recognized that voice too. It belonged to Fychan, the boy David had bested a lifetime ago at Castell y Bere.

"Hurry," the first speaker said, snickering, and David knew the voice now as that of Fychan's friend, Dai.

David cursed his naïveté and stupidity. He'd thought— everyone had thought—that he was safe in Gwynedd, among people who supported him and more importantly, supported his father. That was a mistake.

The cart stopped. Marchudd grabbed David's feet and Fychan his arms and they unceremoniously half-dragged, half-carried him out of the cart. Fychen threw David over his shoulder in a fireman's left, though he wouldn't have called it that. He moved swiftly, not quite running, while David bounced and bobbed on his shoulder, upside down.

What irked David most was that his captors were Welsh. Father was trying to build a network of Welsh to support Wales, and here were three Welshman working against him! Why couldn't they understand that the interests of Wales might supersede their own? Perhaps David was a fine one to talk because the interests of Wales were his own; but what they could hope to gain financially from turning him over to the English was dwarfed by the horror that subjugation to Edward would bring. How could they not know it?

Fychan went on this way for two minutes, with David slowly suffocating in his gag. Upside down, it was hard to breathe through his nose. All the blood had rushed to his head and made him congested. David kicked out at Fychan. *I refuse to die so ignomiously!*

Before that could happen, fortunately, Fychan stopped and dropped David to his feet. With a thrust of his knife, Dai slashed through the bonds around David's ankles.

"Get up," Fychan said.

"Why?" David said, though it came out muffled in the gag.

"On the horse!" Fychan shoved David's shoulder and David staggered to his feet. His hands were still tied so they had to boost him up, pushing and shoving until he balanced in the saddle.

With this change in perspective, the 'farce' to which Marchudd was referring became clear. David was a big person. At six feet two inches, he was taller than most men, and at sixteen and a half, stronger than most too. His abduction had been well planned and executed, but once he was up on the horse, David began to think he had a chance to live through the night. What did they think? That they could get him to ride quietly with them merely because they asked?

They must not have felt too sure of themselves either, because, standing there under the trees and only a short distance from David's camp, they began to argue.

"Have you lost your nerve, then?" Dai, asked in a stage whisper. "We must make haste!"

"Don't fear for me, Dai," Fychan replied. "He's so scared I'm surprised he hasn't pissed his pants. There is nothing to him, now that he has no one to protect him."

"The Prince knighted him on the field of battle!" Dai said. "He's killed many English."

"Fairy tales!" Fychan said.

"Enough!" Marchudd interjected. "We'll bring him to Wrexham as we agreed. King Edward will reward us handsomely for his capture. Edward would prefer him alive and undamaged, if possible, so I suggest you get moving. The boy will be missed soon and we need to be well away before then."

With that, Fychan and Dai mounted their horses and Dai pulled David's forward. A cold feeling settled in David's stomach. It was a matter of weighing the immediate danger he was in, with the unknown variables involved in escape. At the very least, David could simply slide off the horse in a heap on the ground, but

Marchudd might kill him rather than leave him there alive.
Marchudd wouldn't want to risk his own capture no matter what.

If they were caught, Llywelyn would indeed hang them.
David remembered what his father had said more than two years
ago when David had defeated Fychan in that fight: "There was a
time for making an example of a man, and a time for showing
mercy . . . A leader has to be cold in order to mete out true justice."
His father would have no mercy for these men. David couldn't
afford it either.

David decided to keep his options open and wait for a good
opportunity to escape. They trotted on through the night, and
eventually the sky began to lighten. Where were his rescuers? As
the morning wore on, David began to think they weren't coming.
He had excellent trackers among his guard, but given the
efficiency of his imprisonment, they may have left few traces.
Bevyn would try to find David, but the longer he was captive, the
less likely it was that Bevyn would succeed.

By the time they stopped for food and water, David's entire
body ached with the effort of staying upright. The numbness in his
arms had spread such that his upper body trembled from holding
the same position for so many hours and his mouth and jaw had
swollen inside the gag. Fortunately, Marchudd deemed them far
enough away from any possible help that when he pulled David
from the horse, he removed the gag too.

With a grin, Fychan grabbed David's hair and tipped his
head back to pour water down his throat. David coughed and
sputtered, but Fychan kept pouring. David managed to swallow

some, but most of it spilled down his front. Dai laughed at his predicament.

David ignored him. "I need to relieve myself," he said, once he could speak again.

"Piss on yourself, if you have to," Fychan said.

Marchudd sighed and corrected him. "If he fouls himself, we'll have to smell him all the way to Wrexham. Is that what you want?"

Taking a knife from its sheath at his waist, he came over to David. He first put it at David's throat. "I will not hesitate to kill you," he said. "Do you believe me?"

"Yes," David said.

Marchudd nodded and with a flick of his knife, cut the bonds from David's wrists. David relaxed his shoulders which was a tremendous relief, but his hands began to hurt as blood flowed back into them. Marchudd nudged him forward, his knife to David's back, and David walked a short way from the camp. In his head, David ran through the various techniques he'd learned in karate to deal with an assailant with a knife. Unfortunately, in every one, the person without a knife had a high chance of getting cut.

Do I want to risk it? What would Father have me do? David decided to wait a while longer. Maybe tonight, if they were to rest, he would have a better chance when his captors were tired and not as attentive.

Marchudd rebound David's hands, in front of him this time, and they continued the journey. David's company had only traveled fifteen miles from Dolwyddelan before he was captured, so they'd had quite a distance still to go to Dinas Bran. Marchudd had chosen a more northerly path, angling away from the road to Dinas Bran and steering towards Wrexham instead.

The path followed the land up and down, through wooded patches and around craggy blocks. When towards sunset it started to rain, a mixture of hopelessness and hope surged through David. The rain would obliterate their tracks, but David might have an easier time getting away if his captors were miserable.

The rain lasted for several hours, into the evening. Just as David was thinking they'd never take a break, both Marchudd and the rain stopped. After some struggle, Dai managed to start a fire and Marchudd distributed rations from his saddle bags.

"We sleep only a few hours," he said, after untying David's hands and tossing him a dry piece of bread and a skin of water.

David ate and drank what there was, grateful for the fire and the brief rest. Within a few minutes, he lay on his side, waiting for his captors to settle. He hoped Marchudd would overlook the fact that Dai had done a poor job of retying his hands after eating. David was mildly annoyed they thought so little of him, but they must have thought they knew these mountains too well for David to escape.

Fychan had the first watch. Dai and Marchudd fell asleep immediately, or they were good at faking it. David closed his eyes, feigning sleep despite the exhaustion that begged for oblivion. His adrenaline kept him from dropping off. Through slitted eyes, he watched Fychan poke at the fire with a stick. He kept his sword sheathed but held a bare knife on his lap.

David lay still for close to half an hour. Gradually, Fychan's head began to nod. David didn't move. Fychan's head fell forward. Terrified that Fychan would wake up and he would lose his only chance, David sat up. He got to his feet, daring to believe his luck, and was just taking his first step away from the fire when Fychan shot across the five feet between them. With his right hand he grabbed David's throat and pressed the knife to David's belly with his left.

"You thought to leave us, did you?" he whispered.

David could barely speak through the pressure on his throat. "I have to relieve myself," David said. "Would you rather I did that on you?"

Fychan squeezed a little harder, and then relaxed his hold. As David gagged and choked for breath, he twisted the knife into David's stomach, drawing blood.

"I should kill you now," he said. "When you bested me before, it wasn't a fair fight. You only win when you cheat."

"So give me a blade and I'll fight you fairly!" David hissed back, straightening his shoulders and trying to get away from his knife. He left his hands in the loosened rope but held the end in his fist in case it came undone before he was ready.

"Oh no, you don't," Fychan replied, matching David's step backwards with one of his own. "You're worth more alive than dead, and if we fought, you wouldn't live to see tomorrow."

They glared at each other until David forced himself to back down. He let his shoulders slump and tried to look as defeated as possible. Fychan pounced gleefully on his apparent capitulation.

"Ha!" he crowed. "You'll never be the Prince of Wales. We'll not abide a weakling such as you!"

"I need to piss," David said, his head down, though he watched Fychan through his lowered lashes.

"Over there." Fychan jerked his head at a nearby tree.

David walked toward it. Fychan followed, the knife in his right hand, held lightly at David's back. Deciding he could abide this no longer, David took two long strides before Fychan could stop him.

"Hey!" he said.

In the split second it took for Fychan to reach him, David spun around, bashing his right elbow into the flat of the knife and following the spin with a quick grab to Fychan's knife hand with David's newly freed left. Fychan didn't have time to react before David had twisted Fychan's arm up and around, using his momentum to leverage him to his knees.

Fychan screamed and loosened his grip on the knife just enough for David to grasp it with his right hand and jerk it from him. Realizing he was out of time, David didn't hesitate. Stepping behind Fychan, David slashed downward, cutting Fychan's throat and dropping his body to the ground before his blood could touch him. David glanced toward the fire. Dai and Marchudd were just levering themselves to their feet.

David ran.

His goal was to put as much distance between them as possible. David dashed through the bracken and within a hundred yards found himself facing a creek, on the other side of which was a craggy cliff. He had to make an immediate choice: cross the creek or not, go upstream or down, try to find a path through the rock or run along the shore. David crossed the creek, soaking his breeches to the knees, and headed upstream, looking for a path up the cliff.

Settling into a jog, David listened for Marchudd and Dai. They couldn't have ridden easily through the undergrowth, but David didn't know if another path went to this spot. David's sense was that one of the three men knew this region of Wales well. If David was lucky, that person had been Fychan.

Too bad. Within a minute, the crunch of hooves on rock echoed behind David. He threw himself into some bushes. If he could hide for long enough, because Marchudd had neither dog nor bow, they'd give up and leave. Now that David was free, the only way Marchudd could capture him would be to corner him. David swore that wasn't going to happen.

Clip-clop, clip-clop. Marchudd walked his horse past David's position.

"Not here!" Dai shouted, from somewhere downstream.

"Fool! He'll hear us!" Marchudd hissed.

Anxiously David took soft, shallow breaths, certain Marchudd could hear his heart pounding. The sound of it filled David's own ears. Marchudd and Dai conferred in whispers a few yards away, but David couldn't hear their words. *Silence*. David stayed in his bush, praying and waiting. A few minutes later, the clop, clopping of the hooves began again, and gradually moved away down the creek. Still, David didn't move, thinking it a trap. Another ten minutes went by, and then David sensed, rather than saw, a shadow pass his bush and travel up the creek in the opposite direction from the horse.

At last, he couldn't stand it any longer. David eased his head out of the bush. Nobody was near the creek. Taking a chance, he scuttled away from the creek, toward the cliff. Now that the rain had stopped and the moon was up, he could see well enough to detect differences in the shadows along the rock. The moon showed some grassy patches, and what looked like trail, wending its way up through them. David sprinted forward into the rocks, and began to follow the path, climbing up and away from the river.

At the top of the rocky cliff, David faced a rolling landscape of grassland and trees. It might have be green and welcoming in daylight, but would give him little cover. By moonlight, he'd be a sitting duck out there. David couldn't abide the thought of being run down from behind by a man on horseback, but he didn't dare stop moving. He flitted from rock to tree, to rock again, trying not to trip in the hidden holes and roots that pot-marked the landscape, trying continually to move south, back towards the road where his company traveled.

David hiked and jogged and wandered through the long night until, as dawn was breaking, he stumbled out of a copse of trees into a little valley, in the center of which lay five huts. He pulled up short at the sight. He'd known, intellectually, that the people he'd met on his journey through Gwynedd had to live somewhere, but in the thirty-six hours since Marchudd had taken him from the campsite, David had felt completely alone.

He ran to the nearest hut. Before he could knock, the door opened and David fell forward on his knees on the threshold.

"Who is it, Branwen?" a male voice asked.

Surprised faces of the inhabitants of the hut, more than half a dozen of them, looked back at David. The man who'd spoken got to his feet on the other side of the room.

"My lord!" he said.

David blinked. The heat from the fire and the blood pounding in his head blurred his vision. He swayed.

"Help him!" the man said, rushing to David's side. Branwen and the man raised David to his feet, eased him against one wall of the hut, and helped him sit. With his feet splayed out in front of him, David tried to get his balance back.

David blinked. The inhabitants of the hut stared back at him, completely silent, except for the man who remained close by his side.

"My lord, Dafydd?" he asked.

David nodded. "Yes, I'm Dafydd."

"Your captain, Lord Bevyn, was here in this house only last night. He brought news that you'd disappeared. He feared the English had taken you."

David lifted his hand and dropped it, feeling more helpless than ever. "Not the English. The traitors were our own people, Welshman thinking to sell me to Edward."

The man sputtered his outrage, but David turned his head to look at the man's wife who hovered near the fire. "Food? Water? Please?" he asked.

"Yes, yes, Branwen hurry," her husband urged her. "I'm Aeddan ap Owain, and this is my wife Branwen, and our children."

The children gazed at David, their eyes wide and faces pale. One little girl, perhaps about seven, sucked one finger and stared at David with a grave expression on her face. He crooked a finger at her and she came closer.

"Are you going to die?" she asked. "You look like my grandpa did right before he died. He was all white in the face and tired, just like you are."

David smiled and reached for her hand.

"I'm not going to die, *cariad*," he said. "I'm just tired and hungry. If I could stay here a while, and sleep, I will be well tomorrow."

"Yes, yes," Aeddan said. Branwen handed Aeddan a bowl of porridge. He turned to David with it, but as David reached for it, his hands shook so much he knew if he held it, it would spill.

"I—I can't."

Aeddan had seemed flustered before but now his voice deepened with quiet confidence. "Never mind, my lord," he said. "We'll hold it together."

Aeddan leaned forward; David put his hands on the outside of Aeddan's and together they tipped the first sip into David's mouth. The warmth flooded him and he took another drink and then another until his hands stopped shaking. Finally, David was able to take the bowl from Aeddan, who handed him a spoon. Under the watchful eye of Aeddan's family, David ate every drop. When he'd finished, he set the bowl down and leaned his head back against the wall, regarding Aeddan through half-open eyes.

"There were only three men," David said. "One is dead and the others are searching for me. I don't know if they still seek me, but if one or two men approach, possibly on horseback, you must beware. I've no sword and must sleep. I can't be of help."

"My brother-in-law and I fought with you, my lord, the winter we sent Edward home with his tail between his legs," Aeddan said. "I will warn him and the families nearby that you are here. We'll watch until you wake, and then travel with you wherever you need to go."

David lifted a hand to him and he clasped it briefly before letting go.

"Thank you," David said.

One of the drawbacks to David's life in Wales was the almost total lack of privacy. He was never alone, even while sleeping—especially while sleeping. When David lived among the other boys, a dozen of them would sleep in the stable, or the great hall, or an out-of-the-way room somewhere in a castle. Now that David was a prince, Math, or Bevyn, or even Hywel, whom Father had promoted to manservant, was always with him, along with a dozen of his guard close by.

With no privacy at night comes an inability to keep private information private. Everyone knew who snored, who had insomnia, and who was conspicuously absent from their bed when a certain husband was away. What everyone knew about David was that when he slept, he slept deeply. As a child, this had meant he wet the bed routinely (*not* information that he ever wanted anyone in Wales to know— David assumed his sister and mother could keep that a secret) but here in Wales, his fathomless slumber had prompted one of the boys who shared his Latin class to nickname him 'Mortuus', as in one who is dead. Safe at last, in the home of Aeddan ap Owain, David slept the day away.

He woke up once, many hours later. Branwen gave him more food and a flagon of water. "My husband stands watch with his bow," she said. "There've been no strangers near today."

"Thank you," David said, but before he could martial more of a reply, he was asleep again.

Early the next morning, David woke naturally. He lay on a pallet against the far wall. Aeddan must have moved him to allow enough room to walk around the small hut. David gazed at the ceiling, noting that the hut was typical for the Middle Ages, made of wood supports packed with wattle and daub. The floor was dirt, covered by a layer of reed mats. It was simply furnished with a table, two stools, and several benches pushed up against one wall. The fire was the centerpiece of the house, with a hole in the roof above it to let out the smoke. By stretching, David could have touched three of the children who slept near him. The others were scattered across the floor; their parents slept in a small alcove on the opposite side of the room.

His movement caught the attention of the little girl with whom he'd spoken the day before. She curled on her side to talk to him.

"I'm glad you didn't die," she said.

"Me too," David said.

"My name is Gwen."

"That's my sister's name."

Gwen looked confused. "Your sister is named Anna," she said.

David smiled. "I mean my baby sister's name. She's Gwenllian."

"Oh." Gwen stuck a finger in her mouth. "You share the same father."

"Yes," David replied. "The Prince is her father by Elinor, and he's my father by my mother, Marged."

"My lord," someone behind Gwen whispered. David lifted his head to see the bright eyes of her older brother, a boy of twelve, and the oldest of Aeddan and Branwen's children.

"I am Huw ap Aeddan," he said.

"Thank you for sharing your home with me, Huw," David replied. "But it's almost full light and I must leave soon."

"Father and my Uncle Rhys will accompany you," Huw said, "and I get to come too if you will have me."

Sitting up, David half bowed. "I would be honored, young sir," he said, "if you would accompany me on my journey."

Grinning like a madman, Huw climbed out of his covers. David joined him by the fire and while Huw stirred the pot, his father pushed aside his blanket.

"You wish to depart, my lord?"

"As soon as possible, Aeddan," David said. "I understand from Huw that three of you will accompany me."

"Yes, yes," he said, "if that's agreeable, my lord. I have my bow and Rhys and you each have a knife. We have no horse to carry us, but Dinas Bran can be reached in a day of steady walking."

"That's my intent," David said.

Aeddan dressed quickly and was out the door to rouse his brother-in-law. Shortly thereafter, the whole family woke. After a small meal, with a pouch of dried meat and a water skin, they began to walk up and out of the valley, heading east across the crags, making for the main road.

As they walked, David learned something of his companions. Aeddan had told him that he and his brother-in-law had participated in the defeat of the English, and with his great bow across his back, David believed him, though he had no memory of him. His brother-in-law, Rhys, carried a wicked-looking knife, which he said he looked forward to using on anyone who stood in their way. But his true talent was his voice.

"You're a bard?" David asked.

"No, not a bard," he replied, a little ruefully. "I couldn't live that kind of life, always moving from place to place, never laying my head in the same spot twice. My wife wouldn't love me for that. I sing for my own enjoyment and that of my kin."

"Sing for the prince," Aeddan ordered.

Rhys shrugged, and to David's delight, began a long ballad about King Arthur. It was repetitive enough that near the end David joined in on the chorus with Huw.

"You will have a fine voice, my lord," Rhys said, "when it settles more. You sang for us two years ago, but it was a mite different then." He glanced shyly at David, seeing if he would take his gentle teasing without offense.

"It was, wasn't it," David said, thinking that his voice was the least of the changes that had happened over that time.

The song had distracted all four of them, and it seemed that before no time at all they reached the high road to Dinas Bran. As they turned east, however, a lone horseman galloped out of the forest to their left, drawing his sword as he rode.

It was Marchudd. Aeddan took one look and disappeared into the forest behind them.

"Father!" Huw cried.

David didn't look.

"Never mind him, son," Rhys said. "He's doing what needs doing. Keep your attention ahead."

"But—"

"Boy. Obey your uncle," David said.

Marchudd cantered forward, stopping four horse-lengths from David. "You think you can stand against me?" he asked.

Rhys and David had already pulled out their knives and Rhys spoke out of the side of his mouth. "Spread out, my lord. I'll slit the horse's throat if he comes toward you. If you run, he can't catch you."

David understood that Marchudd wanted him to run. Seeing their knives, Marchudd dared not come closer, but if David ran, Marchudd could take him down from above. None of these machinations mattered, however, because Aeddan hadn't run away. He'd merely found better ground for shooting.

Thwt!

An arrow appeared in Marchudd's chest. His face went from astonishment to ghastly white, before he toppled backwards off his horse.

Aeddan returned at a run. "I'm sorry, my lord, if you intended to bring him to Dinas Bran as a captive. I decided he didn't deserve to live."

"You think I mind?" David asked him. "Carry him into the ditch and leave him. We will take his horse. I see my sword hanging from his panniers. I've missed it."

The others wanted David to ride the horse, but he threw Huw up on it instead. The boy had never seen a man killed, and despite his protestations to the contrary, he needed time to recover.

Leaving Marchudd beside the road, the companions set out again. To David's surprise, however, just as when he'd traveled with his company, one by one, people stepped onto the road to walk with them. They weren't very talkative, but every few minutes David would find a different man beside him. He'd introduce himself, David would shake his hand, and then he'd fade into the background to be replaced by another. Bevyn had raised the countryside, so everyone knew what had happened to David, and wanted to make sure he was all right.

The crowd grew from an initial ten, to twenty, to fifty, and still they walked. A family might join the march for a half an hour and then fall off the back of the group to turn for home, only to be replaced by another family coming from the woods. They shared their food and David took some for himself when they offered it. Children ran in every direction. After a while, Huw dismounted from Marchudd's horse to allow smaller children to ride him.

With this train of friends, David progressed towards Dinas Bran at a steady pace so by early afternoon, he approached the end of his journey. The road followed a ridge to the west of the castle, but required that they descend into a valley, through a village nestled along the River Dee, and then up the thousand foot height to the castle.

Over the next few hours they picked their way out of the hills into the valley. At some point, someone at the castle must have grown alarmed at their numbers, because as they reached the valley floor, a host of cavalry appeared on the road around the mountain, flags flying.

"I shall sing a new song in your hall," Rhys said. "If you permit it, my lord, I shall sing of this day."

David turned to the people behind him, now quiet, as they too had noticed the horsemen. "I would like that," David said. "As long as you make Aedden the hero. And Huw." David tousled the boy's hair.

Then David raised his voice so all could hear. "I thank you with all my heart," he said. "Please know that you are welcome to dine at the castle with me this evening. Wales has survived only because of men like you."

Several men nodded, and then came forward one at a time to pay their respects. But by the time David finished greeting the last person, the rest had gone and he stood alone again with Rhys, Aeddan, and Huw.

"The cavalry are upon us," Aeddan said, with a nod for David to look behind him.

And they were. Math's banners streamed in the wind. David strode forward to greet his brother-in-law. When Math saw that it was David and not an enemy, he spurred his horse ahead of his men. He reined him in almost on top of David, dismounted, and embraced him. "By St. Winifred's ear, man!" he said. "You have led us on a merry chase! Your mother and sister have been sick with worry."

"It was not my intent, brother," David said, laughing as Math patted him up and down to make sure he was alive and uninjured. "Did you send word to my father?"

"Bevyn wanted to, but your mother stopped him," Math said. "He meant to resign his position, but she refused him, telling him to find you first. She gave him three days."

"Are our three days expired?" David asked, confused now about how long he'd been away.

"Tonight," Math said abruptly. "Bevyn intends to return tonight." And then, with a bemused grin, he said, "He'll be pleased to see you, my lord."

"It was no more his fault than mine," David said. "He can't blame himself."

"You can't stop him, my lord. He feels responsible, as he should, but not at the cost of his position or his life."

"Is that what people fear? That he will lose his life for his failure?"

"It's been known to happen when a prince is angry," Math said.

"My men should expect mercy, Math, and be surprised when it's not forthcoming, not the other way around."

Turning from him, David waved his companions forward and introduced them.

"Thank you, for your care of Prince Dafydd," Math said formally. "You will be well rewarded."

"We didn't do it for a reward," Aeddan said.

"Of course not," Math replied. "But you have families who are in your charge and you will accept your reward for their sakes, if not your own."

Mollified, Aeddan, and Rhys nodded.

Huw had no such inhibitions. "Are we really going to the castle?" he asked, hopping up and down. "Will we dine in the hall this night?"

Math laughed and patted the boy on the back. "Surely you will. Come. You are my guests."

Math signaled two of his men to come forward, and with David on Marchudd's long-suffering mount, Huw with Math, and Rhys and Aeddan awkwardly riding pillion behind two of Math's men, they rode up to the castle of Dinas Bran.

7

David and Math came through the castle gateway and Meg dashed across the courtyard to greet him.

"We've been so worried," Mom said, throwing her arms around David's waist the moment he dismounted.

"Sorry, Mom. I wasn't as careful as I should've been."

"What are you going to tell your father?" she asked.

"I'll tell him I wasn't careful. He knows that our downfall has always been trusting those who aren't trustworthy. We've never been defeated by the English except when a Welshman opens the door and lets them in."

David looked up at Anna and she took the last step down and into his arms. "Are we ever going to be safe?" she asked.

"No," he said. "I don't think so."

Anna didn't want David to be right, so instead of stewing about it, she took him inside to bathe and change and eat until he couldn't eat anymore. It was pretty wonderful for her to have him in her 'house', to be the lady of the manor, to welcome his companions as heroes, which pleased Huw to no end, and to sit beside Math in the hall, with everyone she loved around her.

It was only later that David described his capture in private to Math, Meg, and Anna. Eventually the story would get out, but Anna didn't want everyone to know it all until Bevyn arrived.

"This isn't an easy thing to hear," Math commented as he sprawled in his chair beside Anna. "If I could never walk alone, I'd go mad."

"That's the problem," David agreed. "We're vulnerable to betrayal by one we thought a friend."

"The alternative is to have no friends," Anna said.

"Not exactly a solution," David said. "Neither practical, nor possible, and even if it were, what kind of life would I live then?"

As the sun faded from the castle walls, the guard shouted that Bevyn and his men were coming. They'd gathered in the valley before making their somber way up the hill. David and Anna climbed the battlements to watch them ride in.

"Bevyn submitted his resignation to Mom, and now he'll submit it to me," David said. "What do I say to him?"

"As you told me once, the stakes are always too high here, David," Anna said. "The sad truth is that Bevyn didn't foresee danger coming from your own company. He did fail to protect you."

"So I should hang him?"

"Of course not," Anna said. "What does our sensei always say? *We learn more from failure than success.*"

214

"He'll learn from this," David said. As his men approached, David walked down the steps and through the gatehouse, to stand alone to wait for them.

They certainly were a disheartened group. They didn't even notice him until one of the men beside Bevyn signaled him to look up. Anna was looking forward to seeing Bevyn's expression when the belief that it was truly David won out over his disbelief that it could be.

There it was.

"Dafydd!" Bevyn roared and spurred his horse forward.

His men cheered another "Dafydd!" in Bevyn's wake, and traveled the hundred yards between them in ten seconds. The wave of men crested and passed around him until they encircled him. Bevyn leaped off his horse and wrapped his arm around David's neck.

"Young pup! Young pup!" he shouted, hammering him on the back.

There was laughter all around, and David greeted each man with a handshake and thanks for diligence in their search. He worked his way through the crowd until he faced Bevyn again. As they looked at each other, silence fell, and slowly Bevyn settled on one knee.

The silence was so complete, Bevyn's words might have carried all the way down to the village. "My life is yours, my lord," he said. "I failed you."

"Justice and mercy, Bevyn," David said, "justice and mercy." And then, "Look at me."

Bevyn raised his head; tears leaked from his eyes.

"You failed me less than you failed yourself. Am I to believe that you would allow such a thing to happen again?"

"Of course not, my lord!"

"I will trust you to see that it doesn't. Stand up, man. The sun sets and I'm hungry again. I would hear your story, and tell you mine."

* * * * *

Meg and Anna sat together in Math's office as Meg wrote to Papa of what had happened to David. It was almost like a poem, the way she wrote it, and Anna longed for the freedom to write what she wanted—a journal, a story, even a letter that didn't have to be carefully crafted—as every scrap of parchment was so precious that it needed to be scraped and reused, treasured until it literally fell apart in her hands. David came to find them before he went to bed, and when he asked to read it, Mom hunched over the letter, at first not wanting him to see it.

She and Anna shared a look, a silent communication in which they told each other how far they'd all come in adapting to the world in which they found themselves; then she nodded and relinquished it. "You should know the truth, David," Mom said. "You of all people need to see it."

David took the paper and read. Anna watched his face. She and Mom had suffered in his absence, Mom sobbing in Anna's arms at David's loss. It wasn't something they could have gotten used to, not ever.

> *. . . Your son came to Dinas Bran today. A host of his people accompanied him. They seem to follow him wherever he goes now. I find that I barely recognize the boy I once knew. I see glimpses of the child, but the man who inhabits his body is someone who bears more resemblance to you than me. Do not think I regret this, Llywelyn, for if he is to become a man, I can think of none better for him to emulate. But the boy is gone, sooner than I would have thought or wished . . .*

When he'd finished, David put down the paper and looked at his mother. "Father is going to freak."

"Again," Anna said.

* * * * *

Aaron surprised Anna in her quarters the next day. He hovered in the doorway of her solar, uncertain. Mom had gone off somewhere and Anna was laboring over a christening dress. She wouldn't have been sewing at all, but apparently the dress was one of those things that she had to do herself or people would talk. As Anna was different enough as it was, she occasionally tried not to call unfavorable attention to herself.

"My lady," Aaron said.

It was the first time Anna had spoken with him since David came home. "What is it, Aaron? Do we have a patient?"

"Not today, my lady. I need to speak to Prince David, but . . ." he paused. "Is your mother near?"

"Not at the moment," Anna said. "Perhaps I can help?"

Aaron bowed his head. "I have something to discuss with Prince David," he hesitated again. "If you could come with me to his rooms, be with me when I talk to him, I would be grateful."

Delighted to put the needlework aside, Anna escorted him to David's room and poked in her head. "Can we talk?" she asked.

David looked up. He was bent over a small table, dictating a letter to a scribe. Handwriting was an art form in the Middle Ages, and as Anna had anticipated, everyone who saw David's had long since deemed it illegible. "Sure," he said, straightening. "Gentlemen."

Bevyn sat in a chair he'd tipped back against the wall, picking at his fingernails with his belt knife. Hywel polished David's armor in one corner. Neither showed any interest in leaving the room. Anna understood completely. Everyone repeatedly reassured themselves that David was back in one piece. Anna had caught Mom hovering outside David's door the previous night. "We almost lost him," she'd whispered.

"Please," David said, trying again.

"Yes, my lord," Bevyn said. "I'll bring a meal when you're finished."

"Thank you, Bevyn," David said. He turned his attention to Aaron who stood in the middle of the floor, shifting from one foot to the other. "What is it?"

With a hand on her belly, Anna settled onto a cushioned chair in the corner and prepared to keep quiet. It was a technique she'd developed in dealing with Math's affairs. If she sat still—the quiet wife—men rarely noticed her presence, but afterwards Math and she would be able to talk as partners about whatever the men had discussed.

"I've kept something from you, my lord," Aaron said. "I accept that telling you of this now might mean my death, but I can no longer withhold this information."

David looked pained. "Don't even say that, Aaron," he said. "Why do my friends keep insisting that I kill them?"

"Just wait, my lord," Aaron said. He took in a deep breath. "It concerns my son, Samuel."

"You mentioned him once," David said.

"I speak rarely of him because he responded to the deaths of his mother and sister by turning from me, and from God. Samuel ran away four years ago and I've had no contact with him since he left." Aaron glanced out of the corner of his eye at Anna. She nodded back, encouragingly.

"I'm sorry," David said.

Aaron swallowed. "What I've kept from you is that a month ago a traveler brought me a letter from Samuel. It informed me that you had a traitor in your midst, that one of your men had made inquiries regarding payment for your capture"

Anna stared at Aaron, shocked.

"And you didn't think to tell me this before?" David asked.

Aaron held out both hands to David in supplication. "I didn't open the letter until after your capture," he said. "It was seeing your mother's fear that prompted me to soften my heart towards Samuel enough to read what he'd written."

Aaron's face had gone gray, and suddenly looked very old. David noticed too. He pointed to a chair and Aaron sat. "Rest a moment," David said. "Then tell me more."

"I cannot explain to you what it means to be Jewish," Aaron said. "We've lived a life apart for centuries, no matter what country took us in. My son never liked that; never wanted it. He fought me and his mother from the time he was five years of age and old enough to run free with the other boys of the town in which we lived. He never followed our teachings well, or any teachings, for that matter.

"Every time King Edward handed down new restrictions against us, he chafed at them more strongly than other members of our community. When his mother died, just after he turned sixteen, he took his rebellion further. Because he was broadly built, with fair skin and hair, he was able to 'pass' as a gentile and so took the path that had always appealed to him. He became a soldier, lying about his ancestry of course in order to do so. While I disowned him, my brother arranged a position for him among the Earl of Lancaster's men.

"However, he *is* still Jewish. He is circumcised, so any gentile seeing him in a state of undress would know his antecedents. This is a constant source of danger to him and makes him wary of everyone.

"Now that he has lived in the world, among those who would revile him if they knew his history, he has seen fear, hatred, and brutality among the gentiles. A soldier's life has shown him what he would not learn from me. In his letter, he apologizes for leaving me and asks my forgiveness. I'm sorry I was not able to find it in my heart to forgive him earlier."

Aaron fell silent, studying the floor.

"We're sorry for your troubles," Anna said. "But is there more?" She moved to the bench next to Aaron and rested a hand on his arm.

"Is that not enough? But yes, there's more."

"Wait a minute," David said. He walked to the door and poked his head into the hallway.

"Yes, my lord?" Bevyn said.

"Ask my mother to come here, if she will," he said. "I need to speak with her."

"Thank you," Aaron said. "Your mother will be most helpful."

"More so than you think," David added.

A few minutes later, Bevyn held the door open for Mom. "What is it?" she asked, settling herself in a chair near the desk.

"Aaron was just telling us that his son has written him with news of a traitor in our midst," Anna said.

"What?" Mom said, starting up from her seat. "Another one besides Marchudd?"

221

"No, no," David said, putting out a hand to stay her, "but Aaron didn't open his son's letter until after Marchudd captured me."

Aaron turned to Mom, regret in his voice. "I told you of my brother, Jacob, while we were at sea," he said. "He and his son, Moses, are physicians for King Edward's brother, Edmund, the Earl of Lancaster. My son, Samuel, who is one of Lancaster's men, wrote to me to warn me of this traitor, knowing that I had found safe haven in Wales.

"Samuel also tells me that there is a rumor that King Edward is preparing for a new pogrom against the Jews. He doesn't know exactly what it is, but the priests in their sermons are inciting hatred at every mass, and he feels there is little time before Edward hands down a new edict. Edward may already have done so."

Mom steepled her hands together and tapped her lips with her fingers.

"It's very difficult to know what to say to this, Aaron," Mom said. "I believe you, but I'm not certain as to what we can do about it."

"Does Samuel expect something specific from us? Or perhaps from me?" David asked.

"Hope, I think," Aaron said. "There is something special about you, my lord, that everyone can see. In both England and Wales, people tell tales of your exploits and deeds. This, combined with your treatment of me, have made you a hero to my son. In truth, I have also come to expect a great deal from you. You and your mother are both wise beyond all expectation. You give my son and me hope for the future."

Anna had been looking into the fire as Aaron spoke, distracted by thoughts his words had prompted, and almost missed Mom's next sentence.

". . . time we tell him the truth?" she said.

"What?" Anna said.

"What truth?" Aaron asked.

"I have wanted to tell Aaron from the first time I met him," Mom said. "He needs to make some decisions about his family and his future, and if we are to help him, he deserves the truth."

"Will he believe us, if we tell him?" Anna asked.

"Believe what?" Aaron said.

The three of them shared a long look, and then David took the plunge. "Believe that the country from which we come exists."

Mom nodded. "Aaron," she said. "We've traveled here from the future. I lived with Prince Llywelyn seventeen years ago and conceived David. I told you the truth about that. I then returned to my time for David's childhood. We are back here again, though how or why we neither know nor understand."

Aaron stared at her.

"Thank you for not immediately accusing us of witchcraft!" she said. "I could take anything but that."

Aaron collected himself. "I don't believe in witches," he said, "but I know of no science or religion that can explain what you've just told me."

"Neither do we, unfortunately," Anna replied. "Believe me, we would gladly hear any logical explanation, but we can't explain what's happened to us. Our superior knowledge doesn't help us in this."

"And . . . when exactly is your time?" Aaron asked, his eyes on David's.

"I was born in November, one thousand, nine hundred and ninety-six years after the birth of Christ," David said.

Aaron put his hand to his head, twisting in his seat. "1996," he breathed.

David gave him time to recover. Aaron sat, his face in his hands. Finally, he looked up. "Somehow, I believe you. I am beyond surprised, yet not surprised at all." He paused again. "You have seen many wonders?" he asked.

He was looking for some kind of confirmation. Mom took up the challenge. "We have vehicles that fly through the air," she said, "and others that travel along the ground, some at hundreds of miles an hour; we have sent men to the moon, and they have sent back pictures of earth, which shows it as an orb, floating in space. In our time, the earth is home to nearly seven billion souls. Our country, the United States of America, exists on a continent that most of Europe has yet to discover. It's a democracy, ruled by a parliament elected by all people in the country, regardless of race, religion, class, or gender. In our country, women have the right to vote in elections, all children must attend school, and I went to a university and studied for many years to receive my doctorate in history."

"It's because of history that we're telling you this now," David said. "In our world, my father was killed at Cilmeri in 1282, and Wales, as a country, ceased to exist."

"In our world," Mom joined in, "in five years, Edward expels the Jewish community from England."

Aaron stared at her, then let out a long breath. "Of everything you've just told me," he said, "it is this last that forces me to believe you. It's such a small number of people, to be perceived as doing such harm." He paused. "I have so many questions I don't know where to begin, except . . . There's a reason you're telling me this now?"

"Your people may have very little time, as your son perceived. You may begin to spread the word among your people that they are welcome in Wales," David said.

"Prince Llywelyn agrees to this?" Aaron asked.

David and Mom exchanged looks. "We've discussed it," Mom hedged. "He's not opposed to the idea."

"It's something we need to explore with him further," David said. "But in the meantime, Wales can provide a safe haven for those who are able to venture here now. Father said he wouldn't object to that."

"Thank you," Aaron said. He stood to leave, but then stopped and sat down again. "My son also writes that on the first of June, the Earl of Lancaster travels to Chester for a meeting with King Edward and the other Marcher lords. Samuel, Jacob, and Moses will travel with him. With your permission, I will meet them, as long as Anna remains well. I don't trust this information to a letter that might never arrive."

David nodded. "I'll send word of this meeting to my father," David replied. "He needs to know of it."

* * * * *

On the twenty-eighth of May, only a day before Aaron intended to leave for Chester, a guard on the wall shouted that a rider—a foreign rider—requested permission to enter. Math and Anna went to find out who it was. The man dismounted and bowed deeply.

"I am Abraham ben Moses," he said. "I'm looking for my uncle, Aaron ben Simon, whom I've heard is within."

"He is," Math said. "I suppose we've been expecting you."

The man raised his eyebrows, but didn't ask questions, just allowed Anna to lead him into the hall.

"Are you okay with this?" Anna asked Math ('okay' was one of the words she couldn't seem to stop using; apparently she said it often enough that other members of the castle had adopted it too).

Math nodded. "I can't predict the future like you can," he said. "But I can see my way clear on this."

"Abraham!" Aaron entered the hall from a rear doorway, David a pace or two behind. In three long strides, Aaron reached Abraham and embraced him. They patted each other on the back, and then stepped away, smiling, though Abraham's quickly faded.

"We are here to impose upon your hospitality, Uncle, and that of your lord, if he will have us," Abraham said, looking past Aaron to David. "The King of England has barred us from London. The Jewish community has fifteen days to leave the city, ten of which have already passed."

"They will lose everything," Aaron breathed. "On such short notice, no one will get a fair price for any of their possessions."

"If such a thing was ever possible," Abraham said. He shook his head. "The edict caught us unawares."

"What is your profession?" David asked.

"I am a wool merchant," Abraham replied, "though in recent years I've worked in the shop of a gentile—ill-paid and ill-respected—except for the money I brought in."

"I'm sorry for your troubles," David said. "But if you have contacts in Europe with whom you do business, you may settle in the village and practice your trade from here. There will be no undue taxes or restrictions on your behavior or your movement."

Abraham stared at him. "Truly?"

"We will restrict usury among your bankers to a maximum of five percent interest," David said. "While they may not feel that is worth their efforts, over the long term, they could earn a living if that profession is their choice. Otherwise, we ask that you accept our hospitality as it is offered: from one free people to another."

Abraham shook his head, opening and closing his mouth but unable to speak. Aaron patted him on the shoulder. "He's the Prince of Wales," Aaron said. "Best take him at his word."

"Sire," Abraham finally managed. "Thank you." He allowed Aaron to lead him to a table and settle him on a bench, an expression of wonder still on his face.

"What is Father going to say?" Anna asked.

"He's not here," David said, "but it's the right thing to do." He glanced at the two men who were too far away to hear him. "But you're right that I probably should discuss it with Father before we get too far down this road."

"I'd have to agree," Math said. "If not for the incident with Marchudd, you'd have gone to him already."

"Then I guess there's no time like the present," David said. His eyes lit and he spun on his heel. "Bevyn!" he bellowed, and disappeared through the front door to the hall.

Anna shared a glance with Math. "My lord," she said. "I think we've work to do too."

He smiled at Anna's uncharacteristic use of his title and reached for her hand. "Abraham?" he said, and gestured towards the door. "I'd like to meet your people."

They rode to the village of Llangollen. Aaron came too because the villagers knew of his work in healing by now, and most had learned to trust him. But his presence was hardly needed. By the time they arrived, Abraham's sons were playing with three of the village boys and one of the women had invited his wife into her home to rest. They'd probably already learned their first words of Welsh.

"One family is not a threat," Math said. "If a dozen were to arrive at once, that might be a different story."

"There may be more than a dozen, in the end," Anna said.

"We will leave tomorrow's troubles for tomorrow."

Within another hour, Abraham had moved his family into a hut that had belonged to the head man's mother who'd died the previous winter.

"We'll leave you in good hands," Math said.

"I think they're a bit overwhelmed by the unexpected hospitality and the foreignness of their circumstances," Anna said to David when she found him later. "As city people, they know nothing of country life, nothing of Wales."

David shrugged. "Like all of us, they'll just have to learn."

8

"You're looking forward to this trip, aren't you?" David asked.

Bevyn rubbed his hands together. "If we are to pay a visit to Gruffydd ap Gwenwynwyn, it will give me a chance to see what that traitorous bastard is up to," he said. "I hear his son and daughter-in-law have fled to her family in England, but he stays for Prince Llywelyn. A dubious proposition at best."

"Gruffydd holds Dolforwyn for us and has reestablished the town," David said. "My father keeps him on a short leash and intended to visit him on his way north. We'll see him on our way south, instead."

Dolforwyn was roughly thirty miles south of Dinas Bran. They made it in two days of easy riding. It was another thirty miles to Buellt, and a further thirty to the flatlands of south Wales, near where David hoped to find his father. Where exactly he was David didn't know, but the people there would direct him. Mom expected that Father's business in the south would take all summer, so even if David stayed a short time with Gruffydd, he should still be able to take part in whatever maneuvers Father was planning.

Gruffydd himself came out of his newly built gatehouse to welcome David's company. After the initial greetings, he brought David into his hall, seated him, and launched into an exposition of everything he'd achieved in the months since David's parents' wedding. Bemused, David leaned back in his chair and listened. Gruffydd was enthusiastic and fiery, pacing back and forth, waving his hands in the air, forcefully presenting his points.

Finally, he swung around to David. "I hear you were taken prisoner for a time," he said.

"Yes," David said. "The ringleader was one of my own men, in fact."

"A bad business," Gruffydd said, shaking his head. "You can never be too careful, even with those you deem most loyal."

David leaned forward. "Is that some kind of warning, Gruffydd?" he asked. "Do you have more to add to that statement?"

"No! No!" He objected, waving his hands again. "I was only making an observation on the perils of leadership."

David sat back, unsatisfied. Father thought Gruffydd had spent too much of his life in the company of the English to work against them so passionately now. Perhaps sensing David's discontent, Gruffydd hastened forward and took a chair in front of him.

"This brings me to some new business; something on which I'd like your opinion," he said.

"I'm happy to help," David said. He'd not thought that Gruffydd would ever want his opinion on anything.

"A week ago, three families of Jews crossed into Wales from England. They found their way here and asked to settle in our village."

"What did you say to them?" David asked.

"Well . . . one is a doctor, and I welcomed him into my household. The other two are both well-educated, but their former profession as goldsmiths is completely useless to me. I made one an overseer of the castle accounts, and the other a scribe. I refuse to waste such knowledge, just because of their religion."

"Excellent!" David said, slapping a hand on the table. "That's exactly as I hoped. We had a similar situation at Dinas Bran. A wool merchant and his family arrived. Math is seeing to establishing his trade on behalf of Wales, instead of England."

"Just be prepared for trouble," Gruffydd said. "Two days ago, my priest railed against Jews as the killers of Christ. I told him if he said another word I'd rip out his tongue."

David blinked. But Gruffydd was serious.

"Come, man!" he said, "If Edward has turned against them, stolen their land, subjected them to unfair laws, they have something in common with us. The enemy of my enemy could be my friend. I say, give them a chance. At the very least, we can line our coffers at their expense if things don't go well."

That had Bevyn laughing. "I like your way of thinking," he said.

David wasn't so sure, but as usual, Gruffydd swung whichever way most benefitted him. In this case, his goals aligned with David's, so he could tolerate him.

"I intend to discuss these developments with my father, who perhaps hasn't heard the latest news. I'm glad to know your position on this," David said.

"You know I've had troubles with Prince Llywelyn, now and again," Gruffydd said—the understatement of the year as far as David was concerned, but he let it go—"but he's not as fickle an overlord as Edward has proved to be. His laws are Welsh laws, and by God, I will stand by him in the face of English oppression as long as need be."

"I will tell my father he has your continued support," David said. "Wales can stand against England, *if* all Welshmen stand with her."

* * * * *

Four days later, they rode for Buellt, accompanied by Gruffydd who wanted to see how the garrison there fared. They arrived as dusk fell on June the fourth in time for the evening meal. As always, David was starving and was pleased that the cook at Buellt was one of the more skilled he'd encountered.

Towards the end of the meal, a man dressed in plain homespun asked for admittance to the hall and permission to speak with David. At David's nod, he strode towards the dais, sure of himself and unafraid. "My lord," he said, bowing as he reached him. "I'm Rhodri ap Tathan. I've heard that you are interested in the movements of our enemies. I have news for you."

David sat forward in his chair. "I'm pleased to see you, Rhodri ap Tathan," he said. "Tell me."

"Humphrey de Bohun, the Earl of Hereford, is on the move," Rhodri said.

Gruffydd stood so quickly he upended his chair. "Hereford!" he said. "Where!"

"He gathers men at his castle of Huntington," Rhodri said.

"Bohun is supposed to be in Chester," David said.

"His men are here," Rhodri replied.

"How many?" Gruffydd asked.

"Twenty knights and many more foot. This news comes from my sister, who is a servant in Hereford's hall." He shrugged. "There may be more but she can't count higher."

David tried not to laugh.

"We're grateful to you, Rhodri. Please accept the hospitality of my hall," Gruffydd said.

Rhodri bowed and turned away. Gruffydd stayed on his feet and called one of his captains to him. "Send out scouts," he ordered. "I want to know the moment Hereford crosses the Dyke." He meant Offa's Dyke, a system of ditches and ramparts that ran the entire north/south length of Wales and was the traditional boundary between England and Wales. Gruffydd turned to David. "Rest easy, my lord. With King Edward and his lords in Chester, little will come of this."

Again, David didn't share Gruffydd's confidence, but didn't
have any suggestions as to what else to do. After the meal,
however, David retired early, uneasy; Buellt made him uneasy, not
only because of the imminent threat of Hereford. David couldn't
forget that this was where his father had almost died and it felt
uncomfortably coincidental that danger loomed here again.

The next morning David lay in bed, wide awake after a
restless night, staring up at the ceiling. Smoke had darkened it,
although someone had recently white-washed the walls
underneath the tapestries. Sparks smoldered in the fireplace,
giving off almost no heat, but as it was June, the room wasn't cold.
David debated with himself, trying to rationalize what he wanted
to do, and finally succumbed to the temptation.

Bevyn was finishing his breakfast when David sat beside
him. "You have always been a most faithful companion, Bevyn,"
David said.

Bevyn wiped his mouth, checking his mustaches at the
same time to ensure they were immaculate, and swallowed. "I have
always endeavored to be of service, my lord."

"Then if you can bear with me," David said, "I ask that you
ride out with me this morning and ask me no questions."

Bevyn gave David a hard look, but nodded. David led him
to the stables. When Bevyn realized that he intended to leave the
castle on horseback, with only Bevyn himself as a guard, however,
he stopped.

"It's not possible, my lord."

"What isn't possible?" David asked.

235

"I won't allow you to ride without a proper escort. You can't go, not with the English so close."

"Fine," David said, "but the men must stay well back when I tell them to let me be."

Bevyn bowed. "Of course, my lord," he said.

David was sure he was smirking beneath his mustaches.

They rode out: Bevyn, seven men, and David. As they trotted across the drawbridge, David looked back, thinking of the Welsh in his old world who'd lost their lives trying to take this castle. It was strongly situated atop a motte, with two Norman baileys defended by six towers and a curtain wall. The twin-towered gatehouse was similar to the gatehouse that guarded Rhuddlan Castle. David turned back to the road and followed it down the hill. They didn't cross the bridge over the river Wye to the north of the castle, but continued west along the Irfon.

They rode perhaps two miles, with David looking from one side to the other all the while. Finally, he stopped, uncertain. Bevyn moved up beside him.

"I can find it for you, my lord," he said.

"What?"

"There's a turn a hundred yards back, if you will permit me to show you."

David studied him. "Please," he said.

David turned around and followed Bevyn to a turn-off David hadn't seen. Taking a left, he led David through a small copse of trees and into a clearing at the base of a small hill. Wild flowers covered it. Spurring his horse forward, David passed

Bevyn and raced to the top and then across the meadow to the other side, where the terrain sloped upwards again. Leaves covered the trees. It looked very different, but David knew he was in the right place. The men all followed him, milling around uncertainly when David stopped half-way up the higher hill to look back. David dismounted and handed the reins to Cadwallon, the youngest and least experienced of his men.

"My lord?" said another, this one Ieuan ap Cynan, a knight in his twenties.

"Hush, man," Bevyn shushed him. "He said 'no questions'."

David squatted in the middle of the slope, trying to find the remains of the tire tracks. It was ridiculous to think they'd still be there after all this time, but Anna *had* skidded.

"It's all right, Bevyn," David said. "Do you know where it is now?"

Bevyn didn't pretend to misunderstand him. He gestured with his head towards the way they'd come in. "Hidden in a thicket, down below," he said.

"Well, let's see it."

They left the horses with Cadwallon, who stared forlornly after them. David led the way back down the hill, walking this time. From the lower meadow, the trees hid all of Cadwallon but his white face. David turned to the spot Bevyn indicated. He didn't know what his men would think, but a twisted part of David looked forward to seeing their faces when they looked at his aunt's van.

Behind the tree Anna had hit were more trees and a thick screen of bushes. Bevyn pushed his way through them, with the rest following, and into a small clearing, maybe the size of a tennis court, with the van smack in the middle of it.

It didn't look too bad, under the circumstances. It was filthy from two years of accumulated dirt, and bigger than David remembered. They stood in a semi-circle around it, and the looks on the men's faces varied from bewilderment (Trahearn) to excited interest (Ieuan) to grim satisfaction (Bevyn).

David walked around the van. The tires had gone soft, but not completely flat. The windscreen had a spider web of cracks across it, but it hadn't fallen out. The airbags rested on the front seats, sadly deflated. David opened the driver-side door and stuck in his head. Anna had left the key in the ignition. *Hmmm.*

Behind David, Bevyn said, "It's a chariot, Trahearn. There's no witchcraft here."

"No, my lord," Trahearn said. "I didn't say there was."

Then Ieuan spoke from his position at the rear of the van. "My lord?" he said. "How is it that a tree fell on it in such a way?"

"We were sliding backwards down the hill when we hit the tree," David said, impressed that he could tell which was the front and which the back.

"Oh," Ieuan said, still thinking hard. "Then why was the chariot not splintered into pieces?"

"Because the people who built it designed the back to crush on impact, to protect the people inside," David said, only listening with half an ear because he was still thinking about the keys.

Ieuan was opening his mouth to ask another question, when Bevyn raised his hand for silence. David froze. He heard . . . nothing. And then, more than heard, he felt the thudding of horses' hooves. As one, the company dropped to their haunches and David scuttled to Bevyn's position. A dozen English cavalry rode across their field of vision, to all appearances preparing to make camp in the meadow, on the other side of the thin screen of bushes.

"Whose men are they?" David asked, silently cursing himself for carelessness, and Gruffydd ap Gwenwynwyn for being incompetent—or a traitor.

"They wear the Earl of Hereford's colors," Bevyn said. "Bohun's men."

David did a quick survey of his men. Ieuan peered through the bushes a few paces away. David sidled over to see what he was looking at. More English. These were hunkered down over something on the ground that David couldn't see from where he crouched.

"Tracks," Ieuan mouthed at David. *Our tracks.*

Then Ieuan whispered, "Cadwaladr ap Seisyll was my great-great-uncle."

"Um," David murmured. He knew all about Cadwaladr ap Cadwallon because he'd flown the dragon banner in the Dark Ages, but David hadn't heard of this Cadwaladr before.

Taking pity on David's ignorance, Ieuan explained. "A hundred years ago, the Marcher lord William de Braose, this Earl of Hereford's ancestor, murdered Seisyll ap Dyfnwal. Braose invited Seisyll to his castle for dinner and then killed him in cold blood. At the same time, he sent men to kill Cadwaladr, Seisyll's son. Fortunately, Cadwaladr had been out hunting and escaped capture, though they killed his wife. Cadwaladr took to the hills and harassed the Braose lands until Braose captured and executed him two years later."

David gazed at him, still not understanding.

He tipped his head at the English knights. "If one man can do so much," he said, "what can nine of us do?"

David had never heard of this Welsh Robin Hood, but Ieuan had a point and it was better than hiding here. The van caught David's attention again. *Ha! I'm sixteen now. I'm legal.*

David scurried to the driver's side door, which he'd left open. He pulled out his belt knife to cut away the airbag; then hopped into the front seat. He turned the key. Nothing happened. Was the battery dead? Even a new one might not last this long unused. David looked at the controls and realized Anna had left it in 'drive'. *Of course she had.* David put his foot on the brake and shifted into park. He turned the key again. It coughed, coughed again, and then started.

David laughed. The miracles of modern science and a Toyota engine. He leaped out of the van and pulled at the sliding door, wanting to hurry because the English could hear the engine. David hoped its unfamiliarity would delay the English response and give them time to get away.

"Get in!" David said in the quietest whisper he could manage that still carried. Everyone had backed away when David had started the engine, but now Ieuan didn't need a second invitation. He climbed inside while Bevyn herded the others in behind him. Everyone should try to fit nine men wearing mail hauberks into a minivan before they die. Fortunately, plate had yet to be invented so the men didn't clank against each other and no one impaled anyone else.

With three across the back, one in the trunk, one in each of the captain's chairs in the second row, Ieuan kneeling between the two front seats, and Bevyn and David in the front, they 'fit'. Once everyone was inside, David eased the sliding door closed and had Bevyn gently latch his door. David climbed back into the driver's seat, shifted into drive, and pressed the gas pedal.

The van rolled across the grass a few feet before David stepped on the brake and shifted into reverse. He backed the van all the way to the rear of the enclosure, and then shifted into drive again.

"Ready?" he asked.

Beyvyn's smile had a wicked look to it. He nodded.

Someone shouted from the back, "Ieuan! Move your head, man. We can't see!"

Ieuan ducked his head, but not so far that he couldn't see himself.

"Okay," David said, and floored it.

The van sped across the grass. David aimed for the branch-covered gap through which Bevyn (and others) had pushed the van to hide it. The van burst through the bushes, already going forty, and rocketed across the clearing, scattering the English and their horses. Thanking his aunt in her absence for buying all-wheel-drive, and glad the van didn't actually hit anyone to slow its momentum, David steadied the wheel. They picked up speed, careened up the incline (which Anna had slid down backwards), kept on across the meadow, and up the higher hill, towards where they'd left the horses.

Near the top, David braked and backed the van between two trees, out of sight of the English.

"Out! Out!" he shouted. He would have liked to drive all the way back to the castle, but he couldn't leave Cadwallon and the horses where they were, and it wasn't as if there was a road suitable for driving on anyway. His company was more flexible on horseback.

David threw himself onto Taranis, took the reins, and then looked back down the hill to where the English cavalry stood unmoving, staring after them. David saluted with a grin, then led his men further up the hill and into the trees until the English were out of sight. None dared follow.

David was prepared to charge off to the castle but Bevyn stopped him. "My lord! Wait!" he said. "We don't know if the English have surrounded Buellt, or if this is only a small advance party. We need care, not speed."

He was right.

"Lead on," David said.

The company circled to the north of the castle without encountering anyone, but a quick foray out from under cover showed that Hereford had indeed surrounded Buellt.

"At least the drawbridge is up," Bevyn said.

"If Gruffydd ap Gwenwynwyn wasn't on our side, we'd have lost the castle already," Ieuan added.

"Who shall we send to my father?" David asked, liking Ieuan's idea of Robin Hood more and more.

"We should all go, my lord," Bevyn answered. "We can do nothing more here."

"We could cause trouble," David said.

Bevyn shook his head. "I disagree, my lord. Better to ensure help comes. Only then can we kill some English."

David wanted to disagree, but couldn't. *Of course he's right. As usual.*

* * * * *

David found his father's men on the edge of the rugged mountain range to the west of Brecon, with Rhys ap Maredudd, his cousin Rhys Wynod, Nicholas de Carew, and their men. They'd camped in a spot that afforded a spectacular view of the lowlands of south Wales. Their grim expressions as David's company rode into the camp, however, couldn't bode well—whether for the Welsh or the English David didn't yet know. Father had retired to his tent to read a missive a messenger had brought in minutes before. Goronwy greeted him, and as Bevyn turned to make disposition of the men, brought David to his father.

Goronwy and David ducked under the tent flap. Llywelyn looked well, but somber. He'd collapsed into a chair, the letter resting on his lap, held in both hands.

"Hereford's men have surrounded Buellt Castle," David said. "They may have already taken it!"

Father straightened in his seat, but didn't answer, merely held out the parchment to David. "It is from the Archbishop of Canterbury," he said. "He thinks it's time to affect a reconciliation between us, Edward, and the Church. He wants to include the Scots for some reason."

David stared at him. His father's words had pulled him up short and he glanced at the paper. It took a moment to shift gears and take in what was written there. "He can't be serious," David said. "Not with Bohun on the offensive." David passed Goronwy the letter.

"Perhaps he doesn't know that the Earl of Hereford is on the offensive," Goronwy said, having quickly scanned the paper. "There's no love lost between Hereford and Edward, and Hereford certainly doesn't confide in the Archbishop."

"But they're all supposed to be meeting in Chester as we speak," David said.

"When is the date set for this new council?" Goronwy asked. "The one the Archbishop is planning."

"The first of August, near Lancaster," Llywelyn said.

"That's some distance for both us and the Scots to travel," Goronwy said.

"Such is my concern," Father said. "I don't trust Edward, even if he promises safe passage. We would be in his country, on his land. Why he doesn't invite us to Shrewsbury and the Scots to Carlisle, I don't know."

"This bears some thinking about," Goronwy said. "Perhaps Rhys would have something to say."

"Ask all the lords to come here," Father agreed.

David was bouncing up and down by now, anxious about Buellt, but before he could bring his father's attention back to his concerns, the other men ducked under the flap and circled Llywelyn.

Goronwy handed Rhys the paper. He scanned it. "You cannot go," Rhys said.

"Edward won't like it if you don't," Carew said, having read it over Rhys' shoulder.

"Perhaps he means to make peace—real peace," Father said. "Is that something I should ignore?"

Goronwy pursed his lips. "I suppose it might be worthwhile to hear him out, if it would bring a true end to this war."

"My concern is your person," Rhys said. "Goronwy has been negotiating on your behalf for months. But Edward asks you to come to Lancaster without confirming he will sign the treaty."

Carew had a finger to his lip. "What does that mean?" he asked. And then . . . "I've changed my mind. I agree with Rhys. You can't go."

"I agree," Father said, "but someone has to. Dafydd must attend without me."

Now it was Goronwy's turn to shake his head. "I would rather you snubbed him, my lord, than put your son's life at risk. He has no right to expect it."

"I'm not suggesting this because I care about Edward or his expectations," Father said. He stood and began to pace around his tent, and when he spoke again, his voice was harsh. "He's going to continue this war, or he's not. He's going to make peace, or he's not."

"It says in the letter that this is at the instigation not of Edward, but of the Archbishop of Canterbury," David said. "It distresses him that you are excommunicate."

"What distresses him is that the people of Wales and its government no longer tithe to his Church!" Rhys said.

"And he misses the power that our money brings," Carew added.

"Ha! You have the better of it," Rhys agreed.

My father's sudden stillness drew everyone's attention. "The Archbishop promises that if I come to Lancaster, he will intercede on my behalf with the Pope," Llywelyn said. "He dangles this as a carrot in front of my nose, as if I were a donkey pulling a cart. He knows how important it is to me, and to Wales, that we are right with God. We and our Cistercian allies defy the Pope, but at what cost to our souls?" Father looked around at the men before him, who, to a man, didn't meet his eyes, their laughter of before regretted.

Llywelyn continued. "Dafydd will go. If that's not enough for the Archbishop—so be it."

Everyone nodded, understanding that the discussion was over and no longer subject to questioning.

"And Buellt, my lord?" asked Goronwy.

"That is now our first concern," Llywelyn said. "I will ride to its defense. How many men besiege it?"

"Bevyn estimates a complete force of one hundred foot and perhaps fifty cavalry. More than enough, given time," David said.

"How many defend?" asked Carew.

"Gwenwynwyn himself, with thirty of the castle garrison, plus forty of mine," David said.

"Oh," said Carew, brightening, "Excellent."

"Hereford will not last if we come behind him," Rhys said. "It's impossible to maintain a siege under those conditions."

"We must move as quickly as we can," Father said. He nodded at Goronwy, who left the tent.

"Father," David said, recalling the other subject they needed to discuss, "do you remember the letter I wrote to you about how Edward was preparing a new edict against the Jews?"

"Yes," he said. "I understand Aaron went to Chester to discuss it with his brother and son."

"Since I wrote you," David said, "Edward evicted the Jews from London."

"I've heard of this," Carew said. "Edward cuts off his nose to spite his face. Would that they established their trades in Wales instead. We could rule the world."

"What? Why do you say that?" Father asked.

"My father had dealings with the Jewish traders in Bristol," Carew said. "They had the best contacts in Europe of any merchants. Their wool, their cloth, their metalwork, was of the finest quality. My father and I may have disagreed about many things, but not this. He always regretted not being able to lure any to his holdings in Wales."

"Why didn't they want to come?" David asked.

"Oh, well . . . they're city people, and Wales has no cities."

"They're coming now," David said.

"Are they? That's news indeed," Carew said. "When and where?"

"A Jewish wool merchant and his family arrived in Dinas Bran before I left," David said, "and three more families have settled at Dolforwyn. There may be more by now. They will come, if we let them and if we spread the word that they are welcome."

"How many Jews live in England?" Father asked, being practical.

"Three thousand? Five thousand?" David said. The other men looked at him. "It's my mother's guess. I don't know how she knows."

Father nodded, his hand to his chin. "We welcome them," he said.

Perhaps the motives were wrong. Once again, it was about a quest for money and power rather than a desire to do the right thing. But this was the thirteenth century, five hundred years before the Bill of Rights. Perhaps Mom was asking too much to champion freedom for all people, regardless of their religion. For now, it was a start.

* * * * *

The next morning, Father finalized his plans. Carew, for all his support, didn't want to break off the pressure he was putting on the southern English castles. Rhys, however willing to fight, felt the same. He did offer to split his force and send twenty-five cavalry with Father.

Then Ieuan explained the story of his great-uncle to David's men, who took to the idea of harassing the Earl of Hereford's holdings with a glee and intensity that was disconcerting. Father thought the small company could distract Hereford and make him reconsider his decision to besiege Buellt. And it would be good fun in the process, David's men thought. Suddenly, David found it terrifying.

The stories of Robin Hood involved bravery and heroism, love and honor, but also the crucial elements of the victorious underdog triumphing over the evil powers that rule the land. *What's not to like?* The Robin Hood concept, placed in the hands of a thirteenth century Welshman, however, became truly blood curdling. Cadwaladr ap Seisyll dropped everything from the story but honor—and revenge.

"My intent is to come behind Hereford's men and break the siege of Buellt," Father said. "If Hereford is concerned about your activities, it could play a role in how quickly he quits the vicinity. You must also be aware that he's likely to retaliate."

"What can he do?" one of the men scoffed.

"He might drive the people north, out of their lands, to make them a burden on us. Or," Father added, "a very real possibility is that he'll put all his effort into hunting you down, just as his grandfather did to Cadwaladr."

"Then we'll retreat into the mountains," David said.

"You'll have to be on constant alert," Carew said. "The Prince's idea is a good one. He should have a role in this fight. I'm all for harassing Hereford where he lives." Then to Llywelyn he said, "We will not fail you, sire. Your southern lords are more than capable of managing a successful campaign. We can continue to hold the lowlands for you, while you see to Powys."

Father put his hand on David's shoulder. "You'll have six weeks before you have to leave for the council with Edward," he said. "Take your men and ride east to the Brecon Mountains. Bohun rules at Brecon Castle, and his vassal, Clifford, at Bronllys and Hay. Use your best judgment as to what will wreak the most havoc in those lands."

If David could come to the council with Edward having shifted the balance of power in the Marches in favor of the Welsh, he could negotiate from a position of greater strength. The defeat of Hereford at Buellt was crucial, and the sooner everyone moved, the better.

9

Meg and Anna sat on a bench against a sheltering wall in the kitchen garden, herbs at their feet and a grape vine running up and over the lattice above their heads, providing shade against the summer heat. They were watching Gwenllian run back and forth along the paths, chasing butterflies. She'd come from Aber with Heledd, arriving in Dinas Bran just after David left.

"There's something to be said for air conditioning," Anna said, just as a suggestion, flapping her fan.

"I've never been heavily pregnant in the summer," Mom said, "but I can appreciate the sentiment."

"Mama!" Gwenllian called, coming to a stop. "Look!" A butterfly had landed on her wrist and was slowly flapping its wings, warming itself in the sun.

"Don't touch it, Gwen," Mom said. "It will fly away if you leave it." It did, and after watching it flutter onto a climbing vine, Gwenllian settled herself under a bush to dig in the dirt with a stick.

Mom and Anna continued to sit contentedly, sharing a moment of peace. "Does Math feel anxious at not going south with David?" Mom asked after a while.

"Yes, of course he does," Anna said. "But Papa told him to hold the north for him and that's what he is doing." She checked the sun, trying to estimate how long before Math returned from the day's patrol.

Just then, Math himself emerged from the shadows of the castle doorway. Anna gathered herself to push to her feet, but he waved her down. "You need to sit," he said.

"What's wrong?" Anna asked.

"Hereford's men have surrounded Buellt."

"David!" Mom surged to her feet, but Math caught her arms.

"Rest easy, Mother," Math said. "It was he who sent the messenger. Dafydd was riding with some of his men at the time, and they've retreated in good order, south, to find Prince Llywelyn."

Mom put her hand to her head and turned away. She walked a few steps, eyes on the ground. "How do I stop caring?" she asked. "How do I stop worrying about him all the time?"

Math shook his head. "You don't," he said simply. "You are his mother." Math smiled down at Anna and put a hand to her belly.

Yes, that is *to be my fate, then.*

"I need your thoughts on a particular matter," Math said.

Meg noted the change in tone and turned back. Math paced around a bit while he gathered his thoughts, clearly restless, and then came to stand in front of Anna.

"I have a situation," he said. "Believe it or not, one of my people has murdered another."

"A murder!" Anna said. "Who?"

"The miller and his apprentice. The apprentice claims he was beaten one too many times by the miller so he walloped him on the head with a wooden staff, killing him."

"In self-defense?" Anna asked.

Math put out a hand and wobbled it in a 'so, so' manner. Anna couldn't remember if he'd done it before or learned it from her.

"Have you heard the witnesses?" Mom asked.

"Yes, dozens," Math said. "They don't change the issue." The way the law worked in Wales was that both the murderer and the family of the victim gathered witnesses who were willing to swear either that the murderer was innocent, or that there were extenuating circumstances such that it was not murder. Math's job, as the judge in the case, was to determine what sort of proof was appropriate, which of the parties were required to produce proof, adjudicate on the case, and then impose the appropriate penalty in accordance with the law.

"What makes this case different?" Anna asked.

"The incident occurred while the two were traveling, just a few miles east of here."

"And?" Mom said.

"And, as the miller's family insists the two were in England, they say English law should apply."

"Isn't that unusual?" Anna asked.

"It's been an unusual summer," Math said, with a glance at Anna's belly, accompanied by another smile.

Yes, yes, yes, I'm having your baby. Hush! But Anna smiled too, as if they shared a secret instead of something that was sticking out for all the world to see.

"So they want the apprentice's head," Mom said.

"By English law, he deserves death. In Wales, he or his family owes a payment of *galanas* to the miller's family."

"Your inclination is to deny the request of the miller's family," Anna said, knowing Math well enough not to ask it as a question.

"Yes," Math said. "We're Welsh, not English."

"If they feel that way, they should take it to an English court," Anna said, "and see if they can get a fair judgment."

"They couldn't," said Math. "They don't speak English and the apprentice is under no obligation to submit to an English decision or appear in court, since he can live freely in Wales."

"So then why are they doing this?" Anna asked.

Mom saw it. "They're seeing how strong you are, Math," she said. "You're a new lord to them, and they're behaving like children, testing their parents and feeling for weaknesses."

"Yes," Math said. "That's what it felt like to me too, but it is possible that the miller's family is within their rights."

"Not in Welsh law," Anna said. "Papa stood up for our people and our laws when he wrote to Edward and refused to give up Wales for lands in England. The miller's family knows that."

"They are looking out for themselves," Math said.

"Then it is your job to look out for them, even if they can't see it," Anna said.

Math held out his hand to Anna and she took it. "Thank you," he said, simply. "I knew the answer, but it is helpful to share my concerns with you." He leaned forward to kiss Anna's cheek, nodded at Meg, and turned on his heel, striding away as he'd come.

When he'd gone, Mom spoke again. Anna heard the tears in her voice and moved closer. "I wouldn't have thought it possible," Meg said.

"Wouldn't have thought what was possible?" Anna asked.

"That a man of this century would look to his wife as Math looks to you." She put her arm around Anna's shoulders and pulled Anna to her. "We've all been very, very lucky."

"What about Papa?"

Mom waved her hand dismissively. "He is the Prince of Wales and no youngster. He's learned over time to listen better, though he still stands on his dignity too much, thinking he has to go it alone."

"A bit like David," Anna said.

"More than a bit," Mom said. "I worry about him too; he has far too great a burden for a sixteen-year old boy, and then he takes on more and more with every month that passes."

"Nobody sees him as a boy," Anna said. "He's a man here, Mom."

"And that makes it worse," Meg said.

* * * * *

Aaron returned from Chester a few days later, near the end of June. He was clearly a bit worse for wear. That night, the four friends gathered in Math's office after the evening meal. Anna sat, very heavily now, on a cushioned bench near the door. That seemed to be *all* she was doing lately. *Sitting; breathing; getting bigger and bigger by the second!*

"As you suggested, my lord, I rode north from Dinas Bran to Ewloe, where I spent the night, before crossing the Dee into Chester. That bridge is well-guarded, but a free flow of Welsh into the city continues."

"But not back again," Anna said, catching the implications of his words.

Aaron glanced at her. "No," he said.

"What happened at the return crossing?" Mom asked.

"The family in front of me, clearly Welsh and with little English, was held up by the guards who reviled them and then appeared ready to arrest the father. So I intervened."

"Oh, Aaron," Mom said. "You could have been killed!"

"I know," Aaron said. "But I was angry. I was able to translate the guards' questions to the Welshman and vice versa. After some dragging of feet, the guards grudgingly let them enter

Wales. The issue, apparently, was that the family admitted to being from Rhuddlan."

"King Edward's former village," Math said.

"It was petty, and I think the guards were bored and amusing themselves at the family's expense."

"But it wasn't funny to the family," Anna said.

"Nor to me," Math added. "England is too close to Dinas Bran for me to feel comfortable with English abuse of Welshman on my doorstep."

"Did the guards bother you afterwards?" Mom asked. "They would have no love for men of your faith either."

"I followed the family across the bridge as if I traveled with them," Aaron said. "It wasn't as if I was going to tell the guards I was Prince Llywelyn's personal physician."

"Wise man," Mom said, dryly. "That wouldn't have gone over well."

"I would say that tensions are high," Aaron concluded.

"As high as they were after Edward's defeat in the Vale of Conwy?" Anna asked.

Aaron nodded. "I'm used to having the priests rail against the Jews, but they're inciting anger against the Welsh as well. Chester is only a stone's throw from Wales. Many Welsh trade in the city, but it was clear that they're not welcomed by many, even for the money they bring in."

"Now *that* is unusual," said Math.

"It feels like it does in the lead-up to a pogrom against the Jews," Aaron said. "My brother reports that Edward and his

Marcher lords are very angry—and I fear that they have something up their sleeve, something we're not going to like."

"And to think a Welshman thought to coerce you into judging a murderer based on English law instead of Welsh," Anna said to Math. "What were they thinking? Why would anyone prefer that Edward ruled here?"

"Because their lives are circumscribed by the small world they live in," Math said. "It's only the Princes who've ever been able to see beyond that very limited perspective."

"And the nobility's own desire for power is very real," Mom said. "It has distracted the common people from recognizing their overriding love of Wales."

"That's changing," Math said. "Llywelyn consolidates his power with each passing week, and more and more of our people are beginning to see what might be possible—what *is* possible, as Welshmen."

"We just need to hang on a while longer," Anna said.

"Yes," Math agreed, "if Edward gives us the chance."

10

At Crychen Forest, Llywelyn turned north to Buellt. With a small compliment of men—the initial nine, plus ten bowman from Llywelyn's force—David rode east, into the rugged mountains of Brecon, from which he'd base his campaign against the castles of Brecon, ruled directly by the Earl of Hereford, and Bronllys and Hay, held by the Clifford family, Hereford's vassals. The area was heavily wooded, with many rivers and streams. Fortunately, one of his bowmen was from the area and could guide the company. Without him, it would have been much more difficult to maneuver.

Brecon Castle sat on a hill, overlooking the confluence of the Usk and Honddu rivers, with a little village crouched at its foot. It was dusk when Bevyn, Ieuan and David first gazed down on the village. Though the sun still shone on the castle, the shadows had fallen on the huts below. As David looked at it, he had a sinking feeling in his stomach. Many of the villagers worked for the English but were not English themselves. Attacking the castle was one thing, but what they were about to perpetrate on the countryside could be hideous.

"We need to be disciplined about this," David said.

"The men know your mind, my lord," Bevyn said. "We can begin by firing the fields. The smoke will bring people out of the houses and reduce the loss of life. We're here to annoy and harass, not to kill Welshman."

And so it began. The fields were still green, this being June, so the fire didn't spread as quickly as it might have in August. As the people left their homes to fight the fires, however, the bowman unleashed their fire arrows—not at the people, but at their houses. This was only the first step. The intent was to cause some damage today, and then retreat, moving down the valley to Bronllys. In a few days, they'd return to cause more damage.

They didn't even stay to see the results of their handiwork.

The next night, it was the same thing again. The town and castle of Bronllys weren't on their guard, not knowing what David's men had done to Brecon. They fired the fields and then the village. Like Brecon, Bronllys was built at the confluence of two rivers (the Llynfi and Dulais), so the rivers limited the spread of the fire, but devastated the village nonetheless. Because only eight miles separated Bronllys and Hay, Bevyn suggested they break the pattern and move on immediately, hitting Hay a few hours before dawn.

Hay was different from the others in that it was a walled town fronting the Wye River on the English border. Llywelyn Fawr had burned the town, once upon a time, before the stone walls were built. Now it was much more defensible. Bevyn, however, saw no reason for that to stop them. The fields were still outside the walls, and the roofs were made of thatch. Like the other villages, it burned. The fire arrows arced through the murky sky. They were as beautiful as fireworks, until they hit.

Even from a distance, David could see the panic they caused. An arrow would hit the thatched roof, begin to smolder, and then catch. The red flames grew, licking at the wood. Each bowman shot only five arrows, but within fifteen minutes, they'd severely damaged the town.

None of the villagers fought back. How could they? There was nobody to fight as David's men disappeared as quickly as they'd come, retreating north along the Wye. At dawn, they turned west and picked their way to the wooded foothills just shy of the plateau of Mynydd Epynt. They camped there the rest of that day to give everyone a well-deserved rest, though Bevyn posted sentries and sent out scouts to ensure that nobody followed or discovered them.

Two scouts traveled to Brecon the next day. On their way there, they met a caravan. Since the burning of the village, Hereford's castellan had evicted them from their land and force them north, hoping to burden Prince Llywelyn with refugees.

"What have you done!" one man shouted when the scouts led them to the camp. "Fields burned; homes fired; a lifetime of labor lost in one night!"

"Are you English or Welsh, man!" barked one of David's men (another Gruffydd), before the peasant could speak again.

"You like living under Bohun's boot, do you? Even if he has no love for Edward, he should not rule in Wales!"

The man shook his fist in Gruffydd's face, not appeased in the slightest.

"Llywelyn, Prince of Wales, invites you to travel north where you will be made welcome," Bevyn said, ignoring the man. "Trust that your sacrifice is not in vain, and we will unite all Wales under his banner."

"And the end justifies the means," David said, though only to myself.

The scouts brought quite different news from the Clifford holdings. The town of Hay was already furiously rebuilding and shoring up its defenses. At Bronllys, the people had deserted the village and moved into the castle proper. Bevyn suggested that they should return there in order to determine their next move. David agreed. The next day they surveyed the damage from a nearby wood.

"We could take the castle, my lord," Ieuan said. "The castellan must be an innocent to have brought the villagers inside. He won't have enough provisions to feed them for long."

"Ieuan is right," Bevyn said. "It would be negligent of us not to take advantage of the opportunity."

"We'll need more men," Ieuan said.

"We'll send word to my father," David said. "We'll keep them penned inside until reinforcements come. When we take it, the man father sends can have the castle as a reward."

The messenger rode to Buellt and back in two days. He returned with exactly what David needed: Madoc, a younger son of Gruffydd ap Gwenwynwyn, and a force of fifteen cavalry and thirty foot soldiers Madoc had force-marched the twenty miles from Buellt.

Madoc brought the news, too, that Buellt was Llywelyn's once again. Hereford's men had fought, but only so they might retreat safely back to England. Gruffydd ap Gwenwynwyn, contrary to David's suspicions, had remained true to Wales.

Bronllys starved in less than two weeks, far more quickly than Bevyn had hoped, though far longer than David thought he could stand. As it turned out, they'd had food for only eight days and had gone hungry for five. David's company were lucky, really, to be in the right place at the right time, unlike the people of Bronllys. As David rode beside Madoc through the gatehouse, the smell and the cries turned his stomach.

"Get these people food!" David ordered.

Madoc looked at him, surprised at his vehemence. In response, David spoke more harshly to him than perhaps he should have. "These are *your* people now," he said. "Their lives are your responsibility. I expect you to see to them as a lord should."

Madoc blinked. "Yes, my lord," he said.

The castle priest came out of the chapel, his arms in the air. "My Prince!" he said. "We thank you for our deliverance from the English usurpers. May God bless and keep you and your father, the Prince of Wales."

David gazed at the weakened peasants, most of whom hadn't the energy to stand. Though these people were Welsh, they couldn't have had any love for him. David felt both guilt and pity. He dismounted and came face to face with the former castellan of Bronllys. He was only a boy, with blonde hair and mild eyes. As he stood before David, ramrod straight, they were red-rimmed, though his chin was set. "My lord," he said. "I am Roger de Clifford. I surrender Bronllys to your keeping."

"Ah. The Clifford heir," Bevyn said. "What's he doing here?"

Roger's father, also named Roger, had died during the English defeat at the Menai Straits in November of 1282, and Llywelyn had word of his grandfather's death in France just recently. A hot rage rose in David. If the fates had been different, this could have been him.

David's hands clenched involuntarily and he had to take a deep breath and let it out. *Who is most to blame for the current situation? Me for attacking the castle, or him for making an emotional decision by allowing them to seek refuge within it?* Perhaps he'd thought Hereford would come to relieve the siege? Perhaps he hadn't known that his people were better off outside the castle walls? Perhaps, not long ago, David would have chosen as he did.

"Relieve him of his sword, get him a horse, so that he may find his way to safety in England," David said to Ieuan.

"What of my men?" Roger asked.

"They will help us rebuild the village."

* * * * *

David's company spent the next week rebuilding the houses they'd burned. David was unused to the manual labor and each night he went to bed with aching shoulders. He was glad to do it. He didn't know if his men felt the same, but there were two sides to every war and it was a lesson he needed not to forget. Unlike his men, David had spent all of his time in Wales on the winning side, without much thought for the peasants who labored for the defeated lords.

Nonetheless, even David was grateful when the time came to head north. Ragged and in need of rest, he reached Buellt in the second week of July. Laborers crawled all over the castle, working to fix the damage done by the English as quickly as possible. David could laugh at the irony of his men spending the last week doing the same thing—except they repaired what they themselves had done.

In the courtyard of Buellt, David dismounted and left Bevyn in charge of the welfare of the men. David's only thought was to see his father and let go of his responsibilities. When he entered the great hall, however, Llywelyn had company: Lord Nicholas de Carew. At David's approach, Carew stood and bowed.

"I'm pleased that you have survived the last few weeks unscathed," he said.

"Are you?" David asked. He walked the last few paces to the table where his father sat and collapsed into a chair.

265

"Dafydd," Father admonished. Their eyes met and Llywelyn's look softened. "I'm glad to see you, son."

Carew very politely ignored the exchange. "My lord, Dafydd," he said. "I am here to request permission that I come with you to Lancaster instead of Goronwy."

David froze, a water goblet half-way to his lips, so surprised he didn't know what to say. "What of Pembroke?" David finally managed, setting down the cup.

"I have left the siege in capable hands," Carew replied. "This is more important."

Father fingered the stem of his goblet but didn't respond.

David sighed, recognizing that his father was leaving the conversation to him. "Why?"

"Because I'm a powerful ally for you, and it will give weight to your negotiations with Edward."

That sounded just about as arrogant as one might expect from Carew. Though that didn't make it less true. David dropped his head into his hands and dug his fingers into his hair. All he really wanted was a bath, a change of clothes, and a long sleep in a bed.

Carew sat down again and picked up his wine. "You don't trust me," he said.

David turned his head to the side and met Carew's eyes. Carew was tall like David, with almost white blond hair, of an age almost equidistant between Llywelyn and David. In truth, David liked Carew, as did Llywelyn.

"No," David said. "I trust half a dozen people and you are not one of them. I would like to trust you. I'm willing to work with you, but I don't understand your motives."

Carew laughed. "My motives are clear. I'm interested in power."

"Edward can give you more of it than we can," David said.

"But Edward is only interested in power too. That means we don't work well together. You, on the other hand, care so little about power it's hard to believe you are a prince. I understand you not at all, but I do trust you. That makes the difference."

David raised his head to look at his father, who lifted his eyebrows and gave him a small smile.

"Fine," David said. "You can come."

"Good," Carew said. "You won't regret it."

* * * * *

David found his father in the stables the next morning, standing in one of the stalls with his back to the door, brushing his horse, Teyrngar, in the dim light. David walked past him to the stall next to his and picked up a brush so he could work on Taranis. They were alone in the stables. That happened so rarely, Father could only have sent everyone away to make it possible.

"Do you miss where you came from?" he asked. He rested his arm across Teyrngar's back and looked at his son over the horse.

"Yes," David said.

267

"There are many wondrous things in your world," Father said.

David studied him, wondering what this was really about, and then shook his head. "It's not the things that I miss, or the people, which is kind of sad if you think about it," David said. "I missed Mom before she came, and I miss knowing what's happening with everyone there. Sure, I would prefer to have books, telephones, good roads, food, central heating, and hot showers available. I could go on and on about the 'things'. The twenty-first century has a lot of . . . well . . . stuff, that makes life a lot easier."

"But you just said that's not what you miss," Father said.

"No," David agreed. "That's not what I miss."

He waited, forcing David to go on.

"What I miss most is the knowledge that it is *here* where reality exists; *here* is where I stand and you can't move me from it. That may sound very strange to you, but when I crossed into this world, everything I thought I believed in was blown apart. I have had to figure out how the world works and what my purpose in it is, but without any of the guideposts that are a normal part of my old world."

"So you would return to your time if you could?" Father asked.

Ah, the real question. "I can't get certainty back by returning to the 21st century and pretending this never happened. How would that work? No," David said. "Even if I could cross through the barrier between our worlds, I would spend the rest of my life looking for a way back. My place is here."

Llywelyn didn't speak for a long minute and he used that time to carefully brush out Teyrngar's mane. "I can't feel guilty for wanting to keep you here," he said. "Wales needs you. I need you."

"I know," David said. "If Edward captures and kills me like he did Uncle Dafydd in the old world, then I might be sorry. But for now, I see what you see."

Father opened his mouth to speak again. David *knew* he was going to say something about how he didn't have long to live. David didn't want to hear it. To forestall him, David changed the subject. "Want to go for a ride in my car?" he asked.

Llywelyn's eyes brightened. "Bevyn will want to come," he said.

"And Ieuan!" David added. "We probably need a few more men, just to be safe."

Llywelyn nodded and David left him so he could round up the men. David found Ieuan first. He was very pleased, as David knew he would be. Fifteen minutes later everyone gathered in the courtyard, ready to ride.

"Let's hope there are no English about today," David said. "You're not superstitious are you? Our stays in Buellt are never uneventful."

Bevyn rolled his eyes. "Lead on, my lord. We'll follow you."

When they reached the meadow, Father dismounted and paced around the spot where he'd almost died. The men fell silent as he began to describe what had happened that night in December when Anna and David first appeared.

"I had close calls before in my younger years," Llywelyn said, "as some of you witnessed, but nothing like this. All my companions were dead, ambushed by the English who poured out of those trees." He pointed up the hill where David had parked the van.

"We were supposed to be meeting the Mortimer boys, but they sent their men against us instead. All my men had fallen in my defense, and I had my back against a tree. In fact, I was going down, having lost my footing in the snow and had landed on my hip, when Dafydd and his sister drove into the meadow in their chariot.

"I can still see it in my mind. Falling and knowing that my life was over, only to have my attackers turn away and themselves fall under the wheels of that incredible machine. One moment I was about to die, and the next, my son and daughter had swept away my enemies."

"God's will," Bevyn said gruffly.

"It *was* God's will," Father said firmly. "And thus, our responsibilities to Wales are all the greater."

Father clapped his hand on David's shoulder. "Now," he said. "I would like a ride in your chariot. I understand from Ieuan that it's the experience of a lifetime."

David led the way up the hill to the spot where the van still sat, undisturbed since the last time. He unlocked it and opened the sliding door. As before, everyone piled in, except this time, David had an idea. Witchcraft couldn't help but haunt them. Maybe there was a way to defuse it.

"Here," David said, handing his father the keys. "You drive."

Llywelyn took them from David, hesitantly, reminding David of Anna. "Are you certain?"

"Sure," David said, figuring the worst he could do was wreck it permanently.

They climbed in. David showed his father how to insert the key and twist it so the van would start. This time the engine caught right away. David explained how to press the brake with his foot and shift into drive.

"Now, press that right lever gently with your foot."

"Like this?" Llywelyn asked, and the van jerked forwards a few feet. Fortunately, Llywelyn removed his foot before the vehicle crashed into a tree.

David had him experiment with the brake and showed him how to steer. After a few more jerks, Llywelyn got the van moving forward. He turned the steering wheel to the right and headed down the hill. As it picked up speed entering the meadow, David glanced back at the men and had to laugh at the looks of utter horror on their faces. Little did they know that when David had driven the van a few weeks ago, it had been his first time too.

"The brake, Dad, the brake!" David said as they got near the far side of the meadow.

Llywelyn found it and managed to stop the van about two feet from the edge. The breath eased out of everyone in the van.

"Maybe you should drive, son," Father said, taking a deep breath himself.

The pair got out of the van, and as they passed each other in front of it Llywelyn put his hand on David's arm. "What's this word, 'Dad?'" he asked.

David laughed, surprised. He'd never called his father that before. In Welsh, 'father' is 'tad', and he'd been comfortable with it, given the similarity in pronunciation.

"It means 'Father,'" David said, "but more familiar. Like Anna's 'papa'."

Llywelyn smiled and David could see that he was pleased. They got back in the van. This time, David eased the van down the hill, back through the brambles, into its little clearing and then turned off the engine. At this point, Ieuan could stand it no longer.

"May I . . . sit there?" he asked.

"Absolutely," David said, opening the door and climbing out to make room for Ieuan. Ieaun scrambled between the front seats and sat down in David's spot. He surveyed the instrument panel, and the other men leaned forward to listen to the subsequent conversation.

"What is that?" Ieuan asked, pointing to the speedometer.

"That tells you how many miles the chariot can go in one hour," David said.

Ieuan studied the panel. "And how fast is that? I can't make out the script."

"Those are Arabic numerals—numbers. They read zero on one end, and one hundred and ten on the other."

"How is that possible?" Ieuan asked.

David hesitated. "Well . . . you would need a very straight and flat road. . ."

"Like the roads the Romans built?" Cadwallon asked from the back. David had included him in the party because he thought the van might lose some of the aura of magic if Cadwallon rode in it. David was probably wrong.

"Yes, exactly like that," David said.

"And what is this?" Ieuan asked.

"The . . ." David searched for the proper word. "The fuel gauge. It tells how much fuel the van carries and thus the driver knows how many miles he can go before he needs more fuel."

"So what is this fuel?" Dad asked.

"Um . . ." Once again David struggled to explain. "The van contains an engine that runs on burning naphtha."

"Oh, naphtha," Dad said and he nodded. 'Naphtha' was a Greek word for petroleum, which was also used in the weapon 'Greek fire'. It was something they had never seen, but many had heard of.

"It really isn't witchcraft," Cadwallon said.

"Of course not," Gruffydd piped up. "Did you not hear the Prince say it was God's will?"

"So," Ieuan said, having thought hard throughout their extraneous conversation, "who built the chariot?"

Oh yeah. That little detail. Silence filled the van. Ieuan looked up, realizing that nobody was answering. David racked his brains for something to say and came up with nothing, but Llywelyn hit upon the answer. And it wasn't even a lie.

"You know of the great Welsh hero, Madoc ap Owain Gwynedd, who sailed west across the sea to a land full of strange peoples, previously unknown to us?"

"Yes, of course, Sire," Ieuan said. This was one of the stories every Welsh child knew from birth.

"Before Dafydd was born," Dad said, "I sent Marged and the children away for their safekeeping. It is from that country that they have come and Madoc's descendents who built this chariot."

Ieuan sighed. "I would like to see that land someday," he said.

"God willing, Ieuan, someday you may," David said. *God willing, I won't—ever again.*

11

The battlements of every castle Anna had lived in since she came to Wales were her favorite places. She could stand on them and see for miles in four directions, feel the wind and the weather, and be alone with her thoughts. Looking down, she had a bird's eye view of the activity in the courtyards, and a detachment from her surroundings that she treasured. With Math beside her being protective, Anna climbed the battlements of Dinas Bran once again to watch David and his company wind their way up the long road to the castle gate. They always had warning when visitors were arriving, which was a good thing when David and his men came. They'd be hungry.

"I don't see Papa's banners," Anna said. "Mom will be disappointed."

"Dafydd doesn't ride Taranis," Math observed. "What other changes are in the wind?" They walked down the stairs to greet the riders as they crossed under the gatehouse.

"Oh, don't look at me that way," Anna said.

"You're huge! *Amazingly huge!*" David said before he'd even dismounted, open-mouthed with astonishment.

"I'm not that fat."

"I didn't say you were fat!" he protested, hugging Anna from a distance, given the size of her belly.

Math and Bevyn consulted about the disposition of David's men, while Anna brought David inside, pleased that he was here again after the upheaval of his last visit. It didn't take long, though, to learn what 'changes' Math was talking about.

"I'll be meeting Edward without Dad."

"Why?" Mom asked. "Surely this will make Edward more angry than he already is."

"The Prince talked with his lords," Carew said. "They agreed that they couldn't risk both the father and the son. The journey is too far into English territory for safety. It's one thing for King Alexander to go—Edward has acknowledged him as king long since. It's quite another for Prince Llywelyn to achieve such a status, upstart that Edward sees him."

Mom was appalled. "So Llywelyn thinks to sacrifice David instead?" she asked.

Aaron turned to her, his expression gentle. "He does no such thing," he said. "One of them must attend, but I think David will be the first to admit that he's not yet ready to assume the responsibilities of rule if something were to happen to his father."

"Absolutely," David said, nodding. "I'm happy to go. If we take the sea route, we can't be ambushed on the road."

Mom didn't appear convinced. "It was bad enough when you were gallivanting about the countryside these last few weeks," she retorted. "At least you were in Wales, among your fellow countrymen, with access to aid and comfort if need be. In England you'll be dependent entirely on your own resources."

"That's the way it has to be," David said.

Mom ground her teeth and muttered under her breath.

"It's okay, Mom," Anna said, in an aside to her. "He's done well so far."

"I want to put my foot down and say he can't go," she said, "but I don't think I can tell him what he can or cannot do, anymore."

And I suspect that's a painful thing for a mother to admit. Anna touched her belly, feeling the baby move and wondering if it was a boy or a girl. *Mom still tells me what to do.* It was curious that she didn't feel as able to tell David.

David wasn't listening to either of them, having turned to Aaron to find out what he'd been up to.

"I know little of what went on in the conference," Aaron said. "Word spread throughout the city, however, of King Edward's anger at your father. Given your successes in the past few weeks, Edward's Marcher lords will be calling for your blood."

"They were doing that before," Math said, "though I agree with Aaron's conclusions. All is not well with England."

"Hereford will not easily forgive his defeat at Buellt," Carew said. "When we meet with Edward, we must take care. Even if Edward seeks an honest exchange, you can be sure that many of his barons do not."

* * * * *

They had a quiet few weeks at Dinas Bran. With each passing day, Anna became more uncomfortable. Unlike in the old world, there were no ultrasounds to perform or exams to make. The midwife's attitude was 'the baby will come when it comes,' and there was nothing anyone could do about it. Mom kept busy by overseeing the boiling of everything in sight. Anything she couldn't boil, she sterilized through fire or by dipping in an alcohol concoction that was so strong, even Math's men wouldn't touch it.

She had explained to Aaron long since, and to the midwife more recently, what her standards for cleanliness were. If someone couldn't get with the program, she was out. In the Middle Ages, most women didn't actually die in childbirth. They died later, from childbed fever caused by unclean conditions and dirty hands during labor. *That will not be me! Dear God, that will not be me!*

Math made himself scarce for the last weeks before Anna's due date—and then during the long two weeks after her due date. He and his men patrolled the Welsh border with England, keeping an eye out for any incursions across the border or a massing of men where there should be none. He didn't want a repeat of what happened at Castell y Bere. He rode out of the castle daily to return at dusk, sweaty and hungry, and too tired to worry much about Anna. She understood him well enough by now to realize that he was suppressing his worry for her by ignoring it, and keeping himself so busy that he had no time to think.

On the nineteenth of July, the day before David intended to head for his castle at Denbigh, Math stayed with Anna all day because Meg cornered him and told him he wasn't allowed to leave the castle. He and Anna spent the day peacefully, wandering in the garden or on the battlements. It was cooler up there with the wind blowing and Anna liked to watch for the return of the men. As evening drew near, she spotted them, glad to see David's banners still flying.

Knowing dinner would be served soon, Math and Anna entered the great hall. The steward greeted Math, coming forward to discuss the disposition of wine and mead that evening. Anna realized that the servants had neglected to strew fresh herbs among the rush mats on the floor and was about to waddle forward to tell them so when David came up behind her, put his arms around her waist (such as it was) and put his cheek to hers.

"Ew! Yuck!" Anna burst out, shoving him away.

He laughed and released her. Anna was turning back to him, to chide him for smelling so disgusting, when she felt a *pop*, like when the pressure is released from a bottle. And then, she . . . *flickered.*

"David!" Anna screamed. He grabbed her hand and spun her around, toward Math, who'd moved at the same instant. Math wrapped his arms around Anna, gasping.

"Hold her," David said. "I'll get Mom."

He raced away while Math patted Anna up and down, making sure she was all there. "What happened?" he asked.

"My water broke," Anna said. "I don't know how to explain it, but I just knew that I would disappear like Mom did if I didn't do something quickly."

"So you screamed," Math said.

"I fought it," Anna said. "I saw blackness before my feet but refused to enter it."

The door opens and closes; opens and closes . . . is it this simple? But now I don't want to go.

And then there was a different kind of abyss before her feet, this one of her and Math's making, as the contractions came on relentlessly. All she could do was surrender to them, giving up herself and everything she'd known before to becoming a mother.

* * * * *

It was nearly three in the morning; Anna had been dozing for an hour or so, with Cadell cuddled against her, nursing on and off. She opened her eyes to find the room lit by one candle burning in its dish on the table near the bed. Math was stretched out beside her, snoring, and Anna thought about elbowing him but decided not to, just glad he was there, and that he'd been there to see Cadell born.

Meg saw her wake and got up from her chair to sit on the edge of the bed. "Do you need anything?" she asked.

"Clean clothes for Cadell and me," Anna said, handing her son to her mother.

I have a son.

Meg cradled Cadell as Anna gingerly sat up, and then stood. Noting the disturbance, Math woke and in a moment was beside his wife, a hand under her elbow. "Careful," he said. He walked Anna to the toilet and back, while a maid changed the sheets and Mom changed Cadell.

"What is it about sons?" Anna said to Math, after she was back in bed. He now sat in a chair under the window, Cadell asleep in his arms. For once Anna had been able to overrule Mom and order her to bed.

"I wouldn't have chided you had you given me a daughter, not like some husbands," he said. "I understand enough to know that it is in God's hands."

"But you're not sorry," Anna said.

"No," he admitted, and then explained. "Think on your father; what it means for him to have your brother to follow after him."

"Gwenllian could never have been enough," Anna said.

"Not here. I can't comprehend what your world must be like if there are more women like you and your mother in it. It seems impossible." He glanced up, having kept his gaze on Cadell's face as they'd talked. "You could have returned to it."

"Maybe," Anna said. "Or maybe the abyss would have taken me somewhere else entirely."

"Thank you for staying," he said.

"I've known for some time what I have here," Anna said, tucking the blanket under her chin. "I have the two of you."

12

According to Mom, Anna did really well and actually had a short, easy labor. She looked pretty terrible, however, when David went into see her at midnight, half an hour after Cadell was born. Her face was red and puffy and it looked like she'd burst some blood vessels in her eyes. David lied, though, and said she looked great.

Cadell was nursing by then, and David didn't want to get too close, but the baby had a nice bunch of black hair, curly like Anna's. Mom assured David that Cadell looked exactly like a newborn should look. Math was so happy David thought his smile would split his face. David hoped he would have been just as happy if Anna had given him a girl, but at least the pressure was now off Anna to produce a son.

David was more concerned about the *flickering*. Mom had been in her sitting room on the second floor, but she'd heard the commotion and met David half-way down the stairs. "It's Anna. Her water broke."

"Okay," Mom had said, totally calm. "I'll get Aaron. You send a groom for the midwife."

She'd turned back upstairs but then David had caught her arm. "We almost lost her, Mom," David said. "I saw her fade out for a second, but I grabbed her hand and she came back."

Mom gasped. "My God. Is Math with her now?"

"Yes," David replied. "I told him not to let her go."

"When I went into labor with you, I was holding Anna and ended up in Pennsylvania. My greatest fear has been that the same thing might happen to her. But how could I prevent it without knowing when her labor would start?"

"I held her and she stayed with me," David said slowly. "Maybe this is a woman-thing. Maybe you and Anna have an ability to shift between worlds, but I don't. Maybe I'm only here because Anna brought me along for the ride."

"Then why didn't she take you with her this time, back to Pennsylvania?"

"I don't know," David said, shaking his head. *Another theory, shot down.*

Everyone was totally absorbed in the baby, and as David felt pretty useless in that department, he only hung around for a few days to make sure everything was really okay before riding north as he'd planned. David was glad that Cadell was taking his mother's mind off worrying about him, but if he stuck around, no doubt she'd start again.

David's impression while at Dinas Bran was that Aaron had seemed somber, but now he thought about it, it was more that he was sad, even dejected. When David quizzed him, he insisted all was well. Finally at Denbigh, David cornered him and demanded he tell him the truth. Was he unwell? Had his son refused to receive him?

"My son is well, my lord. I talked with him for several hours—no more than that as it wouldn't have been wise for him to be seen with me. We arranged to meet in a tavern, as if accidentally. He asks to be remembered to you."

David nodded, and Aaron continued. "It's my brother, my lord. He was much taken aback by the news that Edward had expelled the Jews from London. At first he refused to believe it. But then, it was as if he reversed himself, and the bile and invective he directed against his English masters had both his son and me urging him to quiet his rage. The root of it all, however, is that my brother has a malady that he cannot cure, something that affects his moods and thoughts. Neither of us, despite our experience, know what to do. It's a wasting disease."

"I am sorry, Aaron," David said.

"He's an old man now," Aaron replied, "past fifty years old, but his death will not be an easy one, I fear."

"Will you see him again, once we're in Lancaster?" David asked.

"It seems so, and for that I'm grateful. It might be for the last time."

"You couldn't persuade him to leave his position and come to Wales?"

"No," Aaron said. "He will not come. He spoke of sending Moses, after his death, and I encouraged both of them to consider it well. I warned him that the news from London indicated the extent to which there is no future for Jews in England. I didn't tell him all, of course, for I should have no prior knowledge of Edward's future edicts, but I made my point as clearly as I could. Perhaps in Lancaster, I can make my case again. It would be better for him to die among friends than among enemies."

A few days later, they reached Rhuddlan where the boats were waiting to take them to Lancaster. David had left Taranis behind at Buellt in favor of a new horse, Bedwyr, who was smaller, sturdier, and better able to handle a sea voyage. Still, David found himself missing Taranis—they could talk to each other, and despite what Owain had said long ago at Castell y Bere, Taranis understood American English really well. David gazed across the sea to England, the land of his enemies, and laughed at the thought that three years ago, his enemy had been Bill Morgan (with a Welsh name no less!) who enjoyed tripping and shoving David in the halls at school.

Increasingly, the years between 1285 and 2013 weighed on David. No matter how much he learned about Wales, he was a child of the twenty-first century, not the thirteenth. David knew it wasn't his job to bring Wales all the way to modern times intact. He couldn't transport it into the future single-handedly, but that didn't stop him wanting to. So much had to happen between now and then. At least David was unlikely to see the Black Plague come to Wales—and even that caused him to struggle with himself. Was there some way to warn his descendents of the future? What could they do about it, even if they knew? Perhaps, given some breathing space without war with England, David's family could effect changes over time in education, medicine, science, and perhaps even religion.

For the present journey, David's company had three vessels to carry them to England, all similar to the one Meg had traveled in when she came from Scotland, though larger and designed to carry horses. However, unlike that journey, David had a royal writ of safe passage and his ships would hug the shoreline to avoid whatever weather the sea chose to throw at them. It was late July, and the weather prospects were mild, but with the Irish Sea, one never knew. Aaron confessed that he'd sworn never to set foot on board a ship again. As his Prince, David absolved him of his oath.

They wouldn't actually be meeting in the City of Lancaster, but in the nearby countryside. This was one of the Scot requirements for the meeting, and in truth, the Welsh were happier to meet in the open air rather than inside a walled city and so acquiesced without complaint.

Fortunately, the weather was fair and after a few days, the ships sat off the English coast, preparing to come to shore at the little village of Poulton. Carew, who knew the area, said that it was five miles from there to the English camp. The ships docked at four in the afternoon, giving David plenty of time to establish his camp and send word to Edward that he'd arrived. Happy to be back on dry land, David set out and as Carew predicted, rode out of some wooded hills an hour later to see the English camped at the head of a meadow some distance ahead.

"We should set up over there, sir," Bevyn said, pointing to a spot at the base of the hill. "I don't think it wise to get too close."

"We're going to have to go in there eventually," David said. "With five or twenty-five of us, it makes no difference. We're outnumbered."

"We're always outnumbered," Bevyn grumbled.

David laughed and clapped him on the shoulder. "That's what makes it so much fun!"

"I must think on this," Carew said. "We must consider how to best present ourselves."

David looked over at him. "You think fewer would be better," he guessed.

"Having seen the lay of the land, I'm not happy about committing our entire party to this endeavor," he said. "I discussed this with your father before we left; I would have you lead a small party and leave the rest of the men outside. I don't trust Edward."

They rode another quarter mile and set up camp where Bevyn had indicated. David sent a rider to inform Edward of his arrival, and shortly thereafter, Edward sent word that David was to come to him at his leisure. When David received the message, he was in his tent with Hywel, contemplating his attire. Carew had insisted David arrive in full regalia—armor, sword, and banners—less for protection, than to show Edward the splendor of Welsh nobility.

All David cared about was that it meant donning his mail again. He'd lived in it for all the weeks he was in the south, and had enjoyed the respite from it while on board the ship. Hywel had polished each link until it shone, but that didn't make David any happier about putting it on again.

As soon as Hywel helped David into it, he started sweating. With padding underneath and surcoat over the top to show his colors, the red Welsh dragon on a white background, David was blazingly hot. He couldn't imagine what the European knights were thinking when they wore this in the Holy Land. Hywel buckled on his sword, David drank a flagon of water, and then exited the tent. Only Carew, Bevyn, Gruffydd, and two of Carew's men (Dogfael and Cadoc) would accompany him. Ieuan would stay in camp, in charge of the other men and on guard. If it came to a fight, they would lose, but by remaining out in the open, they could abandon their possessions and flee.

David mounted Bedwyr and, with a nod to his men, rode the short distance to the English camp. The sun was lower now, but in these long English summers, it was hard to tell the hour. It was perhaps seven or eight o'clock, with two more hours until full dark. Given the time, David hoped Edward had finished his evening meal, but as they entered the camp, most of his men were still eating. David dismounted outside a grand pavilion. Its sides and back were closed but the front was open to the evening breeze.

He ducked through the opening. Edward sat at a solitary table some forty feet away. He didn't look up as David entered and his lack of courtesy made David hesitate. *Surely this isn't usual?*

Beside Edward, on a small stool, sat another man whom David would have recognized even if Aaron hadn't warned him what to expect. It was Aaron's brother Jacob, wearing the yellow badge of his religion, acting as the royal food taster. How offensive must that have been to a man whose religion forbade him to eat with gentiles? At larger tables on either side of Edward other men ate, including Uncle Dafydd. He sneered at David from his position at the head of one of them, but didn't speak.

Carew leaned in and whispered that Edmund, the Earl of Lancaster, was to Edward's left, Roger and Edmund Mortimer, Gilbert de Clare, and John Gifford were to his right.

"So the Marcher lords have come too," David said. "What can we expect from them?"

"I can't say," Carew said. "Probably nothing good."

Other men sat at tables along the side walls. Carew didn't see the Archbishop of Canterbury, nor Humphrey de Bohun, the Earl of Hereford. Perhaps they were to arrive later.

David rolled his shoulders and straightened them. "My lord Edward," he said, lifting his chin. "I give you greetings from my father, the Prince of Wales."

Finally, Edward looked up. He jerked his head. Bevyn shouted a warning and Carew and David spun around, reaching for their swords, but too late. Other swords were already at their throats. Not even Bevyn's blade had cleared its sheath.

"Take your hands off your weapons," one of the men ordered. The five men raised their hands, but otherwise didn't move. It would take very little provocation to make these men shove their swords through their throats and David hoped to live a little while longer at least.

Other men relieved David and his men of their swords and knives. While Carew and David had soldiers on either side of them, gripping their arms to contain them, Bevyn and the others were manhandled to the tent posts and tied, their hands behind their backs.

All the while, David kept his gaze on Edward, who still ate his food as nonchalantly as before. David clenched his fists. "There's a certain freedom in finally facing that which you most fear," he said to Carew.

Carew ground his teeth. "Don't do anything rash, my lord. This is my fault. Let me try to speak to the king."

Edward interrupted their conversation. "Separate them!" he said.

David's captors jerked his arms and pulled him away from Carew. David was still trying to get a sense of whether Carew thought Edward's actions were his fault because he'd talked David into coming to England, or whether he was betraying him to Edward but this wasn't how he'd meant it to happen. David saw nothing in Carew's eyes, however, but anger and maybe a touch of fear. Unless they were just mirroring David's own.

Edward went back to his food and eventually the noise level in the tent rose to its previous levels. Edward laughed at something Uncle Dafydd said. He waved his knife around, a parsnip speared through the end. Edward's sojourn in the Holy Land had given him a taste for heavily spiced and sauced foods and David wondered what the meal was. Eventually, Jacob was allowed to leave, but Edward made David stand until he finished eating. Thankful now for his mail armor, David entertained himself with various scenarios for escape. Despite Carew's fears, however, David knew enough not to act until he had no other choice.

Bevyn grumbled behind David and he turned to look at him. Bevyn gave a fearsome grimace and David was glad to see his mustachios were still in place. Bevyn's captors, like David's, had grown bored and David tried to watch them without looking at them directly.

Finally, Edward finished his meal and deigned to look at David. David's captors pushed him forward until he stood some ten feet in front of his companions.

"Well," Edward said, speaking in French. "The time has come."

He leaned back in his chair and rested his boots on the table, newly cleared of dishes.

"Welcome to England." Edward held his hands out expansively. "Though I'd hoped your father would come, you will do very nicely. You will be glad to know that you abdicate the throne today or you die where you stand."

David held his gaze. "No."

A sigh blew around the tent.

"No, you say?" Edward asked. He pulled his feet down and leaned forward. "You don't even want to hear my terms?"

"No," David said again.

Edward laid his hands flat on the table. "You would not trade your inheritance, such as it is, for land in England, yours free and clear?" he asked. "You would not, perhaps, enjoy the adventure of a crusade? You love your rocks and mountains so much, do you?"

"You offered this to my father not long ago," David said. "He gave you his reply. I have given you mine."

At that, Edward stood and pulled his sword from its sheath. He rounded the table and pointed his sword directly at David.

"Edward! What are you doing?" Carew said.

"You think a king shouldn't get his hands dirty?" Edward asked. "I've looked forward to this day for many months, ever since the Vale of Conwy, which I understand was your doing. Did you call upon the weather as well? You and that witch mother of yours?"

"The Welsh need only God to assist us," David said.

"You'll need more than that today," he replied, closing the distance between them. He reached out with his left hand, grasped David's surcoat, and pulled. It ripped and came free. Edward held it in the air, spinning on one heel so everyone could see the red dragon in tatters, before dropping the cloth on the ground and kicking it away. "A king shouldn't ask his men to do that which he's not man enough to do himself."

"He doesn't even have a sword, Edward," Carew said. "You think to kill him in cold blood?"

Edward brought his sword up and saluted Carew with it. "Give the boy his sword back," he said. He gestured to one of the soldiers, who pulled it from its sheath and tossed it at David. David caught the hilt and his guards backed away, leaving David alone in the center of the room, facing Edward.

More comfortable now, David brought his sword up. He was young and strong. His men were hopelessly outnumbered, but if he could hold Edward off long enough, perhaps he would see reason, or his brother would—or perhaps even Uncle Dafydd would intervene, though David wasn't going to hold his breath on that one.

With no warning at all, Edward attacked. David parried his first blows, backing away to gauge what kind of fighter the king was. He was very skilled, which was no surprise given who he was. David held his ground and Edward backed off, sweat dripping down his face. David was sweltering, but so focused on Edward that everything else he saw or felt was as if from a great distance. As Edward attacked and David countered, David had an image of himself back in Castell y Bere with Bevyn shouting instructions and curses at him while he hacked away at Fychan.

David tried every move that he knew and Edward had an answer for them all. The two men fought on, both tiring as the minutes passed, though David less than Edward, who was feeling his age perhaps. David put the king in his mid-forties—no young stripling but with a full head of dark hair and athletic build, David wasn't going to underestimate him.

Edward took a great stride toward David. He tried to trap David against a table to end the fight, but David twisted away. As Edward turned to follow, his foot slipped and he stumbled, falling forward onto one knee. Before he could recover, David swung his sword as hard as he could and swept the king's blade aside. It tumbled across the grass that formed the floor of the tent.

But David didn't finish him. He couldn't really kill the King of England—not in front of his own men and live. Edward knew it too and took advantage.

"Guards!" he yelled.

A soldier with a flail flicked his wrist, wrapped the end of the weapon around David's blade, and pulled. David couldn't recover quickly enough to stop two guards from hemming him in. They grabbed his arms whilst the man on David's right used his free hand to grab his hair and pull back David's head.

Edward got to his feet, recovered his sword, pointed it at David, and smiled.

"This is beneath you, Edward," Carew tried again. "He is a Prince, your own cousin."

Edward kept his sword steady, pointed at David's chest. "He is no prince, Carew!" he said. "He's an upstart bastard; a traitor just as you are. You and I both know traitors deserve death."

"Except for my uncle," David said, his eyes flicking to Uncle Dafydd, still seated at the table.

Edward sneered and Uncle Dafydd started, mouth twisted in an angry moue. Perhaps it was mouthy of him, but Edward was going to kill him regardless of what he said. David ignored his uncle's stutters and returned his concentration to Edward's feet and hands in preparation for the moment the king moved against him.

Edward shifted, the sword two feet from David's throat. "Don't you dare speak of him again," he said. "He's twice the man you are."

"Or twice the traitor," David said.

Then both men moved—David a half a second before the king. Edward stepped forward, his face suffused with anger while David brought his left foot up and drove it sideways into the right knee of the guard on his left. As he fell sideways, David grabbed the guard and pulled him forward, just as Edward slashed at David's head. Instead of hitting David, Edward's sword ripped through the back of the guard's neck.

David continued the spin, swinging the man into the guard on his right, who couldn't withstand the weight. Using the guard's momentum as a pendulum, David twisted around to make space for himself between the tables. Though shocked, Edward's men moved quickly to surround him.

"Stay back! Do not interfere. He's mine!" Edward said.

Again, David stared across the open space at the king. Edward was breathing hard, one hand clenched to his chest, his face pale. *Is he ill?* His sword wavered and Edward hesitated. David didn't.

He strode forward, closing the distance between them in two steps. With the flat of his left hand, safely covered by his half-glove gauntlet, David batted the blade of Edward's sword away and then drove his right fist into the king's face. Edward staggered back, falling into the table behind him, blood pouring from his nose. David grasped the sword he'd dropped and held it to Edward's throat.

The nobles had gotten to their feet in an uproar, but above the noise, someone said, "Do not kill him, I beg you."

David glanced to his left. Edmund, Edward's brother, had risen unsteadily to his feet, his hand out, beseeching him. David gazed down at Edward. "A prince does not kill another, Edward," David said, stepping back. He pointed the sword to the ground.

Edward looked up at David, and the loathing on his face caused David to take another step back. "You have not won, cur. I am too ill to fight tonight." Edward nodded to the men behind David. "Bind him," he said. "I will deal with him tomorrow."

But David wasn't going down without a fight. He swung around to hold them off. This time, however, they didn't make the mistake of trying to grab him. Instead, a soldier held his knife to Carew's throat. Carew's eyes met David's as silence descended on the tent.

"You can escape, my lord," Carew said. "I am only one man. You are Wales."

David couldn't do it and couldn't think of a way out, not that wouldn't end in Carew's death as well as David's own. Twenty Englishmen still stood between him and the door. David lowered his sword and a mass of guards crowded him. Once again, they stripped his sword from his hand. This time, they bound David as they had his men. By the time David was trussed, Edward was gone and the tent all but deserted. Only two guards remained, standing sentry at the entrance to the tent. David wished then that he had his mother's talent for laughing at impossible situations, but the skill seemed to have deserted him.

Edward's soldiers had tethered David to a post at least ten feet from the rest, his hands tied behind his back. The tent flaps were closed and David could see nothing of the camp outside. Carew stared at his feet, unable to meet David's eyes.

"You should have run, my lord," Bevyn said.

"I wouldn't have gotten far and you know it," David said. "Besides, we're not dead yet."

"You fought well," Bevyn said. His grudging admission almost made David smile.

Still, he didn't regret his decision not to abandon his companions. Exhausted, David slid down the pole and sat with his back against the post and his feet splayed in front of him. He leaned his head back, trying to relax, and found himself replaying the fight in his head. *What should I have done differently? How am I going to salvage this situation, without losing my life or the lives of my men?* The light outside had faded during David's fight with Edward, and now the candles flickered, close to going out.

Soon it was full dark, with a single candle guttering in its dish. The wind gusted outside, but no other noise penetrated the tent. At one point, the changing of the guard caught David's attention. One of the guards left, and the second was replaced by a third man.

Then, Carew spoke. "I didn't betray you, my lord," he said. In his agitation, he had reverted to French, and David answered in the same language.

"I thought it only for a heartbeat, Carew," David said. "I apologize for thinking it at all."

"I underestimated their hatred of you," Carew continued, not really hearing David. "I never seriously considered that Edward would seek to murder you in his own pavilion. What would King Alexander of Scotland think of that? No ruler would ever trust him again. That is why a king doesn't kill a king, my lord. It's not out of honor that he refrains, but because the price he pays, even if he succeeds, is too high."

"That hasn't stopped the English from killing us before," David said. "Cadwaladr ap Seisyll is a case in point."

"Yes," Carew sighed.

"And English kings have hanged Welsh captives when they outlived their usefulness or as punishment for their father's deeds."

"Yes," Carew agreed, "but never the son of the Prince of Wales."

"There's always a first time," David said. "But I swear to you that prince will not be me."

"You should have let them kill me and won free yourself," Carew said. "Now we will all die . . ."

He broke off. David's attention had wandered and Carew followed David's gaze. The soldier at the entrance to the tent was conversing with someone outside the flap. The soldier gave an abrupt nod before he closed the flap, turned toward David, and pulled a knife from his belt. David tried to scramble to his feet but the bindings hindered his movement and he only managed to reach his knees. Eyes wide, David watched the knife come towards him. Beyond, Carew's face showed what David could only interpret as pity.

"My lord, it's time," the soldier said.

And then leaned down and cut David's bonds.

"I'm sorry, my lord," the man continued. "I would have released you sooner, but you were safer inside the tent. But now it's time to move."

"Who are you?" David asked. He flexed his hands. They throbbed as the blood rushed back into them.

"Samuel ben Aaron," the soldier said. He cut through the rope that held David's feet and turned to do the same for Carew.

Free, David ran to Bevyn. "Tell me you have a knife up your sleeve," he said.

"Of course, I do," Bevyn said. "Bloody maddening that Edward's lackeys were upon me before I could reach it." David slipped it out.

Samuel spoke again. "You must leave here at once," he said. "I've strapped your weapons to your horses, which are tethered just outside. Hurry!"

"Where are our guards?" David asked. "Are they drunk?"

"A great sickness has overtaken the camp," Aaron said. "Everyone is ill."

Before David could ask for more of an explanation, Bevyn put a hand to his arm, listening hard to the sounds outside. Carew doused the candle, leaving them in darkness. David lifted a corner of the flap and peered outside. Proof of Samuel's words lay before him.

Chaos reigned in the camp. What David had heard as wind was actually a chorus of moaning men. Whatever the source of the sickness, David wasn't going to waste this chance. As one, he and his companions threw themselves on their mounts and spurred them to the exit. As David rode the last yards to freedom, a soldier reached for him in supplication. David didn't stop.

They pounded across the grass towards their camp. "Sentries!" Bevyn called, "Prince Dafydd returns!"

"My lord!" Ieuan ran to catch David's reins. "What's happened?"

David dismounted in front of him. "It was a trap," he said. "Edward never intended to make peace with us. We've spent the last hours bound, but Aaron's son released us." David gestured to Samuel, who pulled up and dismounted.

"I recommend we don't dally," Carew said.

"What sickness is this?" asked Aaron, his question for Samuel.

Samuel shifted from one foot to another. He glanced at David and then back to his father.

"Tell us," David said.

"I was among those who patrolled the exterior of the camp this evening. My shift ended after you arrived. I reported to my commander, intending to seek out my dinner, when Moses waylaid me. He insisted that I dine with him and Uncle.

"I'd never dined with them before, seeing as how we disguised the intimacy of our acquaintance as a matter of course. I was shocked that he wanted to draw attention to our relationship by having me eat with them. But Moses told me that Uncle Jacob desired that I come to his tent and argued for it most insistently.

"So I joined them. Having fulfilled his obligations to Edmund as food taster, Jacob arrived a few moments after I. We ate our meal and conversed over our wine for a time, but it was not long before Jacob became ill.

"Moses stood over his father as he retched on the ground. I asked what was wrong and he said, 'Open the flap. See what's happening in the camp.' I did as he asked. The camp . . . well," Samuel gestured helplessly. "You saw it. One man crawled to Jacob's door. I bent down to hear his words and he said, 'the King . . . the Earl . . .ill . . . please help them.'"

Samuel paused. Aaron and he stared at each other. "Finish it, Samuel," Aaron said.

"Jacob poisoned everyone. He used every poison in his collection: water hemlock among the parsnips, belladonna in the wine, Herba Paris in the stew, foxglove, henbane, nightshade, mandrake, monkshood . . . none could withstand it. The combination would look to those who come after like plague."

"Yet it's not plague," David said.

"No," Samuel agreed. "But it kills just the same."

Carew took a step towards Samuel. "The King is dead?" he asked.

Samuel nodded. "The King is dead."

* * * * *

The next morning, Carew and David stood at the edge of a copse of trees and looked toward the English camp, some two hundred yards away. As they watched, the Scot force galloped into the valley and across the meadow. They reached the English camp and, noting the absence of sentries, milled around in confusion before one of them dismounted.

The camp was silent, and David could practically feel the uncertainty coming off the Scot cavalryman. Then, a tent flap inside the camp swung up and a man appeared. Aaron hissed from behind David. "I know you told me to stay with the ship," Aaron said. "But I had to see. Forgive me."

The Scot spoke to Moses. The conversation was short. The cavalryman backed away, calling to his men. He mounted his horse and his entire company galloped back the way they'd come, the dust kicked up from their horses' hooves hovering in the still air behind them.

"The story will spread as quickly as men can tell it," Carew said. "Soon, the English will notice their king is missing, and someone will send a force to the camp. It will probably not happen today, however, and by the time it does, any trace of Jacob's work will have disappeared."

Once the Scots were out of sight, Moses left the camp. "Your father will call it murder," Aaron said.

"It was murder," David said, "but he'll feel no dismay at Edward's death either. My Uncle Dafydd, however . . ." David trailed off. Dafydd had betrayed Llywelyn too many times, but his death was still not going to be easy to encompass.

Aaron nodded. "Please excuse me, my lord." He headed down the hill to intercept Moses.

"And what do you say?" Carew asked when Aaron was out of earshot.

David hesitated, and then decided to trust Carew with the truth. "Even now, this constant killing is something I find hard to accept," he said. "I fear for my own soul, and the soul of every man who marches with me. To take another's life becomes easier the more one does it and I ask myself what kind of man I will be when it begins to come more easily. Yet, I fear that I cannot become the kind of ruler I need to be, unless it does."

Carew reached out a hand and gripped David's shoulder. "You worry needlessly, my lord. There are none in Wales who share your fears. They see only a son, who walks in his father's footsteps and fills them."

David looked once more upon the devastation in Edward's camp, and then turned Bedwyr towards the village of Poulton and the boats.

"Come," David said. "Let's go home."

Historical Background

Llywelyn Fawr, the great Prince of Wales, had two sons: Dafydd and Gruffydd. Dafydd became Prince when his father died in 1240, but died himself in 1246. Gruffydd had already died in 1244 while attempting to escape from the Tower of London where King Henry had imprisoned him. That left Gruffydd's four sons to split power in Wales: Owain, Llywelyn, Dafydd, and Rhodri. Of those four, only Llywelyn was old enough, determined enough— and free—to step into his uncle's shoes.

By 1282, when the events of *Footsteps in Time* take place, Dafydd had grown from the eight year old boy he was in 1246, to a forty-four year old man who'd spent half his life supporting Llywelyn, and half his life fighting him. Dafydd grew up in the Tower of London, a close companion to Edward, King Henry's son and the future King of England. Only a year apart in age, their love never wavered, and the hate that grew between them after Dafydd revolted in 1282 was a product of two powerful, egotistical, arrogant men on opposites sides in war.

Dafydd rebelled against Llywelyn's rule three times: first in 1255 when he allied with his eldest brother, Owain, and was defeated by Llywelyn in the Battle of Bryn Derwin; second, in 1263 when he defected to England for no apparent reason any historian can discern; and thirdly, in 1274 when he conspired with Gruffydd ap Gwenwynwyn of Powys and his son, Owain, to assassinate Llywelyn. The timely intervention of a snowstorm averted the attempt. Dafydd, as in 1263, fled to England, and to Edward.

Each time, Llywelyn either forgave Dafydd outright, or was forced by the terms of a peace treaty with the English to accept him back in Wales. That Dafydd started the war against Edward in 1282 only reveals his fickle nature. Dafydd's betrayal wounded Edward to the point that he would never forgive him. Instead, when the English finally captured Dafydd in 1283, Edward had him hanged, drawn, and quartered, and dragged through the streets of Shrewsbury, the first man of noble standing to achieve such a death. Edward was practicing, apparently, for William Wallace.

As to the fate of Llywelyn, *Footsteps in Time* is a work of fiction. In our history, Llywelyn died on December 11, 1282:

> *And then Llywelyn ap Gruffydd left Dafydd, his brother, guarding Gwynedd; and he himself and his host went to gain possession of Powys and Buellt. And he gained possession as far as Llanganten. And thereupon he sent his men and his steward to receive the homage of the men of Brycheiniog, and the prince was left with but a few men with him. And then Edmund Mortimer and Gruffydd ap Gwenwynwyn, and with them the king's host, came upon them without warning; and then Llywelyn and his*

foremost men were slain on the day of Damasus the Pope, a fortnight to the day from Christmas day; and that was a Friday.

—*The Chronicle of the Princes,*
Peniarth Manuscript 20

At Llywelyn's death, Wales fell to English rule. Edward declared his own son, Edward II, the new Prince of Wales.

As to the fate of the Jews, they'd lived in England during the Roman and Anglo-Saxon periods, but not as an organized community. King John confirmed a charter in 1201 (for which he received 4000 marks) that stated: "John, by the grace of God, &c. Know that we have granted to all the Jews of England and Normandy to have freely and honourably residence in our land, and to hold all that from us, which they held from King Henry, our father's grandfather, and all that now they reasonably hold in land and fees and mortgages and goods, and that they have all their liberties and customs just as they had them in the time of the aforesaid King Henry, our father's grandfather, better and more quietly and more honourably."

This goodwill, if it ever existed, had disintegrated by the time of Edward I. As king, he cast a long shadow over the thirteenth century and historians have generally viewed him favorably, in large part because they see his reign as good for *England* as a country (meaning he was stubborn, vibrant, and never backed down from a fight), if not anyone else. But one of his most heinous acts, in addition to conquering Wales, was the expulsion of the Jews from England in 1290.

Edward, and his father before him, began with a series of pograms designed to reduce the Jews' ability to secure a livelihood. He and his predecessors encouraged the Jews to become physicians, merchants, bankers, and traders but they were not allowed to own land. Through apprenticeship and education, which was of supreme importance to the Jewish community, many Jews accumulated a great deal of wealth, in disproportion to their routinely uneducated gentile counterparts. Of course, this engendered animosity among gentiles, who saw only the wealth, and not the effort to attain it.

This did not stop the gentiles from borrowing money from the Jews, however, and Edward allowed the Jews in England to charge interest on loans. In turn, Edward would exact huge taxes from them. As the taxes became more burdensome, it forced them to both raise the interest rates which they charged their debtors, and to call in those loans when taxed to excess. If the Jews refused to pay Edward, they were punished. In 1278, Edward arrested 600 Jewish men upon charges of coin clipping and hanged 270 of them. Edward then claimed their wealth for himself, to the tune of over 16,000 pounds.

That equaled 10% of the annual income of the entire realm. The money Edward took from the Jews compensated for the huge expenses involved in the 1277 war against Prince Llywelyn (see how this is all related?).

Once Edward had taken all their money, he had no more use for them, and began to pass more laws restricting their activities. They had to wear specific clothing and badges, could not own land, practice money lending, join any guild or business, or pass on their assets to their children. England was the first country to complete the pogram by expelling the Jews from the country (though some did pay bribes to stay). France and Germany followed suit in short order. (see my web page for citations: http://www.sarahwoodbury.com/?p=179)

* * * * *

My sources in writing this book are many, both traditional and online, and include:

A History of Wales, John Davies.
Castles of the Welsh Princes, Paul R. Davis
An Imperial Possession: Britain in the Roman Empire, David Mattingly
Welsh Castles, Adrian Pettifer
Llywelyn ap Gruffudd: Prince of Wales, J. Beverley Smith.

Smith's book, in particular, is an exhaustive and meticulous accounting of Prince Llywelyn's life. Any discrepancies between the events described in his book and my own, are a result of my error or embellishment, not his.

No understanding of this history of this era of Wales would be complete without the novels of Edith Pargeter (also writing as Ellis Peters) and Sharon Kay Penman:

The Brothers Gwynedd of Quartet, Edith Pargeter
Falls the Shadow, Sharon Kay Penman
The Reckoning, Sharon Kay Penman

For sources online, see:

http://www.castlewales.com/
http://www.earlybritishkingdoms.com/index.html
http://www.maryjones.us/ctexts/index_welsh.html
http://www. Garthcelyn.com/index.html
http://www.visionofbritain.org.uk/index.jsp

Acknowledgments

I have many people to thank, not only for their assistance with *Footsteps in Time*, but who have helped make my books better and my life sane for the last five years.

First and foremost, thank you to my family: my husband Dan, who five years ago told me to give it five years and see if I still loved it. I still do. Thank you for your infinite patience with having a writer as a wife. To my four kids, Brynne, Carew, Gareth, and Taran, who have been nothing but encouraging, despite the fact that their mother spends half her life in medieval Wales. Thank you to my parents, for passing along their love of history, and particularly to my father, who died in 2011 but was one of my most ardent fans.

Thanks to my beautiful writing partner, Anna Elliott, who has made this journey with me from nearly the beginning. And thank you to my readers, without whom, none of this would be possible.

About the Author

With two historian parents, Sarah couldn't help but develop an interest in the past. She went on to get more than enough education herself (in anthropology) and began writing fiction when the stories in her head overflowed and demanded she let them out. Her interest in Wales stems from her own ancestry and the year she lived in England when she fell in love with the country, language, and people. She even convinced her husband to give all four of their children Welsh names.

She makes her home in Oregon.

www.sarahwoodbury.com

Made in the USA
Lexington, KY
19 November 2012